"Do you think we were in love when we were kids?"

Cassie straightened. "What? I mean, I loved you. I looked up to you. But romance?" She raised her eyebrows at him. "Do you?" Granted, she'd considered herself in "love" with Brent Preston, so Cassie at eighteen had been a horrible judge of men and romance in general.

Considering her recent relationships, she might not have gotten better, either.

"That was my reaction, too." Marcus pointed at her face. Cassie wondered what it was doing. Shock had taken over. "Then one of the guys at Concord Court asked me if the way we left things then... If it would have hurt so much if it hadn't been love."

Cassie stared hard at the dirt under her shoes as she considered that. "I don't know. Family can hurt like that, too."

If they'd been in love then, what did that mean for them now?

Dear Reader,

I love to hear stories about friendships that have spanned decades, like the women who met on the bus on the first day of high school and whose kids are now best friends, too. It's difficult to maintain those relationships over time and distance, so most of us lose touch.

Cassie Brooks and Marcus Bryant were as close as family growing up, next-door neighbors and best friends. One decision, one argument and words neither would take back sent them in different directions. But when Cassie needs help planning the class reunion that could be the key to a story that can change her career, Marcus is the only person in the world she trusts to help. Time and distance have changed them. That friendship is there, but this time, they're ready for something more.

To find out more about my books and what's coming next, enter fun giveaways, or meet my dog, Jack, please visit me at cherylharperbooks.com. I'm also on Facebook (cherylharperromance) and Twitter, @cherylharperbks.

Cheryl Harper

HEARTWARMING

Second Chance Love

———

Cheryl Harper

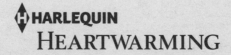

HARLEQUIN
HEARTWARMING

HARLEQUIN®
HEARTWARMING™

ISBN-13: 978-1-335-42665-9

Recycling programs
for this product may
not exist in your area.

Second Chance Love

This edition published by arrangement with Harlequin Books S.A.

For questions and comments about the quality of this book,
please contact us at CustomerService@Harlequin.com.

Harlequin Enterprises ULC
22 Adelaide St. West, 41st Floor
Toronto, Ontario M5H 4E3, Canada
www.Harlequin.com

Printed in U.S.A.

Cheryl Harper discovered her love for books and words as a little girl, thanks to a mother who made countless library trips, and an introduction to Laura Ingalls Wilder's Little House books. Whether the stories she reads are set in the prairie, the American West, Regency England or Earth a hundred years in the future, Cheryl enjoys strong characters who make her laugh. Now Cheryl spends her days searching for the right words while she stares out the window and her dog, Jack, snoozes beside her. And she considers herself very lucky to do so.

For more information about Cheryl's books, visit her online at cherylharperbooks.com or follow her on Twitter, @cherylharperbks.

Books by Cheryl Harper

Harlequin Heartwarming

Veterans' Road

Her Holiday Reunion
The Doctor and the Matchmaker
The Dalmatian Dilemma
A Soldier Saved

Otter Lake Ranger Station

Her Unexpected Hero
Her Heart's Bargain
Saving the Single Dad
Smoky Mountain Sweethearts

Visit the Author Profile page
at Harlequin.com for more titles.

To old friends who remember my last perm and make sure I can never forget it, either.

CHAPTER ONE

CASSIE BROOKS GRIMACED as she shook her hand over the trash can, trying to loosen the napkin that was stuck to it. She had no idea what sort of pastry was covered in icing that adhered as well as glue, but someone in the ten-o'clock story meeting had gotten some on his napkin.

Then he hadn't thrown it in the trash can— some people clean up their own messes, but Dan O'Malley was not one of those people. There were also people who came along behind to clean up for them. Otherwise, unfortunate souls like Dan O'Malley's beleaguered assistant would have to do it, and Cassie had a long history of stepping in when someone needed help.

"What are you doing?" Dan asked as he frowned at her from the doorway. "I told you to follow me to my office. I need to ask you something."

And we both could have gone straight there if you ever cleaned up after yourself, but here we are.

Cassie smiled sweetly. "Coming, boss." His assistant mouthed her thanks as Cassie scooped up her calendar and her notebook. They were planning stories for the next weekly issue of *Miami Beat*, the online magazine that tried to capture the rhythm of southern Florida. Writing the weird and quirky local-interest stories was her assignment and her calling.

Finding her spot after several career false starts had been a relief. She loved her job. Every day was a good day.

Even if she now had icing melded to her hand.

"Close the door," Dan said as he stepped behind his desk. The shiny row of awards lining the window that looked out on the big, open newsroom was a monument to why Dan didn't have to do the small jobs. He was *Miami Beat*'s version of a rock star. Transforming a weekly circular into a real online magazine that generated a million views monthly had been his life's work. Dan had deep roots in southern Florida, and he used them to tell the stories that people wanted to read. *Miami Beat* ran like a newspaper, with news stories, sports for kids of all ages, community events and enough local color to keep it all interesting.

And so far, *Miami Beat* was profitable. Advertisers kept showing up because the readers did. Cassie was proud to claim part of that success.

She had been working in classified sales when Dan had walked through the door at *Miami Beat*, and she'd hung on for the bumpy ride with him as editor because she loved her stories. He'd opened the door for Cassie. She would never forget that, either.

A clump of icing could be forgiven. She knotted her hand into a fist to keep from getting the gunk on her clothes and asked, "What's up?"

Dan glanced over his shoulder into the newsroom. "You have any sources over at Preston Banking and Loan?"

The urge to pretend to smoke a cigarette and say *Preston. That's a name I haven't heard in years* was strong, perhaps because she watched too many old detective movies.

"No, sir. Not my beat. Too boring." The

image of her number-one crush from her freshman through junior years in high school floated through her brain, but Brent Preston wasn't a source of hers. If he remembered her, he'd be polite, but he'd never have the urge to spill any secrets to her.

Brent had always been polite.

That made it much easier to convince people to do what he wanted.

Cassie had learned that lesson the hard way as a senior at Sawgrass High School, home of the Manatees, but the allure of the golden boy was strong. Even now, she was afraid the scalding blush that she'd battled whenever Brent Preston brushed against her in the hallway of Sawgrass High would return. At this point there should be a remedy to successfully treat acting like a fool in front of a cute boy. But no one, not even the homeopathic life coach she'd interviewed three months ago, had told her about one.

Dan was studying her closely, as if he suspected she wasn't telling the whole truth. That expression was important for good reporting.

"What kind of story are you working?" Cassie asked, setting her calendar down to flip through her notebook. Nothing in her notes seemed to line up with the bank or the family.

Dan shook his head. "You know I don't trust anonymous tips. Those are the wild tales you chase down for us." He ran a hand along his jaw. "But this could be big, the kind of story that rocks more than Miami society, because of the bank's history and presence throughout Florida. It's been a long time since I sank my teeth into something juicy like this." He pulled his chair out and dropped into it. The hiss of air escaping as the seat sank under his weight whistled through the quiet room. "Fraud. Someone at the bank is stealing. Or might be. Whoever he was, he didn't want to make the call."

Cassie whistled soundlessly, her lips pursed to suggest a whistle even though she'd never learned how. "An employee? Or management?" The family in trouble? That could be big.

"The message that came in through the anonymous tip line didn't go into specifics," Dan said. He held up his hand to tick off points. "Didn't fit the usual pattern of old and cranky or distinctly weird or plain suspicious."

Cassie jotted down a note to avoid frowning. Those *weird* calls? They were transferred directly to her, and they were a source of some of her favorite interviews. Lots of people clicked over to read all about those callers, but his tone did not suggest respect.

At all.

"Also didn't leave a name or number for follow-up. Usually means it's fake. Found some discrepancies in loan paperwork, unusual approvals and fast payoffs. No names were given, though," Dan said.

The Preston Bank dated back more than a century. Family wealth and community goodwill that old were powerful. Few people would want to take them on, young or old. This would be a big story. "Couldn't they call the police?" They'd be the pros at solving the problem, wouldn't they?

Dan dipped his chin and gave her the *Get real* glower. "That right there is why you'll never make it to managing editor." He tapped the nameplate on the front of his desk. "Thinking too small. Your whole reputation could be made with a story this size. All you'd have to do is gather enough evidence to convince the family or board of directors or banking regulators to take a look. We're reporters, not investigators."

The urge to argue was strong. It sounded like they'd have to be *both* reporters *and* investigators in this case.

And nothing Dan said suggested what would happen if they launched the story against an innocent person. Preston Bank was big enough to crush *Miami Beat*, but the magazine was big enough to draw attention and possibly stronger journalistic allies. It could be a war.

Writing about the first-grade teacher who'd made it her life's work to teach American Sign Language to every single class she led was easy. Fulfilling.

Those stories didn't provoke powerful people to decide to ruin her life, either.

"But you don't have a connection, even though I vaguely remember you telling me a story about how the Prestons built your high school a new football field when it came time for their son to quarterback the team. That's okay. I'll keep hunting. I know you'd do anything you could, because we've been friends for a long time, ever since I gave you your first story to write. Maybe Anonymous will call back." Dan tapped his pen against the coffee-splotched notepad near his keyboard.

Cassie had finally reached the age where she understood this was how people got her, how they convinced her to do more work while they took more credit.

However, seeing his manipulation didn't mean it didn't work. Guilt turned in her stomach.

Dan picked up his pen and clicked his mouse to wake up his computer screen. The silence stretched out in the room until Dan cut his eyes in her direction. "Did you need something, Brooks?"

She was dismissed. "No, sir."

Make a clean getaway, Cassie. Say no and avoid the war. Avoid Brent Preston completely.

"That's right...slink away," Cassie muttered as she picked up her notebook and opened the door. After she dropped her things at her desk, she made a straight line for the bathroom and sighed as warm water washed away the sticky mess on her hand. The idea of a career-making story used to drive Cassie. She'd graduated college with the need to right wrongs, but it had mellowed into a warm glow that took over when she exposed random acts of kindness or got to celebrate people who made a difference in their community.

But her stories had failed to impress the one man she'd been focused on her whole life. To her father, *online magazine* was a kind of oxymoron. News should be in print, smudge his hands and include a crossword to complete in ink.

Breaking a big story might change his mind.

"Maybe it's not too late," she said to her reflection in the mirror over the sink.

"Talking to yourself," Dan's assistant said as she stepped out of one of the three hideously pink stalls in the bathroom. "The sign of a creative mind, my dear."

"Thank you for being kind. *Creative mind* I will claim." Cassie reached up to tighten her ponytail. "Rosa, at what age do you think it's too late to become a star?"

Rosa studied Cassie. "On the stage? As a singer? How do you mean?"

If she answered that with enough information for Rosa to guess she meant a star reporter, one who might someday pick up one of the awards that lined Dan's window, would that make them both sad or…

Rosa sniffed. "Doesn't matter. I'd say as long as there's life left in the old girl, she can be a star." Her eyes narrowed. "So long as she is very, very ambitious. Do you know anyone that ambitious?"

Cassie returned her stare to the mirror and had to face the hard truth. "Nah."

Rosa pursed her lips. "Dan, though, he can take the smallest bits of ambition and talent and turn them into the kind of story that makes a change. If you wanted to do that, to right a wrong, he could help. It's all in your perspective, don't you know?"

She did. She really did. And the idea of having her name on a story that reached real national news… It was right there, a sparkle on the edge of her vision. She'd almost let it disappear.

"He's got his issues, no question, number one being how aware he is of his own talent," Rosa said, "but he's generous with the spotlight. I'd say he'd assist that old girl get to where she needed to go, as long as there was a story there." She reached for the door handle. "You can pass that along to her."

Cassie nodded as she followed Rosa out of the bathroom.

Still deep in thought as she sat down at her desk, Cassie picked up her phone and scrolled through all the social-media alerts. They'd become almost unbearable since someone had put her in the Sawgrass High School Class Reunion group for her year. If she ever found out who that person was, she'd have some stern words.

Possibly a glop of industrial-strength pastry icing, too.

High school had been fine. Not terrible, not wonderful. A reunion probably wouldn't be unbearable. But the person she most wanted to see in the world did not want to see her.

Cassie stretched back in her chair as she read the automated messages being sent by the account. "Lots of excitement for cold punch and receding hairlines, my fellow Sawgrass High Manatees," she muttered. When Brent Preston's face popped up, more rugged with a few lines but still as handsome as it had been at eighteen, Cassie paused to read his post.

"Hello, Class of 2001. Are you excited for our reunion? Can you believe it's been twenty years? Join me in the old Sawgrass gym. I plan to recreate that enchanted garden, only make it bigger and better than the one I brought you when we were seniors. Sign up to let us know you're coming!"

Cassie closed her eyes as she slowly set her phone down. The enchanted garden he'd brought them? Right. He had paid the bill, but she'd done all the work.

Over and over, she'd obliged Brent Preston, but that prom and the nightmare of pulling it together for him after he'd waited beyond the last minute had burned any misplaced affection she'd felt for him to ash. What a gift that had been. By the time graduation arrived, she'd battled the urge to back into his car in the seniors' parking lot. There was a good chance she didn't need a reminder to avoid Brent Preston.

But was this the door she needed to open to pursue Dan's story? Brent Preston was part of the management team for the family bank.

Or would she just get a lot of headache for zero payoff like at prom?

At seventeen, she'd imagined Brent Preston glancing up from whatever backdrop he was painting to admire her creativity and hard work. Since she'd never won him over with her looks, she'd hoped he might be deeper than he appeared and fall for things like *personality* and *intelligence* when she came in to save him in his hour of need.

Except Brent Preston hadn't even shown up until it was time for the show to go on. Apparently, he didn't do behind-the-scenes hard labor.

Instead, Cassie had dragged every person she could call a friend into a race against the clock.

They'd only managed what they had because of Marcus Bryant.

The boy next door. Her hero. The guy she hadn't spoken to since he'd joined the Air Force. If she and Marcus were still friends, she'd get his opinion on the wisdom of approaching Brent Preston as a source. Even now, after years of not talking to him, she'd respect his advice.

But Marcus had made it clear that he wasn't interested in renewing their friendship. He'd been back in Miami for a year and had never reached out.

Cassie spun her phone in a circle in the only clear spot on top of her desk as she entered a web search for *Southern Florida Landscape Design*. Miss Shirley had said the name of Marcus's new business so often that it was easy to remember.

A simple website popped up, but there were no images of the owners, only four sets of Befores and Afters to show what the company was capable of. Cassie frowned as she studied every page of the site. They'd worked some real-estate flips and had one corporate account at Concord Court.

What if Marcus was planning to attend their high-school reunion? Cassie didn't hesitate to answer her own question. He wasn't. She'd bet her next big scoop that his answer would be no.

But his business could benefit from that network. Sawgrass High had been fully middle-class, with a few outliers like Brent Preston, and most of them had stayed close to home. That meant lots of houses and businesses that might need Southern Florida Landscape Design.

Almost as much as she needed Marcus Bryant if she decided to approach Brent Preston.

"Cassie, this might be a real sign of progress." She grinned. She hadn't immediately jumped into the fire by promising Dan she'd find leads for their story or contact Brent Preston to pursue a half-baked plan. No, she needed to get Marcus on board first, and she'd already come up with her pitch. Teenage Cassie could never manage that.

First, she'd sell Marcus on the volunteering to decorate for the reunion because it would be so good for his new business. Then she'd offer their services to Brent.

When her plan worked, she'd have her old friend back, and she'd have a logical excuse to nose around Preston Bank. Dan wouldn't need to know about her involvement until she could give him good information.

The first step, finding Marcus, would be easy.

Every step after that would be tricky, but not impossible.

After a check over her shoulder at Dan's office, Cassie grabbed her purse from the bottom drawer of her desk. "Rosa, I need to run a quick errand, check something for a story, if Dan comes looking for me."

Rosa contemplated Cassie for a few moments and eventually shrugged. "If he notices, I'll tell him. Otherwise, see what you can do, star."

Cassie laughed under her breath as she

weaved through the desks in the open room. Her place in the world was nice, comfortable, with lots of good people. Going back to high school held no attraction.

Except she might be able to tell a big story.

So, she would swallow her pride and track down Marcus Bryant by the end of the day.

Even if she never got the courage to fix what had broken between them, she could see his face, know that he'd come back home okay. Remembering how to breathe freely again was worth doing some snooping.

The drive to the apartment complex where she'd grown up was quick. Her father still lived in the three-bedroom unit he and Cassie had moved into after her mother died when she was seven. It had been a great place to grow up, due mainly to the family across the wide, covered walkway. The Bryants still lived right next door, and Miss Shirley kept Cassie in the loop on all of Marcus's movements.

As expected, her father and Miss Shirley were playing dominoes while Marcus's father reclined nearby with a paper over his face. Mister Marcus was a skilled napper.

"Why aren't you at work?" her father asked

as Cassie stepped up onto the walkway next to their table. "It's the middle of a weekday."

"I am working, Daddy," Cassie said as she kissed his cheek. He didn't look up but absently patted her back. "Working an important lead." She relaxed as Miss Shirley stood to wrap her arms around her in the best hug. Cassie rested her chin on Miss Shirley's shoulder for a moment, missing her mom, and enjoyed the warm greeting.

There was no doubt who had convinced her father to get himself to the barber, either. Cassie would add that to the endless list of things she owed the Bryants for. He'd always preferred casual over dressy, with a buzz cut and a smooth jaw. Since his retirement, that had changed and it was harder to ignore that her father was…older. Not old.

"Did you eat your lunch today, Cassandra?" Miss Shirley asked as she plopped down into her chair. "You always forget to eat."

She had, but it was still early. "No, ma'am. I haven't forgotten today." Not yet.

Her father crossed his arms over his chest, his shoulders almost as broad as they'd been when she was little enough for him to rough-house with after he finished his day delivering furniture. That playfulness had gone away when her mother died. Everything had gotten serious then.

"What work are you doing here?" He was always worried she was one step away from being fired.

Probably because he didn't understand why anyone would pay her to write the stories she did in the first place.

"I would have called, but you never answer your phone." Cassie waved her cell. "Where is the phone I got you, Daddy?"

He twitched a shoulder. "Inside. It's charging."

"Has been for at least twenty-four hours. Should be fully charged any second. I warned him I was going to give his phone number to a friend at church, and now that phone will never see the light of day again. He'll *lose* it like he did the last one as soon as he thinks he can get away with it," Miss Shirley said as she rolled her eyes at Cassie.

"Last thing I need is another woman watching over me," her father muttered and dropped a domino on the table. "I said the last blind date was the last blind date, and I meant it."

Mister Marcus raised his newspaper as if he had something to say, but Miss Shirley raised her eyebrow. The paper dropped back over Mister Marcus's face. Then she asked, "You need our help with this work, honey? What is it?"

"Actually, I was hoping you could tell me where Marcus is today. I need his assistance." Cassie shoved her hands in the back pockets of her jeans and tried to look extremely innocent.

"Been a hundred years since I've seen that expression on your face, baby." Miss Shirley exhaled slowly. "I always knew you were about to execute mischief then." She stared up at Cassie over her drugstore cheater glasses. "Nothing has changed, has it?"

Cassie tried to smooth away the frown that would give her away until Mister Marcus raised the corner of his newspaper again. "Boy could stand some mischief. He's working over at the new library building on Ninety-Seventh. Volunteering." Mister Marcus dropped the newspaper over his face again.

Miss Shirley straightened the last domino she'd put down. "You want his phone number? I don't give it out to everyone." She sniffed.

"No, ma'am," Cassie said and choked down

a laugh as Miss Shirley's eyes met hers. Her outrage was clear. She didn't make the offer to most people, so she expected it to be snapped up this time. "I'd rather surprise him today." She and Miss Shirley exchanged a stare. Cassie was mentally sending the *Do not call him and warn him I'm coming* vibe. She wasn't sure what Shirley was saying, so she motioned with her hand. "I'll head over there now to say hello."

"Mm-hmm," Miss Shirley muttered.

"Bye, Daddy!"

"Hurry up and get back to work!" Her father waved, and Cassie repeated her usual mantra of reassurance. His concern over her job and her bills and her money was how he showed love. She could be okay with that.

Cassie pulled over at a taco truck and bought enough for lunch and a bribe, and then parked in the nearly empty lot of the library. She made a mental note to find out how soon the doors would open to the public. It would be nice to bring positive attention to her old neighborhood. Then Marcus Bryant stepped around the corner of the building, a thin tree of some kind clutched in his arms, his muscles bulging and flecked with sweat from Florida's spring sunshine, and Cassie nearly dropped her tacos.

She needed that remedy against acting like a fool ASAP.

This was Marcus, her buddy, her confidant, her number-one pal, the guy who'd introduced her to skateboarding and endured her boy-band phase and kept all the kids in line while their parents worked. He'd been her brother and her lifeline.

Some things were the same. The way he frowned in concentration, his complete focus on the job at hand. His crisp, closely cropped dark curls. The worn spots on the knees of his jeans.

And the urge she had to smile when she saw him was still there.

But Marcus had changed.

He'd changed.

The urge to smack her forehead was strong. Of course, he'd changed. She had, too.

What did it mean that the prospect of seeing Brent Preston again left her bored, a little cold, but watching Marcus hard at work, muscles flexing...

She was on the verge of stammering and blushing harder than she ever had at seventeen. This fever? Yeah, it had her worried she was about to relapse.

CHAPTER TWO

As MARCUS BRYANT placed the second red maple into the long bed lining the full-sun side of the new library, he ignored his grumbling stomach. Breakfast had been more than six hours ago, back when the sun was rising instead of beating down on his shoulders. Eventually, he'd have to figure out how to keep himself fed and watered as he worked, not just the plants and trees.

He might also learn how to make a profit one day, instead of barely covering expenses and hoping for so-called positive exposure. Zeke Mason had signed him up for this. His partner, the one guy in the world who'd stick his neck out on an unknown, was back in the office, working on payroll.

So yeah, Marcus had gotten the better end of that deal, but he needed food soon.

He turned the tree carefully in the hole he'd prepared and wondered if he was hallucinating.

The smell of food… Some kind of Mexican food…

He yanked up the shovel, brushed dirt in to secure the root ball and mounded up the mulch before turning on the outdoor spigot. Marcus took a drink out of the hose, ignored the memory of his mother shouting at him to never do that because who knew what was in that water and wet the dirt around the tree. The urge to spray himself down with cold water was strong, but when the new tree was soaked, he'd pack up for the day.

Get a taco, maybe.

Marcus bent down to pick up the trash that had accumulated while he'd filled and mulched the bed.

When he straightened, he could sense someone watching him, so he turned his head.

Cassandra Brooks was standing next to the first maple he'd planted, her feet sliding in the mulch that he'd carefully mounded and soaked. She was about half a second from falling onto the curb herself or pulling his beautiful, kind-of-pricey tree down with her.

And she had a bag in her hands.

"Please step away from that tree." Marcus

hurried to catch her arm before she took a tumble and immediately had a sense of déjà vu. He'd spent about ten years catching her before she hit asphalt. How strange was it that they'd fall right back into their old patterns after years of distance?

"Thanks." Cassie shook her arm to remind him to let go. She used to have to do the same thing. His reflexes had always been good, but coming down from saving her from hurting herself had taken a minute.

"I'd ask how you found me, but we both know my mama keeps no secrets." Marcus shook his head as water poured off the second tree's mound of mulch. He hurried to turn it off. The need to conserve water was one of the reasons he studied Florida's native plants and pushed his clients hard to stick with them.

Even the clients who paid nothing for his advice, like this library.

"I promise not to tell her I saw you drinking from the hose after we both swore, hands over our hearts when we were thirteen, we'd never do that again." Cassie smiled. "You know you can trust me to keep your secrets, don't you?" Her smile faded as she waited for him to respond.

He tipped his chin up. He didn't have a good answer for that, and it didn't matter anymore. They weren't anything to each other. Not now.

"How about you start with what you're doing here, instead." Marcus picked up his shovel and the tools he'd used before moving over to the flashy truck with the fancy new logo splashed along the side. The truck was beautiful.

The loan he'd signed his name to, secured with his business partner's equity, kept him awake at night. Zeke was a businessman who was ready to expand his company, but he was putting a lot of faith in Marcus, a guy who liked plants, drawing and working for himself. Landscape design was Marcus's answer on what to do with those skills, but he wasn't sure he'd proven himself to the level of signing loans.

"I have tacos and a business proposition. Are you interested?" Cassie asked with a broad grin. That had been her standard method of operation as long as he'd known her: wide-eyed optimism and a beautiful smile.

"I'm kinda busy. Call the office and make

an appointment. I'll come out and give you an estimate." Marcus checked to make sure everything in the truck was secure and realized he had no idea what her situation was. "I'm assuming this a residential request." She was some kind of reporter, so it probably wasn't commercial.

"It's bigger." She shook the bag at him. "I have your favorite tacos."

Marcus pulled his shirt up to wipe the sweat off his forehead. When it dropped, Cassie had pivoted a quarter-turn away. It was the stance of someone who definitely had never been interested in looking at his stomach ever.

Or someone who wanted him to believe that.

"I need something to drink. No hose. My mother will sense I'm breaking a promise and arrive in a cloud of fire and smoke." Marcus propped a hand on the driver's-side door.

"I'll get us drinks. You finish up here. We could meet over at the basketball court," Cassie said.

Marcus opened the door and reached in to start the truck so that the air conditioning could do its thing.

The corner of Cassie's mouth curled upward. "I don't have a basketball on me, so you won't be forced to watch me shoot basket after basket while I try to improve my free throws. We aren't in high school anymore," Cassie said.

She'd tried out for the basketball team every year and always failed to make the cut. It was a sign of growth she'd given it up.

"You never have been able to come out and ask for whatever it is you want, have you?" Marcus shook his head. "Fine. Get drinks. Lots of water. Meet me there in fifteen." He wouldn't mind seeing the old park. He and his brother and sister had grown up there.

With Cassie.

He held out his hand to take the bag of food, but she pulled it back. "I need this for collateral." Then she was trotting back across the small parking lot, sunshine gleaming off the sway of her ponytail. That hadn't changed. Cassie Brooks had moved into the apartment complex with a long, brown ponytail, too. Her jeans and T-shirt were less business casual than he'd expect from a newspaper reporter.

He should have paid closer attention when his mother had tried to tell him what Cassie was doing. Marcus knew Cassie's father still lived next door to his parents. They'd grown as close as the kids in both families had years ago.

As he finished packing up and checked the roots of both trees, Marcus remembered all the times he and Cassie Brooks had negotiated favors. She'd been the one asking, and he'd been the one in charge of all the kids in their corner of the complex. If she needed support with a plan, he could provide the helping hands.

Another thing that hadn't changed: Cassie Brooks was cute. Too cute. A smile cute enough to get whatever it was that she wanted, except the one jerk who'd disappointed her over and over. In high school, Cassie had called in favors to attract Brent Preston's attention with that pretty smile. Brent had been oblivious to it and the crush she'd had.

But Marcus had watched it all. He should just ignore it now.

Her request that he change his mind about the Air Force had been the only time Marcus had been able to tell her no. That single *no* had been the end of their friendship.

Until she needed him, apparently.

He tightened his grip on the steering wheel and made the short trip to the park they'd walked to almost every afternoon after school. Cassie had shot free throws until she'd gotten frustrated. Then she'd hopped on her skateboard. The Bryant kids all had to wear helmets. His mother had passed by one afternoon and spotted them without helmets, because helmets weren't cool at the skate park, and the punishment had settled into their bones. Cassie's father? He'd never worried about his girl breaking her head.

Why was that? Marcus had never thought to ask.

When he parked, he saw Cassie at the concrete picnic table under the shade tree.

That had been their table.

She was sitting on top of it, legs curled under her.

"They make seats for a reason," he said as he crossed the gravel to join her, the echo of his mother's voice strong in his ears.

"Okay, Miss Shirley." Cassie held out a big bottle of water and then offered him the bag of tacos.

Marcus drank the whole contents of the bottle and ate three tacos while he waited for her to make her case for whatever it was she wanted. Cassie seemed to be content to gather up the garbage and shoot it at the trash can. When she made the first and third shots, she cheered for herself. Then she scrambled to get her missed shot into the can.

Marcus opened the second bottle of water and shook his head at the three remaining. She'd taken him at his word about the drinks.

As he opened his mouth to ask *What's this about?* Cassie blurted, "Are you going to the reunion? I know you've gotten announcements about it."

Marcus balled up the final taco wrapper and handed it to her to shoot into the bin. He rolled his eyes when she made it and pretended to be the crowd going wild. "Have I got you to thank for that? I was convinced my mother was out there, signing me up for stuff without my permission. Reunions aren't my thing."

"Obviously. You moved back to town and didn't even contact me." Cassie scrambled off the table. "Which is cool. It's been a while." She inhaled slowly. "I don't know how they tracked us down, but it might benefit us both."

Marcus rested his elbows on the table.

"Please tell me this has nothing to do with Brent Preston because…" He shook his head. There was no way she was still pining for that dude. All three of them, Cassie, Marcus and Brent, had lived complete lives since high school. They were all different people. No way could a crush be sustained over decades and distance.

Then he met Cassie's eyes and realized he'd tumbled right back into…that. Whatever it was, time and distance meant nothing.

"I've got a lot going on, Cassie. I need to be concentrating on the business. I won't be taking time out for the reunion, no." He stood and turned to walk toward his truck. "You still skating?"

Cassie was moving to cut off his retreat, but she slid to a stop on the gravel. "Am I still skating?" She snorted. "Of course I am. I left my board in the trunk. I didn't want to make you feel bad because you can't keep up anymore." Then she raised her eyebrows.

The urge to slip deeper under her wave was strong. Instead of arguing about who couldn't keep up or telling her how silly it was to reconnect with Brent Preston, Marcus said, "Thanks for the food."

Cassie hurried to press one hand to the center of his chest. Had she ever touched him that way? Maybe the day she'd stormed into his parents' apartment to tell him how ridiculous tossing away his Florida A&M scholarship was. September 25, 2001. That had been the last time she'd talked to him. He'd packed up his dorm room, left Tallahassee and headed home. She'd been a freshman at Sawgrass University and waiting tables in their favorite pizza joint. That day she'd touched him.

He could still remember the way her face had transformed from joy at the surprise of seeing him home from school to...tears and then anger.

She'd begged him to change his mind. Enlisting to fight would only get him killed. He was no superhero.

He could still remember her words and her expression: fear, desperation and anger.

If anyone could have gotten him to change his mind, it might have been Cassie. He'd followed her lead on some bad ideas, like stepping in to decorate for their senior prom with one week's notice.

Then she'd made it clear that she didn't

want to hear from him again. He'd given her what she'd asked for.

But here she was.

"Please, listen." Cassie tugged on the bottom of her T-shirt. "I want to contact Brent Preston to tell him that you and I will take over the decorations for the reunion."

He wasn't going to have a single thing to do with Cassie Brooks pursuing Brent Preston again. That mistake was made only once in a lifetime. She waved her hands as he moved to step around her.

"Think of the publicity it'll mean for your business. Enchanted Garden, Marcus. That's the theme. It's perfect for you." She fluttered her eyelashes like a cartoon flirt. "You'll put up signs everywhere, hand out business cards like confetti. Oh, people love confetti. We'll make actual confetti of your cards if you like." She leaned forward. "Think of how many contacts that means, Marcus, and people who would be inclined to use your services because of the connection you already have. People like Brent Preston. People with money. What new business owner can turn his back on leads like that?" Then she folded her hands under her chin and made big eyes at him.

He crossed his arms over his chest. "What do you get out of this?" If she was honest about her intention to reconnect with Brent Preston, he'd… What? What would he do?

Cassie shoved her hands into her pockets. That used to be a sign that she was working on a lie. "You know how I felt about Brent. It'll be nice to see if there's any…" She shrugged and left the sentence hanging there in the air.

The truth he hadn't expected and certainly didn't want.

"Let me think about it, talk it over with my partner." Who would say yes so quickly that he'd stir up a breeze in their cramped office.

She wanted to argue. It was easy to see that in the firm set of her jaw.

What did it mean that he could still read her face so easily?

"Cherry on top. I'll write up a story for *Miami Beat*, the most successful online magazine in the Miami area, about the local hero who is building a new business with the assistance of Concord Court's new business lab." She shrugged. "It's a story with a couple of strong angles. I know I can get this done. Free advertising, Marcus, at the reunion and in *Miami Beat*. Opportunities like this don't come along often."

Then her shrewd-businessperson mask melted into the wicked grin of the girl who always knew when she had him right where she needed him. Her hand stretched out between them, and she wriggled her fingers to show she was ready to shake on the deal.

Everything she said was true. The exposure could be big, and it would cost him nothing but time. Adding more accounts, actual paying customers, might make it easier to sleep at night and cover his monthly truck payment.

If he did this, they'd need a lot more hands.

Finding someone to loan them the plants they'd require had been the biggest hurdle the last time they'd done this. The reunion decorations would have to be bigger and better if they were advertising his business.

"You're going to get us more volunteers, Cas. I'll see if I can set a rental agreement up with the nurseries we've been using. They might do it for publicity, too. Brent Preston is going to give us a budget, and I don't do anything but decorate. No meetings. No paperwork. I'll bring in plants. I'll help with construction. I'll plaster the place with my signs. But I will not meet with Brent Preston." Marcus held his hand out but didn't take hers until she agreed.

"Just like prom. I'll handle everything else. You bring the enchantment." Her hand slipped against his. The shiver of awareness that had always surprised him when Cassie touched him showed up right on schedule. When he stepped back, Marcus made a fist with that hand and pulled out his wallet with the other. He offered her a business card. "Text me when you have more details, like how much money we're working with." He waited for her to agree before he let the card go.

Then he moved back to the truck, got in and left the park without looking to see what Cassie was doing. He wasn't her friend or her stand-in big brother or whatever they'd been to each other. He didn't have to warn her about wasting any more time on Brent Preston.

Cassie was an adult. She could make her own mistakes.

All he had to do was work hard and make his venture grow. Cassie Brooks was a tempo-rary distraction. Once the reunion was over, they could go back to being acquaintances linked by history, the place they called home and his mother's gossip.

CHAPTER THREE

THREE DAYS LATER, Cassie was seated in the expansive lobby of the Preston Bank headquarters, waiting for the tall, mostly disapproving receptionist to call her name for her appointment with Brent Preston.

When the receptionist answered a call, Cassie sneakily pinched the too-tight band on her skirt and tried to shift it away from the rift it was cutting in the soft skin of her stomach. The *Miami Beat* dress code was easy: make it jeans as long as they're clean. She hadn't worn this suit since the job interview for a local public-relations firm. How long had it been since she'd considered doing anything other than quirky news for *Miami Beat*? Five years? Longer?

Cassie leaned back. That the skirt fit as well as it did after five years was a victory, a nice boost of confidence for her upcoming meeting. The receptionist connected the call and returned to watching Cassie to make sure…well, there was nothing to steal in the stark, expensive lobby of the bank's executive suite, but the power of her stare might stop a robbery in its tracks.

Since Cassie was here to scout for sources, she asked, "Have you heard of *Miami Beat*? It's an online magazine. We do lots of stories on Miami events, news, business, things like that. Do you read it?" This was the moment when Cassie remembered she had business cards with the website, her email…lots of useful contact information.

Where were they?

In her desk. At work.

"Read?" The receptionist arched an eyebrow. "I do not read." Her shock that anyone might suspect it of her was contained within that one superb arch.

"Oh, it's…" Cassie pointed at her tablet. "I mean, I could show it to you, if you were interested." Silence was her answer, so Cassie nodded. If the receptionist had never heard of the magazine, she wasn't Dan's source.

Silence might not be golden here, but it was the only option left. Cassie picked at the cuticle on her left thumb and waited. Silently.

"Miss Brooks, he will see you now," the receptionist said politely, although the full hiss of her *s* sounds meant the delivery was creepier than expected. "Please step onto the elevator. I will send you up."

Cassie brushed down her skirt while she tried to place the accent. Eastern Europe by way of Transylvania? Cassie clutched her tablet in both hands and watched the number over the elevator door light up. Being a Preston came with benefits, obviously. The high-rise tower that housed the bank's headquarters had a penthouse level for the family's offices. That much she'd been able to pick up while she'd been eavesdropping in the lobby.

The elevator's glass walls showed a panoramic view of Bayfront Park and the ocean beyond it. The park ran along choice Miami waterfront. Even in winter, there was a lot of foot traffic, and today the tourists and locals blended into a blur as the elevator rose. If she'd been nervous before about her foray into hard-hitting journalism, the swanky surroundings turned up the anxiety.

The elevator door opened into a heavily paneled hallway.

"Casserole! Long time, girl!" Brent Preston hurried through one of the open doors, his arms held open wide.

Caught off guard that he remembered her, much less the terrible nickname he'd given her—possibly the worst in the long history of puns based on given names—Cassie relaxed into his hug but didn't return it.

If Brent had ever greeted her like that when they were in high school, her heart might have stopped beating out of sheer joy.

Now, it was like faking her way through an introduction with someone who remembered her name but whom she couldn't place. She pasted on a wide grin to show how happy and completely comfortable she was in the situation, a clear *fake it till you make it* opportunity.

Brent was still handsome, still golden in the all-American-athlete kind of way, and time had been kind to him.

When he stepped back, Cassie realized the immunity to his good looks she'd feared lost was holding strong.

Nice.

She could actually pull this off.

"You're wondering why I asked you to come," Brent said as he trotted behind his desk, his finger pointing at the comfortable armchair in front of it. Cassie took the seat and swallowed the argument that she'd reached out to him via the social-media group and he'd told her to make an appointment for today at this time. He'd done zero asking.

"The reunion," they both said at the same time.

Brent waggled his finger. "I'll tell you, you had me worried, waiting until the last minute like this, but then I remembered you did the same thing with prom. I knew you'd come through." Brent laughed long and loud. "You always were so smart, Casserole. The way you organized that prom, that was impressive. I promised that this reunion would be bigger, so you've got your work cut out for you." He braced an elbow on the desk and leaned forward. "I'm telling you the truth, if I'd known the class president was in charge of either of these things, I wouldn't have let my father push me into running. 'Looks good on college transcripts, son.'" He rolled his eyes, like *What are you gonna do, right?*

"So does the Preston name when you go to the same college where your great-grandfather built a library," Brent continued. "You always were such a lifesaver. Glad to have you in my corner." He flashed the golden smile that had always worked on Cassie and every female who fell within its beam.

"You know what, Brent? I'd love to." Cassie opened up the website on her tablet. "But I'd like to talk about an exchange. I work for *Miami Beat*. You know it, right?" Cassie turned the tablet to face him, showing an advertisement for Preston Bank's zero-down home loans. "I do local-interest stories. I want to write about the reunion and our class president, then and now. What do you say? I'll help with planning. You give me time for an interview to finish the story before the reunion." She'd been thinking about this since she'd gotten Marcus to sign on to do the decor. She needed time to become a face at Preston Bank. Maybe the anonymous caller would see her and understand she could be trusted, or maybe Brent Preston would lower his guard and say something he shouldn't. She didn't need the whole story, just the loose thread that Dan could pull. "Do you have time to give me a tour of the office, introduce me to some key players who might give me a quote about—" Cassie shrugged "—how great it is to work here?" She needed access and a list of possible contacts. She'd pass them along to Dan, who would want to take care of the heavy lifting, anyway.

Brent leaned back in his chair and studied her face. Was he trying to determine if she knew about the bank's management issues, whether she was a threat? This didn't worry Cassie. No one ever saw her as a threat.

"Why has it taken you this long to ask? We were friends in high school. We should have already done this. Think of how a high-profile story like this will impact your career," he said magnanimously. Cassie ignored the irritation that flared at his generous concern for her career—now that she'd reminded him she was alive—and reminded herself that this interview was the reason she was wading into this mess.

"Do you have time today?" Cassie asked. "For the tour? I'll need to come back with a photographer to get a shot of you and to do an in-depth interview. I'd like to talk about what it means to belong in this community, with history. We can talk about the old days and new ways Brent Preston is tied to Miami. I'll get some quotes from employees to sprinkle

in. I shouldn't need any of your time for that."
That was her goal: time to roam the halls of
Preston Bank unsupervised.

Brent wiggled his mouse to check his calendar. "Thirty minutes or so." He raised an
eyebrow.

Cassie nodded. "Yes. That's a great start.
For anything else I need, you can hand me off
to someone else, and I'll set up another time."

Brent tapped his fingers on his desk in a
rhythm that was familiar even after all these
years. "You sure you have time for all this?
Reunion is two weeks away."

Cassie blinked. Did he think she was going
to stop doing her job until the reunion was
over? "Oh, you know how the newspaper
business is. The deadlines never stop. I'm a
professional. Besides, you're going to round
up lots of volunteers for the day of. That's
when most of the work will be done." She
smiled innocently. "That's where you shine,
Brent. You pull people together."

He tilted his head to the side to evaluate
that and finally pointed at her. "Yes, ma'am.
That will be my role: getting volunteers and
telling them when and where to show up."

"And writing the check," Cassie added sweetly.

This time, she believed his grin was genuine when he said, "Oh, you know the banking business. The check-writing never stops. I'm a pro."

The little flutter she felt at how…normal and real he seemed at that instant caught Cassie's attention.

Time to get started.

"Good. I talked to Marcus Bryant this week. He's opening his own landscape-design business with a partner. In exchange for the publicity, he's going to take the lead on the decor. All we need is a budget for decorations, food and entertainment." Cassie shrugged. It sounded so easy. The amount of work that would be required to put this together in a couple of weeks should require a longer sentence.

Brent Preston inhaled slowly as he evaluated her words carefully, an effect she didn't want.

She was the same old Cassie, everyone's best friend and number-one volunteer. Nothing else to see here.

"I want final approval on the story you run," Brent said.

His request surprised her. Seems she hadn't convinced him she was completely harmless yet.

Fortunately, she'd answered this demand before.

Cassie shook her head. "Sorry. In the past, that requirement has ruined deadlines. My boss won't agree to that." Part of her answer was true. They had missed the deadline to post the magazine because of the homeopathic life coach. He'd hated the photograph chosen and demanded a reshoot. Luckily, the staff photographer had numerous shots to choose from, and the magazine had posted only a couple of hours past the usual deadline.

Cassie didn't know whether Dan would agree to giving away the final approval because she hadn't asked him. She hadn't hinted she might have the source he wanted. Until she knew how this was going to shake out, everyone in her life was on a need-to-know basis, and she was the only one with clearance.

Putting it in those terms wasn't strictly necessary, but it did give her a Woodward-and-Bernstein kind of thrill.

"You can trust me. Have you read any of my pieces?" Cassie said as she pulled up her story of the week and slid it across his desk. "Come on. I wrote about the candidate for mayor who wants a clothing-optional platform." Nothing about this conversation with Brent could match the awkwardness of conducting an interview about policy reform while her subject was completely naked. Getting a usable photograph everyone could agree on for that story had taken some time and careful cropping.

Yes. It was a good example, meant to lower his guard.

If the receptionist had spared a glance, she might have deigned to read such a surprising story.

"And, of course, you should definitely come down to set up for the party. I'll get the staff photographer down there to take pictures of it all. That will give this story a new flavor, make it different from the rest of the Preston family's coverage." Did Brent Preston want to stand out from the family? Hard to say. Cassie imagined coming up with a new angle was unusual enough that it could catch his attention.

Plus, he had no desire to be bothered with the details of the reunion. That was her ace, the card he couldn't beat.

"Fine." Brent pushed her tablet back across the desk without reading the piece. That always stung a bit. Whether it was her father, who was like the receptionist and didn't read anything unless he had to, or new acquaintances, people remembered *Miami Beat*'s big stories, not hers. Which was fine. At least those stories had been told now. "Give my assistant your email address. She's got all the information on the budget and what to do to access the funds. She'll also review the receipts for all purchases. She can schedule the photography and the follow-up interview." And Cassie didn't need to be bothering him with anything else until then. That was the tone underneath his words, crystal clear in his delivery.

He delegated like a busy professional. Was Brent doing any of his own work here at the bank? If not, she needed to spend more time searching for leads with the men and women performing the bank's business instead of Brent.

He was her opening. Cassie had to build from there.

Brent pointed at the door. "Let's go take a quick tour, get you started."

He didn't wait for her agreement but stood and walked out into the hallway. Cassie trailed along behind him, took notes and shook hands as he introduced her to the management team. She managed to make an appointment with the head of Bank Operations, which might give her some insight into the bank's internal processes. All in all, the tour was too fast and like being introduced to the family for the first time by a boyfriend, but it was a good step in the right direction.

"Here we are, back at my office." Brent pointed at the closed door opposite his. "Jane will have everything else you need. Don't forget to make another appointment to finish your interview with me. And I'll see you at the reunion." Because that was the extent of the hard work Brent Preston, Class President, was going to put in.

It would be sad if Cassie had been disappointed by that.

Instead, she was relieved. Planning the reunion with Brent would be irritating and feel like work. Cassie was already anticipating her next meeting with Marcus. If she could get the budget numbers, she could push that meeting up to today and avoid manufacturing another reason to surprise Marcus at a job.

Now that she'd broken the ice with him, she was anxious to watch it thaw.

"Good to see you, Brent." It had been. She had no leftover crush. Except for that one flutter at seeing his real smile, Cassie felt none of the awkward giddiness that had swamped her when she'd run into Brent Preston in the hallways of Sawgrass High School. All good news.

Was he as irritating as he had been after the prom, when she'd realized what a user he was? Not quite, but the edge was there. She needed to keep Marcus and Brent separated because Marcus had never been able to stomach anyone with an attitude of superiority. Brent Preston had been at the top of his list there.

Nothing she'd seen in the thirty minutes she'd waited three days for had changed Cassie's impression of Brent Preston.

But if someone was stealing from the bank, especially if it turned out to be someone in the executive management team, any affection she might have had for Brent Preston would have made it harder to tell the story.

What a relief she didn't have to worry about that.

She waved as she stepped out into the silent hallway and tapped on the doorframe of the office across from Brent's.

The beautiful woman seated behind the desk glanced up from her screen. "Yes?"

"Are you Brent's assistant? He asked me to give you my email so you could send budget numbers for his high-school reunion project," Cassie said as she wished again that she'd remembered to put business cards in her wallet. She did that once a year, whether she'd given out the previous year's or not. A serious journalist should go through more than three cards a year. To be fair, Cassie didn't want some of the people she interviewed to have her number. The guy who'd been collecting boa constrictors for ten years? Yeah, not a guy she wanted calling out of the blue.

"Actually, I'm the chief fiscal officer for Preston's residential-loan business. But here I sit, conveniently close for the president to treat me like an assistant." She handed Cassie a pad of sticky notes. "Write down your name and email address. I'll send a budget and the form I want you to use to submit receipts." She didn't offer a card, but the small stack on her desk was within reach, so Cassie picked one up. Jane Wynn.

"Chief Fiscal Officer." Cassie studied the files on Jane Wynn's desk. That person would have access to all kinds of secure information, right? "That sounds important." Given time, she might have come up with a hard-hitting investigative question, but she had to go with that.

Jane Wynn's slow blink confirmed Cassie's suspicion about the level of her interrogation.

"To build out the story about Brent Preston and the family bank, I need to know something about how it works." Cassie pulled out her phone to record. "Can you give me the overview of your position?"

Jane leaned back in her chair and huffed out a breath. "You mean in addition to whatever odds and ends Brent clutters up my day with?" She tapped the stack of files. "Reports. I read a lot of reports. It's my job to monitor the bank's residential loan performance and make adjustments when necessary."

Cassie nodded as if she had any clue what that might entail. "Do you approve loans?"

"The branches have loan officers and a solid approval process that accounts for the majority, but when there are special circumstances, they land on my desk." She stared hard at the pile in her inbox.

Special circumstances. Those would open up the door for irregularities, wouldn't they?

Before Cassie could form the next question, Jane held out her hand for the note.

"Please also let me know when I can return to do a follow-up interview. Brent said you could make the appointment." Cassie handed back the pad and watched her rip off the top note and stab it with a thumbtack to the messy bulletin board behind her desk. Aggressively.

"Here's a credit card. There is a limit. I can change that limit up or down." Jane met her stare steadily to make sure Cassie got the message. "Scan and email all receipts with the total in the subject line and a description of the purchase in the message."

When Brent Preston had been the only employee of Preston Bank she knew, Cassie had wondered if he was secretly smarter and better at business than she suspected. He'd have to be to keep the family business thriving, right?

Having met Jane, Cassie understood that Brent or someone else at Preston Bank was good at hiring the best people. There was no way Cassie would try to fudge the budget for this reunion under any circumstances, but with Jane Wynn and the receptionist downstairs being so skilled at mean stares, only a fool would try stealing from this bank.

The urge to press her luck and try to get Jane to spill any gossip was strong, but that would be a mistake. Ready to make her escape and to change from her skirt back into comfortable jeans, Cassie stepped away.

"I enjoyed the sign-language story. I learned in middle school because a new girl moved in and I wanted to be able to say hello." Jane straightened the stacks on her desk. "Thanks for the encouraging news that other people care about teaching it."

Cassie blinked until she absorbed the information that not only did Jane read *Miami Beat* but she'd enjoyed that story well enough to remember the person who'd written it. Amazing. "Wow, thanks. I love hearing that."

Jane had returned to frowning at her computer screen, so Cassie made the short trip back to the elevator. The doors were standing open, as if an all-seeing eye had been waiting for her exit.

The elevator bypassed the Preston Bank executive lobby and went all the way to the ground floor of the building. Her business there was done, obviously. Cassie scrounged around in her purse to pull out her valet ticket and considered what she'd accomplished while she waited for her car.

She'd contacted Brent Preston and ironed out their agreement.

She'd eliminated the receptionist as Dan's anonymous source.

She'd met the woman who was currently stuck with doing all the work Brent Preston took credit for. Jane Wynn might be the most important piece, but was she the suspect or a source? Was now the time to talk to Dan? She wasn't sure how to proceed.

Cassie chewed her lips.

Waiting until she had a chance to interview more employees at the bank made more sense than telling Dan she'd struck out this early. She'd get another chance to bat.

Talking with Marcus again might jog some

creative ideas. If she told him the real reason she'd volunteered them both for party planning, what would he say? Cassie wasn't sure, but she had a good excuse to drop into his life again today. Eventually, those would run out.

Every step in her class reunion plan was leading her back to him.

Why? Because Cassie had missed him. Untangling the mess of their friendship wasn't going to be easy, but she'd never have another chance like this again.

Find the bank story.

Reconnect with Marcus.

Two big plans in motion. Definitely not her strong suit, but she knew which one mattered most. Finding Marcus would be easy. Convincing him to forget their past would be the challenge.

CHAPTER FOUR

MARCUS DROPPED THE pencil he'd been squeezing like a lifeline and shook his hand. Pins and needles in his fingers suggested he'd been lost in thought longer than he realized. Cassie Brooks had always been able to distract him that way.

"How are the plans coming along for the house Impact is flipping over on Taylor?" Zeke asked from his corner of the small office they'd recently moved into. After they decided to join forces to launch Southern Florida Landscape Design, they'd run the operation out of Zeke's garage for a few months, but building a business plan and getting the bank loan had changed everything.

Business was steady, growing slowly, but having overhead like this? Another reason to lose sleep.

Not that he'd say anything like that to Zeke.

Marcus studied the paper he'd spread out

on his drafting table. "Good. I priced shrubs over at Pascual's this morning to finish up the budget. I wanted to sketch everything out before I do the final schematics. I'll be ready for the meeting next week." The jobs for Impact, the small company flipping houses in Homestead, would never make them rich, but they'd been the first professional outfit to partner with him and Zeke, so Marcus was determined to do the best job he could. Loyalty still mattered, as far as he was concerned. "If we get the chance, we need to suggest setting up a contract again. It hasn't been six months yet, but they've seen what we can do. Having a guarantee of business every month will make it easier to breathe." He hoped that was true.

"I only asked because I wanted to remind you that I was still here, sitting in the corner, watching you stare into space," Zeke said as he shook his head. "Worries me when you do that, but you're right. It's time to get serious about making a real agreement."

"Worries you? You are sounding like my mama right now." Marcus stood and stretched his arms. How long had he been hunched over, doing nothing but thinking?

"I'll take that as a compliment. Miss Shirley is pretty sharp." Zeke pointed at the trucks parked outside, each one with the new logo on the side. "A fleet we're building. Looks nice."

So far, except for Marcus's truck, it was a fleet Zeke was financing. That was the problem, but Marcus wasn't going to say it. It was Friday afternoon. No time for an argument he never won.

They both moved to stand next to the window of the converted garage they'd decided fit their needs perfectly. It still said *German Auto* on the sign. That was the next improvement on the list.

"Want to tell me what the problem is or keep on worrying it?" Zeke asked. He studied Marcus closely. Zeke was good with people probably because he could read them.

"Same as always, wondering how long it'll take for all this exposure work to turn into money. I'm adding another project, barely covering expenses, while you carry us. This reunion is going to be a headache. Not sure the contacts will be worth it." Also, the time he wasted thinking about Cassie's smile and swinging ponytail was seriously eating into his productivity.

"Who secured the loan for the garage?" Zeke held up a finger. He didn't need an answer. "Who found the most reliable team I have to ramp up our third crew? Those veterans you pulled in do good work. Who is dealing with the new business lab at Concord Court and found us an actual web designer? We're going to have a great website, one that can take information for bids instead of showing a few photos and a phone number." Zeke crossed his arms across his chest. "Your problem is that you're too impatient. Want everything right now. What would Principal Ramos say?"

Marcus rolled his eyes. "Bringing out the big guns, huh?" Principal Ramos had been in charge of Sawgrass High School for thirty years before his retirement. He and Zeke had both been Manatees, and they'd shared stories about how Principal Ramos had supported them after graduation. He'd been Zeke's first regular client and still frequently made referrals.

"Are you sorry we expanded so quickly?" Marcus asked, determined to withstand the answer stoically, no matter what it was.

Honestly, what he wanted to know was if

his business partner regretted taking Marcus on at all, but he was not ready for that answer.

Zeke snorted. "You know how long I had this business?"

"Twenty years," they said in unison.

Marcus chuckled as Zeke narrowed his eyes. "Fine, smart guy, but in my book, that's not 'quickly.' I've been building and waiting until the right time. The minute you walked in the door and offered to build your own lawn crew if I'd hire you on, I knew the right person had arrived. Taking those courses at the university, all of that was building up to this." Zeke pointed at the window. "The trucks. The building. The exposure. Ain't nothing quickly about it."

Marcus nodded. It was logical when Zeke said it. If he could only remember that late at night.

"It's late. It's Friday. All the bills are paid, and we've got next week lined up. We're on track." Zeke wagged his finger "Important business lesson here. Learn when it's quitting time. I'm done for the week, and I'm going home. You should do the same."

Marcus knew he was right. His projects

were in good shape. There was no reason to hang around.

Except sometimes he liked to sit behind his desk, squeezed in next to his drafting table, and enjoy how his life had changed since he'd left the Air Force. It was a lot easier to do that when Zeke wasn't watching him like a hawk.

"Or, better yet, go out somewhere. Call up your buddies, hit a bar, whatever it is single people do nowadays," Zeke said with a wave of his hand as if it was simple.

Since Marcus had never been one for bars and had never been one of the successful singles in love, he had no idea what they were doing nowadays. He found his dates like he found his jobs: referrals. Friends introduced him. At this point, he should give Brisa Montero, who had helped him settle in at Concord Court, permission to give matchmaking another try.

She liked to think she was an expert. Except she seemed bad at it.

Which was hard to believe because she was good at so many things.

Would Zeke's wife be a better source?

Before he could ask, Cassie turned into the driveway. She parked and flipped her visor down to check the mirror. Was she worried about her makeup? Marcus had seen her in every stage of hair and makeup…but he hadn't spent time with her in years. Were they back to worrying about things like that? He held a hand up to check his breath.

Zeke's eyebrows shot up. "Oh, it's like that, is it? You're checking to see if you need a mint?" He hooted as if that was the funniest thing he'd seen all day. It probably was. "Maybe you aren't as single this weekend as you were last weekend?"

"Don't you want good breath to meet a customer, Zeke?" Marcus asked and fought the urge to shush the man. Shushing would turn up the volume on the laughter.

"She's checking her lipstick. You're checking your breath. This does not sound like a client relationship we're building here." Zeke looked determined to get information.

He ran out of time to force Zeke into polite behavior because Cassie pulled the door open. Instead of the casual Cassie who'd surprised him out of the blue, today she was wearing a suit. With a skirt. With low heels and bare legs. That might be closer to what Marcus imagined reporters wore every day to work, but he was trying to remember if he'd ever seen her so polished. It didn't fit his memory of her as a girl, but it was a clue to how she'd changed.

Warm sunshine followed Cassie inside as she paused in the doorway. Her eyes would need a minute to adjust. It was sort of like walking into a cave. Dark wood paneling. Brown furniture. Concrete floor. And seriously ugly plastic blinds that had no place anywhere but a landfill.

After the *German Auto* sign outside was updated, the office was the next on the improvement list.

"Hi," Cassie said as she smoothed her hair behind an ear. "You guys are seriously hard to find. Is the sign some kind of defensive maneuver?" She motioned over her shoulder. "I passed you twice before I saw your truck."

Zeke held out his hand. "Leftover from the previous owner, but we're almost ready to upgrade. We do not want you to have any trouble finding us." His grin was slow. It never failed to fluster single women. Marcus had seen him use it more than once.

Cassie slipped her hand into his, and the sparkle in her eyes was proof that she was not immune to Zeke's power, either. "I'm Cassie. I'm an old friend of Marcus's." Then she frowned. "Wait, is your name Zeke… something. I'm sorry. I'm good with names and faces, normally."

"Sawgrass High, Class of 1997, Cassie." Zeke held her hand until she took it back. "What a pleasure to meet you. You must be the one working on your class reunion. Marcus told me all about it."

Her eyes darted to meet his, which was nice. Marcus was starting to wonder if she even remembered he was standing there. Zeke could do that.

"That's me." She motioned vaguely to indicate the office. "Nice place. I hope I'm not keeping you."

"What are you doing here? We don't have an appointment." Marcus was ready to get them all back in motion. "Zeke, you can go ahead and leave. I'll lock up." Would he listen or insist on hanging around and charming Cassie? He could never tell when Zeke was going to be ornery just because he could.

"Been a long day. I need a hot shower and cold beer. Cassie, I hope we'll have a chance to talk again. Drop by when Marcus is out of the office. You can tell me embarrassing stories about him." Zeke paused in the doorway and shot Marcus a teasing glance, held up his hand to check his breath and then grinned as he backed out the door.

Cassie waited for the door to close behind him before she said, "Sorry to drop in. I bet you're ready to get home." She moved over to read the diploma his mother had insisted he frame and hang on the wall as soon as they'd closed on the office. To most people, it wasn't that big an accomplishment, finishing college, not anymore. Some truly unimpressive people managed to skate through and earn a degree in business, but he was proud. He'd done it against his mother's advice. She had expected him to find a steady job, use his military experience, and pick up a regular paycheck. Miss Shirley valued career security. His plan to become a landscape designer in business for himself? Not secure at all. That they both agreed on.

That's why he would never tell his mother that he was anything less than completely satisfied with the state of his business. He didn't want to confirm her fear or listen to *I told you so.*

Marcus forced himself to relax his shoulders. He'd tensed as soon as he'd recognized Cassie's car. "No rush. I like to unwind, finish up the last-minute stuff so I don't worry about it over the weekend. Zeke's nothing but a distraction. Gotta wait for him to leave, anyway."

He watched her meander over to the project board they'd built. One side listed their regular lawn-care customers, the standing jobs Zeke had lined up, along with the schedules of the crews they were running. When Marcus had big jobs—someday—he would be able to slot them into this schedule and pull from those crews when needed. So far, he'd managed all his planting and volunteer work on his own.

On the other side, he'd pinned photos of various building exposures, showing sunlight, ground slope and elevation from all directions, and his sketches for each of his projects in progress. Now that the library job was finished, he'd take those pictures down, put them in a binder, and file it behind his desk. That was the system he thought would work best, but he was still planning. He didn't want to ever forget the projects he'd completed. Someday, he wanted to be able to look back and remember the beginning so he'd know how far he'd come.

"These drawings are great, Marcus," Cassie said softly. "Do you remember that time we got in trouble in geometry because you were drawing a cartoon and I was laughing? Miss Shirley refused to let either of us go to the park for a whole week. I'm not sure how she knew when I was sneaking out, but she did."

"Yeah," Marcus said, "Mama has a sixth sense. Always knows somebody is about to act out."

Cassie nodded. "What was the cartoon called?"

"I don't think we decided on the title before we were caught. Ray the Rhombus was stuck in an angle of depression, as I remember it." Marcus laughed. It had been a long time since he'd thought of that. He and Cassie had both been good students, but leaving them too much time to get into trouble had always been a problem, especially when they were seated next to each other.

"Ray the Rhombus." She laughed. "We were weird kids."

When their joking ended, she cleared her

throat. "I wanted to drop by to let you know that I met with Brent today at the bank. We have a credit card, a loose budget, and his promise to send volunteers our way. My plan is to book the caterer and DJ, rent the tables and all that first thing so we can spend everything else on decorations. I called the school and set an appointment to take a look at the old gym on Monday afternoon after school lets out. Will that work for you?"

She fidgeted with her skirt, and Marcus wondered how often she dressed the way she had today. He preferred the Cassie he remembered, jeans-and-sneaks Cassie, her hair flying behind her as she practiced skateboard tricks.

"Sure. Late afternoon is good." Marcus was impressed with how much planning she'd already done. As a kid, she'd leaped first and expected to build the parachute on the way down. "Meet you there about four?"

Cassie nodded and looked uncertainly over her shoulder. Was she trying to find a graceful exit or…

"In case you were wondering," Cassie said before clearing her throat again. "Brent was his old self. Called me *Casserole*." Her disgusted expression was cute, but his irritation squashed the amusement he felt.

"I hope you didn't expect him to be pining away for you." *Because he only knew you existed when he needed you.*

Those last words burned, but Marcus couldn't say them.

"Nah, I'm surprised he remembered that much," Cassie said. "But that's good, too."

Good because she could work with that, or what? Marcus wasn't going to ask. He refused to be pulled into this crush thing again. They were too old for that now.

Cassie shook her head, as if she'd changed her mind about something she meant to say, and turned back for the door.

Before Marcus second guessed himself, he blurted, "Don't book the caterer and DJ yet. Meet with Brisa at Concord Court. She's building a list of veterans and their businesses." Marcus crossed his arms over his chest. "If we can send the job to one of them, I would appreciate it."

Cassie stopped in front of the framed photo his mother had plastered up next to his college diploma. In it, he was wearing his Air

Force dress uniform while his mom and dad stood next to him.

It was impossible to read Cassie's expression as she studied it. Eventually, her head tipped to the side. "Great photo. Your mother is your biggest fan."

Cassie was right, but something about her words, the serious expression, reminded him of the way she'd begged him to change his mind. Her tears and her request that he not join the Air Force, that he stay here, had been burned into his memory. Over time, he'd stopped pulling the memory up because the hurt never lessened, but it was still there.

"Her son's a hero. I don't blame her for being proud." Cassie straightened her shoulders. "Good suggestion about finding vets if we can. It will certainly strengthen the reach of the story."

Marcus knew she was right, but the idea that her attention was on the story instead of growing those businesses brought him up short. Before he could find the right words to point out the problem, Cassie had opened the door. "See you at the gym on Monday, Marcus."

Then she was gone. He moved to the door

to watch her pull out of the parking spot and drive away.

He wasn't sure what he'd expected of the next time he saw Cassie Brooks. More than once since their final argument, he'd considered tracking her down, calling her, just to... know how she was. For years, they'd shared every day in some way—school, the park, the same group of friends and several plans to get out of trouble that it was good his mama never found out about.

In his mind, that was who he wanted her to be, but it didn't square up with the person who'd abandoned him when he needed her. That hurt was still fresh some days. When he thought about the loneliness and fear of leaving home for the first time, he couldn't help remembering that Cassie had let him go through it without her.

She'd always been the cheerful one of the group, ready to pitch in for any mischief or assistance she could provide. Traces of that Cassie were still there, but this new attempt to impress Brent Preston and the focus on her job over the people... She'd changed more than he'd expected. They weren't the same people. He needed to remember that. He'd agreed to lend a hand because it would benefit his business. Cassie had known exactly the right way to convince him.

She wasn't stuck in the past, unless he counted this rekindling of interest in Brent Preston.

The kids who had built that friendship were gone, and they weren't coming back.

Why did that make him sad?

CHAPTER FIVE

CASSIE COULDN'T REMEMBER feeling as nervous and excited about walking into a high-school building as she felt on Monday afternoon while she waited outside Sawgrass High's practice gym.

Since she'd graduated, the school had been gifted with funds to build a state-of-the-art sports complex that held the basketball court, complete with a high-tech scoreboard and seats for three thousand fans, upgraded locker rooms and a fancy weight room. The man who had replaced Principal Ramos had been happy to tell her all about it when she'd gotten the quick tour after accepting a set of keys on loan until the reunion. The keys were secured by a promise of Brent Preston's, of course.

"His name still opens doors," Cassie muttered to herself as she studied her phone. She hadn't gotten a message from Marcus, but he didn't have her number. Should she call him?

Cassie chewed her thumbnail as she contemplated her options.

First, he wasn't even late yet. Excitement had her fifteen minutes early, and she had no one to blame but herself.

Second, if Marcus had changed his mind, what would she do? In the old days, begging, pleading, cajoling or threatening might have been her first step. She'd been proud of herself for skipping straight ahead to logic and sound business principles this time.

If he turned those down, she was out of ideas.

How would she pull this off on her own?

The principal had been much less interested in showing off the old practice gym that hadn't been remodeled or updated. His vague description of where the light switches might be had made that clear. A smart person would already be investigating what they had to work with. Cassie was sitting in the hot sunshine, worrying.

It didn't matter where the switches were if there was no plan. Marcus was the man with the plan. She'd have to disappoint Brent Preston and disappoint her boss, Dan. And her father would be in there somewhere, too, in the disappointment mix.

"Oh, no, not the thumbnail. Things must be bad," Marcus said as he stepped up next to the concrete planter she'd climbed on top of to wait.

Relief spread over Cassie like a cool waterfall.

"Old habits die hard, I guess." She smiled at him. It was so easy to be happy when Marcus was around. No matter what her problems were, he had this attitude of calm certainty.

As if he never doubted that there was a solution to every problem.

Cassie had forgotten about that reassurance.

"I was afraid you'd decided you were too busy today." Cassie untangled her legs, prepared to jump off the planter and get to business. He was doubtless pressed for time, and she was going to do everything she could to make sure he didn't regret agreeing to her request.

Marcus stepped up close enough that she couldn't jump down, not unless she was prepared to crash into him. "We might need to talk about that, Cassie. Exactly what am I helping you do? What's your goal to win Brent's affection this time?"

His dry delivery reminded her of how often he'd listened to her talk about Brent Preston when they were kids. Sure, it was silly now, the crush she'd had, but then? Crushes were what high-school kids were supposed to do.

Did he think she was still that girl? That she hadn't matured a bit?

The urge to tell him about the story was strong, but it felt unfair and unethical to spread a rumor about Preston Bank with zero confirmation. Also, she was already walking a fine line with her own conscience about trading on the relationship with Brent to try to find said evidence.

Would Marcus understand all that?

Her old friend would. He would also have good advice on how to go about investigating the story.

But she didn't know Marcus anymore.

The old Cassie would never have worried that he'd back out.

At least she understood that two decades had brought about some changes in Marcus.

The boy was a man now. Expecting him to be the same was naive.

She was disappointed to realize Marcus wasn't giving her the same consideration, but that letdown changed nothing about the circumstances. He'd asked a question. He would wait for an answer.

"Good question. When I was a kid, I gave Brent more credit than he deserved." Cassie met Marcus's stare to make sure her point had time to land. He was older, more mature. So was she. "No plans to reignite my old love from afar. One *Casserole* was enough to answer that question." She put her hand over her heart the way she used to when she was trying to convince him she was telling the truth, the whole truth. "I am here to get this party planned, to promote your business and to forget that Brent Preston will take every bit of credit again."

Marcus's lips thinned. Did he think she was lying?

"And your story. Don't forget the story. The one you need all those angles to sell."

Relieved that he did seem willing to acknowledge that she'd grown up, Cassie grinned. Marcus didn't smile in response.

"Well, yes, it is my job," Cassie said slowly, unsure why he seemed almost angry as he reminded her.

"Right." Marcus shook his head as he stepped back. Had she said something wrong? She waited for him to add words to make it easier to understand, but he turned to stare at the gym.

"I've got keys. Brent got us permission to come and go as we need to in order to plan, and the week of the reunion we can have the gym all day every day. They mainly use it for warming up, sometimes practice and PE classes now." Cassie jingled the key ring that would open the main doors, locker rooms and restrooms. "Not sure how this gym ever cleared Brent's standards for one of his parties, but I would guess there's not much we can do to damage it. The principal handed over the keys and told me to track down a custodian if I need assistance."

Marcus paused at the door and waited for her to unlock it. When he didn't say anything, Cassie glanced up at his face. "This is going to be hard work if you aren't going to talk to me, Marcus."

He opened his mouth but changed his mind

about whatever he intended to say. "Let's see what we're working with."

Arguing had never been the best way to convince Marcus to open up. When they were kids and he'd been worried about a test or annoyed at his mother, Cassie had learned that making him lighten up had been the only way to make him talk. Luckily, she'd been good at that. Tricks on her skateboard, trash-talking on the basketball court… That had been the route to ease under Marcus's guard.

As soon as the gym door swung open, Cassie realized the first hurdle they were going to have to jump in enchanting the gym. "Decades of sweaty jerseys… The smell has seeped in. A portion of your decorating budget is going to be sprayed away in the form of Sea Breeze air freshener." Cassie spotted the light switches and went to flip every one. When each of the overhead lights hummed to life, she said, "All the light bulbs work." Then she spun slowly in a circle to survey the bare-bones gym. "But I can't tell if that works in our favor or not. Darkness might be a gift. We could call it *mood lighting*."

Marcus didn't answer as he stepped out onto the floor. Cassie watched him do a slow turn to match hers. "The good thing is..." His words trailed off, and she had to laugh. Filling in that blank wouldn't be easy. When he faced her, his lips were twitching, too. "The good thing is we have lots of space to work with and an almost-blank canvas." He lifted his chin. "I almost pulled that off. You want to believe me, don't you?"

"I do. I want to, and I do believe you," Cassie murmured as she watched him pull a small notebook from his shirt pocket. Why was she locked in on his hands with that small notebook? It was like a symbol that Marcus was in control of the situation. More relief settled into her bones.

"Should we talk about the big idea? Or the areas we'll need to set up..." When they'd done this as kids, she'd been the big-idea person, but Marcus had proven then that he was so much more creative than she was.

"We should start outside the gym, set the mood on the walkway in." Marcus pointed with his pencil. Before she could ask any of her questions, he added, "Six arches? We could string netting between them and cover it with vines and small twinkle lights."

Cassie was immediately struck by the romantic picture. "I love it. We can set the registration table up outside. I was thinking we'd have everyone write their own name tag, and we could pin them on with flowers. I don't know, a carnation or something."

Marcus didn't wrinkle his nose, but the impression that he wanted to was clear.

"Not carnations. We can do better than that," he murmured. "But it could add some color if we had a sign printed. You know, *Class of 2001 Reunion* or something like that, but with some bold flowers, bright colors." He jotted down a note and moved closer to center court.

Disappointed not to get a better reaction to her name-tag suggestion, Cassie trailed behind him. "For prom, we had a refreshment table and a stage. I was thinking I'd rent those and some standing tables for people to congregate around. If we do that, we'll need centerpieces."

"I did this cool thing for Concord Court for New Year's Eve. Brisa wanted a celebration in the courtyard with some kind of countdown. We used these strings of those old-fashioned bulbs, Edison bulbs?" Marcus stopped to wait for her to acknowledge that she understood what he meant. "They give off a warm glow. If we did something like that here, we might be able to keep the mood lighting plan. Turn the lights off, string up lights to outline the dance floor." He paced a line back and forth as he plotted out his imagined dance floor. Cassie was disappointed again to be left in the dust, but it was amazing to watch him think and plan as he walked. When they were kids, he'd done the same, but it had been the big, wild movements of a kid burning off energy.

Today, he was a professional plotting out solutions as he worked.

"Might be too dark. It's a big gym." Why did she say that in such a low tone? Was she disturbing the genius at work? She had a point to make, but she didn't want to startle away his inspiration.

"You're right," he said and tilted his head back to study the ceiling. Cassie held his agreement tightly and waited for his next move. "Those rafters are steel, right?" He motioned with his pencil.

Cassie peered up at the rafters. She knew what rafters were, but she couldn't say what they were made of. Not wood. Probably. "Sure." Agreeing with him was easy.

"The challenge will be getting up there, but more white lights, the nets like we're using outside. When we put them up there, they could be a starry night." Marcus jotted down a note.

As if that was decided. The plan would include stringing lights... How high up were those rafters? A thousand feet in the air? Stringing lights at a height that would definitely hurt her when she fell was not on her list of enchanted things. They hadn't even attempted that in the hotel ballroom they'd decorated for prom.

"Need to check with the custodian to see if they have a ladder here tall enough to reach." Marcus made another note and then glanced at her. "You can do that, right?"

Maddie cleared her throat. "Do you mean hang the lights or find the custodian, because..."

Marcus blinked slowly. "No way are you climbing a ladder in my presence, Cassie. Do you remember the time you stepped backward off the moving truck in the apartment complex? The ramp we were using to help the Lees move in slipped and you went down. On your back. I've never seen anything like that before or since."

Cassie would never forget it, but she'd sort of hoped the audience that had watched her bounce on concrete had gone on with their busy lives. "You cursed at Miss Shirley when she didn't move fast enough to check on me."

Marcus huffed out a breath. "And it's a testament to how scared we all were that I'm still alive. That was the only time my mouth got ahead of me that way."

Cassie chuckled. "Good thing I landed on my butt. I could have been hurt otherwise." His snort instantly took her back to afternoons trailing Marcus. "Right, might have broken something."

Relieved that they could still do this, she said, "The white lights instead of the dance-floor lights? Not sure that's enough light, either."

Marcus shook his head. "No, both. Lights in the rafters for extra boost, but the dance-floor lights are more intimate. The more lights, the better, right? But keep it dark enough to hide the gym, light where we want the enchantment." He flipped his pencil in the air. "What do you think?"

"As long as I keep both feet on the ground, I love it. I will check with the custodian about the ladder, and if the school doesn't have one, I'll find out where we can rent one." Cassie pulled her phone out and made herself a note. Both of them could be organized.

"Ten standing tables. Four of the longer tables for food, a couple more for registration," Marcus murmured. "We can get chairs, too. Pulling out the bleachers for seating will remind everyone that we're in a funky gym. We can arrange them in groups."

When she looked up, he pointed at her phone to remind her to make a note. She shook her head but followed along. She didn't want to forget anything. They'd scrambled until the last minute to pull together on their prom night. For the reunion, they both needed plenty of time to circulate.

"For the table centerpieces, what do you think about orchids? They could be door prizes, too." Marcus crossed his arms as he stared out over the gym floor. Standing next to him, being dazzled by imaginary lights overhead and orchids scattered throughout, Cassie was impressed. "You have a talent for this."

When he startled and turned her way, Cassie wondered if he was embarrassed at the compliment. Didn't matter. It was completely true.

"I mean it! You've always been so good at finding answers, especially when we were kids and the biggest problems we had were sneaking past Miss Shirley to make sure we caught the ice-cream truck." Cassie squeezed his hand, the one gripping the notebook. "It's no wonder you were such a success in the Air Force. You're going to do great things with your own business, too. I'm lucky I convinced you to say yes to this."

Marcus stared at their hands until Cassie let go. She would have stayed there longer, the two of them, connected that way in the hot, stinky gym.

Because that touch was enough to remind her of the ache of missing him. In the early days, when the pain was fresh, missing him had been almost enough to tempt her to break her word and ask his mother for a way to contact him.

She'd managed not to because she'd wanted him to miss her enough to come home, to leave the Air Force as soon as he could. Eventually, the ache had faded and she realized he had to make whatever he thought of as the right decisions for his life, regardless of what she wanted.

That was a good thing because it had taken too long for him to come home.

"Did she ever find out your dad was the one slipping us enough money to fund the ice-cream habit?" Marcus asked as he stepped back.

The question helped Cassie gain her footing, too. Old friends. Best friends.

"I doubt there's anything your mother doesn't know, but she's never said anything to me about it." Cassie wrinkled her nose. "It's almost like she didn't mind that we ate ice cream before dinner as much as she said she did."

He nodded. "Agreeing to let us have it, that might have made her look soft."

"Sneaking around taught us problem-solving skills and stealth," Cassie added.

They both laughed.

"It's a good thing my sister moved back to Miami after her divorce," Marcus said. "If Mama was able to concentrate all of her attention on getting me settled, as she calls it, for too much longer, we would be fighting."

Cassie agreed. She'd been visiting her father when his sister, Tasha, had brought her kids over to swim in the apartment complex. "Tash's twins are so cute. Have you seen them swimming? One of them—I can't tell them apart yet, but I think it was Bran—he made a break for it while Tash's back was turned and had both feet in the pool before she could stop him. His screams when he had to get out of the water! And the way he glared up at Tash as she scolded him about not waiting for her. She has her hands full." Cassie covered her ears with her hands. Even her father had been forced to come find out what the noise was about. Which reminded her. She grabbed Marcus's arm. "You aren't going to believe this. Your mama is setting my father up on blind dates." It was wild. All she could do was shake her head.

He glanced over at her, and she was happy to see pleasure on his face until it faded. The conversation had been so sweet, like they'd stepped back in time into their old spots.

"I couldn't do this without you, you know," Cassie said softly. Even if she couldn't smooth over their history before the reunion was over, she wanted him to know she appreciated his talent and his help. When she realized she was still holding his arm, she forced herself to let go.

"You could, but I kind of like that you think you couldn't." Marcus tapped his pencil on his notebook. "You didn't have any trouble picking up after I left, going on with your life, building this career you love so much." He moved toward the women's bathroom next to the exit and touched the door. "Do we dare inspect this?"

This career you love so much. There was something she didn't recognize in his tone. Bitterness? No, couldn't be.

He pointed at the bathroom door.

"I don't want to go in there, but I can't ethically allow people into this gym until we know how bad it is." She also wanted to argue with him about how easily she'd moved on without him. Some days, she still felt like the kid who'd lost the support she'd always leaned on.

Having him back, even if they weren't friends anymore, restored some of that balance. But this was not the place for pouring out her feelings. Marcus had never been big on it when she'd done it as a kid.

Of course, her feelings had been about her father or Brent Preston too often, back then.

He tipped his chin up and waited for her to straighten her shoulders. They'd done that before, too, pumping each other up when needed. "It has to be done."

They both pressed their hands on the door and pushed. When she stepped inside, Cassie was relieved. "Out-of-date institutional bathroom. Old but clean enough. We can fix this."

Marcus stared. "If the men's bathroom is this good, we'll have escaped true horror." Then he tapped her hand. "Better double your air-freshener order."

They were both chuckling as they finished walking through the gym. All in all, strategic darkness would be their main goal, with plenty of lights and enough greenery to create enchanted focal points.

Marcus flipped the light switches before they stepped out of the gym. He waited until she locked the door and yanked the handle to make sure it was secure. "For the photo backdrop, I was thinking we could do potted trees. An iron gate or—"

"We'll definitely need props so people can take goofy pictures." Cassie waited for him to agree and noticed his confused frown. "You know, mustaches, hats, visual puns about flowers and gardens or weeds. I'll need to do some brainstorming for that." She'd been trying, but the best she could come up with was a play on herbs or vegetables. *Kind of a big dill* and *Thyme to celery-brate* were funny. They were not enchanted at all.

"Do you think we could get a fountain for the punch bowl?" Cassie asked as she pulled her phone up to make a note.

His sigh was quiet, but she could still hear it.

"What? You have a better idea?" She knew he did. He'd been improving everything she'd tossed out all afternoon.

Cassie hadn't decided how she felt about the fact that he was better at enchanted things than she was.

"No, people will enjoy both of those things. I forgot what it was like to work with you." Marcus dropped his notebook into his pocket. "I bring the framework. You supply the fun."

Cassie blinked as she considered his words. It almost sounded like a bad thing when he said it that way. "I…" She wanted to defend herself but she wasn't sure how.

"I've missed that fun." Marcus grinned at her. "That's all."

His words were a direct hit. A warm glow spread throughout her chest, and Cassie's cheeks flushed with delight. It was enough to make her shy.

With her oldest friend in the world.

It took a minute for her to catch her breath and build up her nerve, but when she did, Cassie slipped her arm around his waist. She'd done the same thing day in and day out when they were kids. This time, Marcus's spine snapped straight, but he wrapped his arm around her shoulders before she could pull away.

Before the moment passed, Cassie said, "I've missed you."

He squeezed her and cleared his throat. "We're going to plan an amazing party together. Brent Preston is going to be so proud of himself when it's all over."

Then he moved away.

Cassie wasn't ready to say goodbye. "So I was thinking…" What was she thinking? She'd started this with no way to finish it.

Marcus stopped next to his truck, one eyebrow raised. Waiting for her to figure out where she was going.

That brought back old memories, too.

"I need to get the rentals, the caterer, all that lined up so we can order the plants and... everything." True. All that was true. And this wasn't the first time she'd told him, she reminded herself. Cassie licked her lips. "Do you have time to meet me at Concord Court? I can get names for the businesses we might use, and you can introduce me around, so I can outline my thoughts on the story I want to write. Multitasking for the win!"

Marcus opened the door. "You're good at multitasking. Planning this party without taking your eyes off the real prize, Brent Preston and your stories." He slid into the seat. "I'll text you with a time, if that's okay. Let me look at the jobs I've got this week and set something up with Brisa Montero at the Court."

"Sure, whatever is easiest for you." Cassie wanted some other way to slow down his exit, but she had to agree. "Do you want my phone number?"

He shook his head and held up his phone.

"My mother made sure I had it plugged into my phone as soon as I landed back in Miami. I'll text you." Then he shut the door and pulled out of the parking spot.

Cassie watched him leave and tried to be happy with how much they'd accomplished this afternoon. They had a plan for the reunion, and things were closer to normal between them. Some of the distance was gone.

But the knowledge that he'd had her phone number a year without using it...

That said more about where they were than she liked.

If Cassie wanted to change their relationship from *used to be friends* to something new and better, she only had two more weeks to get it done.

CHAPTER SIX

MARCUS KNEW EXACTLY how this visit to see his parents would go. His mother would ask questions, drilling down and down until she could put her finger on whatever it was that might be bothering him. His father would listen until he got tired of the discussion. At that point, he would explain how Marcus and his mother were both wrong and go turn on the television.

By the end of the dinner, everyone would be exhausted, but he would promise to meet them again on the next Wednesday night.

And the leftovers were absolutely worth it.

He'd wrapped up the meeting with Impact promptly at five. He and Zeke had pretended to be long-time well-established business owners as they'd loaded up to go back to their office, but they'd celebrated with multiple high fives in the parking lot under the *German Auto* sign.

The builder, Richard Terrence, had approved Marcus's plans for the latest flip and agreed to negotiate a contract. A real contract.

Zeke's company had been mowing and raking lawns on all the houses Impact had for rent for years, until Marcus had convinced his buddy to aim higher. Bargain pricing had convinced Terrence to give investing in the landscaping to raise sale prices a shot. Enhancing the curb appeal had added value to each flipped house, earning Marcus time to learn the business side and prove himself.

Up until this point, he and Zeke had been happy enough to shake hands on deals because they'd been small potatoes, but the new plan was to negotiate a full contract for a year. The guarantee of work on a certain number of houses would make planning expansion easier for Zeke and Marcus, and he and Zeke could provide easy full-service lawn maintenance for Impact's rental properties and higher value for their flips.

These jobs could give him the freedom to show how sustainable landscaping practices could be beautiful, too.

So maybe this dinner would go differently

than usual. He could show his mother that his business, the one she was convinced would leave him hungry and hunting for real work, was growing.

Marcus yanked off his tie before he slid out of the truck. His parents had gotten used to seeing him in a variety of work clothes, but a tie might send his mother into a swoon. Every time he gave in to her urging, reminding, requesting, hinting and generally pestering him to go with her to church, she took great pride in straightening his tie.

As he rolled up his sleeves and walked up the sidewalk, he realized Cassie's father was sitting out on the small patio that faced his parents'. "Evening, Mr. B. Nice night." While Cassie had been rolled into his family like a second daughter, mainly because she'd been seeking a mother, he'd never gotten quite as comfortable with her father. Every kid in the complex had settled on Mr. B as his name.

When Marcus had moved back home, Cassie's father had insisted Marcus call him Brian.

At Mr. Brooks's immediate scowl, Marcus cleared his throat. "Sorry. Still gets caught right there sometimes. It's a nice night, *Brian*."

Cassie's father peered at him over the top of his reading glasses. "Yep, 'tis." Then he dropped the folded newspaper he'd been studying on the small table next to him. "Must be Wednesday. I smell pot roast and chocolate cake."

"Yes, sir. I expect you'll see some leftovers." Everyone knew the routine. No matter how many times his mother invited him over for their family dinner, Cassie's dad refused.

But he never said no to leftovers.

"Sure I can't get you to join us?" Marcus asked, already deep into the traditions of the evening.

As Marcus knew he would, Mr. B pursed his lips. "No, family time's important. Couldn't intrude. Your mama and daddy are lucky you and Tasha come around." His sister's schedule working nights meant Marcus was the center of attention on Wednesday nights, but she got her own time on Saturday mornings. Did Cassie's dad sound lonely?

Then he remembered Cassie mentioning blind dates.

Since that was uncomfortably close to the way he'd been considering asking Brisa or Zeke's wife to take his dating life in hand,

Marcus realized he and Mr. B might have something in common.

If he had to guess, Cassie would make herself a nuisance if she was convinced her father needed her. Was that the old Cassie? Maybe this was another way she'd changed. Or it might only be that her father was lonely when she wasn't there. Marcus had spent enough time on his own, staring up at the ceiling of his town home, to understand how that could happen. "Had a good chance to catch up with Cassie this week. Sounds like work's going well."

"I guess it might be this time," Mr. B said, but Marcus wasn't sure the older man believed it. Resignation filled his voice. "Took long enough for her to find her spot. Teaching. Marketing. Temp jobs when that fell through. Then she landed at this online thing. Interviewing *characters*, as she calls 'em, makes her happy."

Why didn't her father sound happy about that himself?

Marcus eyed the distance to his parents' door and wondered if he should make an awkward escape. The mood was somber, and he wasn't sure why or what to do about it.

Before Marcus could think of anything to say, Cassie's father stood up. "I'll call her and make sure all this reunion work isn't messing with her deadlines. She always did take on too much. If the girl could focus, she'd be unstoppable. I worry about the kid. When I'm gone, who's going to look out for her?" He stretched slowly and Marcus judged that, even if he was retired now, he hadn't changed much from his delivery days. His hairline was receding. *But that happened to most of us.*

"You know Cassie is family, Brian." That time it rolled out a bit more smoothly. "Always will be," Marcus added. Then he realized it was true. No matter what the status of their friendship was, if Cassie was ever in real trouble, she could count on him. For that matter, she could count on his parents, too.

Her father grunted. "You ever look back and think *Shoulda done that differently*, Marcus?" His lips twisted. "It's almost like holing myself up after my wife died was a mistake, and now here I am, waiting for my leftovers. Don't even have a boss depending on me anymore. Can hide in this apartment forever if I want to." He shrugged. Marcus wondered if he should call Cassie and tell her... What would he say? "Ignore my rambling, or at least tell yourself not to forget how to live in the real world. Work is important, so is family, but a man owes himself something more, too." Eventually, Mr. Brooks remembered he had an audience. "Go eat dinner, son."

Relieved to have an exit, Marcus nodded. Before he knocked on his parents' door, Mr. Brooks said, "We sure are glad to have you home again. Your mama and daddy missed you, and I'm glad Cassie finagled you for this party she's planning. Never had to worry about the girl when you were here. Never doubted your drive." He waved as he stepped inside his apartment and shut the door.

Marcus didn't have time to knock. His mother was staring at him across the threshold, one hand on her hip. "Food is getting cold. Are you planning to come inside?"

The urge to give her a smart answer, something along the lines of *No. Could you make me a to-go plate?* died a swift death as she raised an eyebrow. It was a dare.

There was no way he'd accept it. "Just making conversation with Mr. B, Mama." Marcus kissed her cheek and then hugged his father's neck as he closed the door behind himself.

"He seemed…" Sad. Quiet. Confused by his daughter. "Not himself."

That wasn't quite right, because Mr. Brooks had always been quiet, but tonight there had been weight to it.

"Anniversaries. They catch you off guard, I think." His father untied the frilly apron he always wore when he cooked before he turned off the radio. That had been how his parents always cooked: together, talking and laughing, while music filled in the background. "Birthdays. Holidays. When you lose someone, I know those days hit hard. This is the day his wife passed."

"Well, now, how did you remember that?" his mother asked as she pointed Marcus to his usual seat. When his brother and sister and their families came for the holidays, this table groaned under the weight of food, plates and silverware. These weeknight dinners were casual, only the three of them, although there was still enough food to feed an army or four adults for at least a week.

"I pay attention," his father said slowly before pressing a kiss to his mother's lips. He held her chair out, waited for her to take a seat and then settled in his usual spot at her right hand. "Been neighbors for almost three decades. Happens like clockwork, though this might be the worst I've ever seen it. Guessing that before his retirement, he had his job and his routine to take his mind off what he'd lost. Now? He has us, and we are not enough." He shook out his napkin and settled the cloth over his lap. "I always ask myself how I'd go on if I had to face the same kind of anniversary."

Marcus watched his parents tangle their fingers together. Whatever ups and downs came, they'd always held hands like that.

"I'm glad you asked. I'll tell you how to go on. Mourn for ten years, then find a lovely woman who is almost as amazing as I am and marry her," his mother said sweetly before fluffing her halo of natural curls with her free hand. "I give you permission to be happy, not quite as happy as we have been but only a fraction less."

Marcus watched his father slowly place an elbow on the table as he weighed her words. "Ten whole years? At our age?"

Laughing would have been a mistake, so Marcus coughed into his napkin.

"Five years," his mother said slowly, "but

no less. Don't wait too long, either. That's what happened to Brian. He waited too long to get back to living, and now it's a big scary thing." She waved her hands in the air. "Who warned him? I did, but did he listen? No. Does anyone ever listen?" She missed the way Marcus and his father mouthed *No* in response. "So it is what it is. Now we do it the hard way. I have warned the single ladies at church that he will not be an easy nut to crack, and may the best woman win."

Marcus exchanged a glance with his father. His father answered with a wink, and that was that. They passed dishes and filled their plates. Marcus tried to eat efficiently before his mother started asking questions.

"Aren't you glad to see Cassie again?" she asked as she buttered the yeast rolls that were his father's specialty. "Your old friend."

Marcus was not fooled by her nonchalant tone. "Do I have you to thank for that, Mama? I'm not sure how I feel about it yet." He'd been fine without Cassie in his life. They'd both been fine apart.

"You, a grown man, can say no as easily as yes," his father said. He poured sweet tea into their glasses before sipping. "If you don't wish to be caught up in Cassie's plans, it is a simple thing."

Marcus stifled a sigh as he watched them both chew oh so innocently.

"Mr. Brooks mentioned Cassie has taken a while to find her career." Marcus stared at his plate as he tried not to give away too much of what he thought. He wasn't certain, really, but the emotions he could name were uncomfortable. Like worry. "Why didn't you tell me more about what she was up to while I was gone?" He had no doubt his mother had kept the whole apartment complex in the loop about his own accomplishments.

"Don't you remember?" his mother asked. "You were in Biloxi, working on your technical training. I tried to tell you a funny story about Cassie..." She stared at the ceiling as she tried to remember the story. "Oh, I can't remember. Was it about her classes?" She waved a hand. "Doesn't matter. It's not important." She pointed at him, her perfectly manicured finger wagging. "What is important is how you snapped at me that she'd decided you weren't friends anymore, so you didn't have to waste your time with any more Cassie stories." She blinked slowly at him. "I took you at your word. I had no idea it would last so long."

When Marcus's father cleared his throat, Marcus understood they'd discussed his tone and his demand more than once. "Of all the things I snap at you about, you decide to grant that one." Shaking his head, Marcus served himself another slice of pot roast. He wasn't sure whether he was happy or sad his mother had followed his request. When he'd been at Keesler, working through the Command and Control tech training, he'd been overwhelmed. He'd been afraid he was in over his head. Having a friend like Cassie, one who had never once doubted his ability to do anything, would have been sweet.

But she'd ended their friendship.

Because he'd enlisted.

Marcus had felt a duty to join the military. To step up when he thought he was needed most.

And Cassie had turned her back on him when he needed her most.

That didn't mean he'd forgotten the ache of missing his best friend or the twist of jealousy he'd felt when his mother had tried to pass along her funny Cassie story. "It was a date. She'd been set up by her roommate, but before she was introduced to the guy in the bar, the guy tried to pick her up, offering to ditch his blind date." Namely Cassie.

She'd always had terrible luck with men.

That had been little comfort at the time.

His mother considered that. "I cannot say if that's the right story, but it does sound like our girl." She pasted on the innocent look again, but Marcus didn't miss the knowing glance his parents exchanged. Did he want to know what that was about?

"She's had a collection of jobs, but she's done fine at all of them," his father said. "Brian's worried because he wants good things for her. That's what we parents do, hope our kids do better than we did." He popped the last bite of his roll in his mouth, satisfied with his wisdom and his baking, no doubt.

Marcus leaned back. "I guess I've missed too much. Cassie is focused on this job of hers." *Focus*. There was the word Mr. Brooks had brought up. "Like, at the expense of helping people, which surprised me."

His mother straightened in her seat. "No, son. I don't know what you've misunderstood, but you got something wrong. That girl, the one thing that has not changed is that she'll drop everything to help someone. Remember that summer I worked two jobs to save up money for Tasha's braces? Cassie skateboarded down to the daycare every afternoon to help me clean up after lunchtime. Made her father lose sleep, that did—all the traffic—but she wouldn't change her mind." His mother smiled. "He trailed her in his delivery truck, whenever he had the chance, to make sure she didn't cross against the traffic light or do some other foolish thing. She never did."

Marcus had been working retail at the big-box store that summer, so he'd missed that part of the story, but it didn't surprise him, any of it. "Cassie takes risks, but they aren't foolish risks." He'd seen it in action. That was why he knew her better than his parents or her father did, even though it had been years.

"And sometimes she needs people watching over her because of those risks. Her father has. We have. You have. But I would bet the money I made that summer that those risks are taken to assist others, not herself." His mother gave him a firm nod, probably because she believed he was proving her point, as she stood and took his empty plate. "Chew on that while I cut the cake."

His father chuckled as Marcus turned toward him. "She's cute when she's right."

Marcus had to laugh at his dad's expression.

When his mother returned with three big slices of cake, Marcus said, "I should have told Mr. Brooks how Cassie talked me into stepping up. She's smart. The big ideas haven't changed." He closed his eyes as the first bite of moist cake hit his tongue. No matter how inquisitive his mother could be, there was no way he'd skip this dinner as long as her chocolate cake was on the menu.

"Neither has her ability to find and win the support she needs for those plans," his father said.

His mother bent her head closer. "What about your friendship? Has it changed?" The gleam in her eye made him nervous.

"Well…" Marcus turned to his father, hoping for an ally, but he was waiting expectantly, too.

"We haven't seen each other since we were teenagers. Of course that friendship has changed." No one could expect otherwise, could they?

"Are you still mad at the girl?" his mother asked.

Marcus pinched a pleat in the gold tablecloth his mother always pulled out for their sit-down dinners. Was he mad? Could a grown man stay mad for decades like that?

"No," he said slowly, "but…"

"But you haven't forgiven or forgotten, have you?" His father sighed, as if that was the confirmation of what he'd expected all along. "She hurt you. That's different than losing touch."

Marcus wanted to argue. Adults were supposed to have thick skins, to be tough enough not to let things get to them.

"I needed her, and she wasn't there," Marcus said.

Because if he couldn't admit his true emotions to his parents, who could he trust?

This time, he ignored the glance his parents shared. "Can I have a piece of cake to take home, Mama?"

Her slow grin eased some of the awkwardness he was experiencing about confessing his feelings.

"Two slices, one for you and one for Zeke," his mother said as she stood to serve up his to-go request.

"Got some good news today," Marcus said, reminded of the whole reason he'd been looking forward to this particular meeting with his parents. "We're going to sign a contract with Impact, the home remodeler and house flipper, for a guaranteed number of residential projects annually. We still need to negotiate the terms, but the owners are happy with my plans and our installations." He straightened his shoulders. That contract was real, measurable success that contributed to the long-term growth of Southern Florida Landscape Design.

Their reaction was gratifying. The whoops might have alarmed the neighbors, but how his dad clapped his hand on his shoulder and his mother hugged his neck were exactly what Marcus wanted. He wanted them to be proud of him. He wanted them to have faith in his success.

"My baby boy, a real honest-to-goodness business entrepreneur," his mother said as she put her hand on his head.

Like she had when he was six and bouncing in his chair at the dinner table.

She'd been the one who asked him to re-evaluate going into business for himself, but when he'd moved forward without her approval, she'd come around and supported him however she could. His parents had done the same thing when he'd enlisted. They'd been afraid, but they hadn't left him alone.

Seeing their pride made him feel as vulnerable as that six-year-old he'd once been.

So far, they'd had a good night. No one was annoyed, and his mother had not mentioned finding a date or eligible singles at her church.

Maybe setting up Mr. Brooks was keeping her occupied.

"Okay," Marcus said as he stood, "that's my cue to leave." He took the container his mother had placed near his elbow. "Unless you're going to let me load the dishwasher."

His mother waved her hands. "Not this time. Go get some rest."

That was her answer every time.

Marcus had almost made it all the way to freedom when his father said, "Something you can do for me, son." He waited until Marcus agreed. It didn't matter what the request was. There was no way Marcus would say no. His father draped his arm over his mother's shoulders. "Give some thought to how friendships can change. Other than dying out, I mean."

Watching his mother giggle like a schoolgirl was uncomfortable.

"Your mama and I were classmates, fairly good friends, until senior year. Can't point to what it was exactly, but everything changed." His father held up his hand and wiggled his wedding band. "And that change made everything better. Couldn't have taken the steps I did or built this life we have without that change."

Marcus propped one hand on his hip as he worked to decipher exactly what they were saying.

Were they encouraging him to view Cassie as a woman…a woman he would date, fall in love with and marry? He tried to rub away the frown, but his forehead kept wrinkling.

"'Night, Mama, Daddy." He escaped into the breezeway between the apartments and did not look at the Brooks apartment as he walked by.

He'd had a good dinner and shared the good news about his business with his parents.

Though they'd gotten the last word in and left him plenty to think about.

Because there was no way he'd be able to forget their suggestion that he take another look at Cassie, the woman he'd just met but had known forever.

CHAPTER SEVEN

ON THURSDAY, CASSIE watched the Preston Bank teller she'd been talking to finish up with the customer who'd walked into the Bayfront Tower lobby location. All in all, she'd been impressed with what she had seen of the executive offices. She'd asked to spend some time downstairs to ditch her escort, a nice guy who had the number of Preston Bank locations, employees and small-business loans memorized and ready to quote at the drop of a hat. He'd worked his way up from teller over the course of twelve years, so he had a lot of stories to share—all of them positive about Preston Bank, its managers and the family at the top.

She'd spent the better part of a day interviewing Brent Preston's coworkers, and all she had to show for it were several recordings to transcribe and admittedly sparse notes. The teller she'd locked in on, Michelle, was young, smart and beautiful. The easy way she and the other tellers conversed between serving customers made Cassie believe they liked each other. No secrets about who to avoid here.

"So you said you started here a year ago," Cassie said as she flipped back through her notebook. "Have you thought much about what the next step in your career is?"

If Michelle was ambitious, she'd be careful to understand how to operate within the bank's structure.

"Thanks to the educational reimbursement program the bank offers, I'll finish my degree in a year. Then I'll have the background I need to apply for one of the loan-officer positions." Michelle pointed at the branch manager's office. "Kina thinks that I'll be good at the sales piece that's part of that, working with realtors to find first-time home buyers, that kind of thing."

Cassie jotted down a note to ask Brent about management training at the bank. Michelle's story was common. More than once, an employee had told Cassie about a manager seeing potential in them and encouraging them to aim higher in the bank.

"Preston Bank must be a good place to work if you're planning your next step here," Cassie said as she very carefully did not look up with a pointed, interrogative stare like a detective might.

"Yeah, it's a good place. Being family-owned makes a difference. Plus, they're local, the branches are all in southern Florida, so it's easy to identify the community the bank serves. The pay and benefits are competitive. I like that they've invested in my future." Michelle shrugged. "It's a good job. I came here from waiting tables and took a pay cut to have the regular hours, but now I'm making more and I'll have a degree."

It did sound like Preston Bank invested in its employees. That seemed rare these days.

Cassie chewed her thumbnail as she evaluated and tossed out any follow-up questions. Michelle was a dead end. Another customer entered the bank and Michelle greeted them, so Cassie waved her notepad and mouthed *Thank you*.

Determined to make some progress on the story, Cassie returned to the executive lobby and asked to see Jane Wynn. She'd been the only Preston Bank employee who had given off any disgruntled vibe. The receptionist called to see if she was available and then said slowly, "Ms. Wynn has no extra time for Brent Preston's special projects today." Then, even the cool, superior receptionist winced and whispered, "Sorry."

Cassie inwardly winced. Disgruntled vibe, indeed. "Okay, I'll call and make an appointment. Could you point me to the closest restroom?"

Maybe she could stall there until other inspiration hit. Cassie didn't want to lose this opportunity to snoop around.

The receptionist motioned with her head. "That hallway, on your right."

As she opened the door to the restroom, Cassie was immediately impressed with the difference between the building's public restroom and the executive level's. Gleaming wood paneling lined an anteroom with a cushy couch and two plump armchairs. When she paused, barely-there strains of classical music added to the atmosphere. Were all management bathrooms like this?

Curious to see the rest of the setup, Cassie moved over to the archway that led to the sinks where she could see a massive floral arrangement. Were those fresh flowers?

She paused when she saw the reflections of two women, their heads bent close together in the universal sign of "juicy gossip exchange in progress."

If she strained, she might be able to...

"Has Brent seen the plans yet?" the petite blonde asked. "If we move forward without his okay, this could be a mess. We do not want a mess."

The brunette shook her head. "Not when there's so much on the line. I need this job here."

The blonde nodded. "If only the possible payout wasn't so huge, having Brent owing us."

"I've got a few options for him to choose from. I'm going to drop them on his desk while Jane's out for lunch." The brunette checked over her shoulder for any company and Cassie cringed further back. "She's too suspicious. I'm not sure how we've managed this far without her catching on, but we're too close to the big day to get sloppy now."

When they both turned toward the mirror to check makeup and hair, Cassie had the feeling her time had run out. Next, they'd be coming her direction to leave, so she carefully shifted the handles of her tote on her shoulder and tiptoed to the beautiful, heavy door. Once she was back out in the hallway, she took a deep breath and resumed normal activity, hurrying past the receptionist with a wave and pretending everything was completely normal until she was outside on the sidewalk.

The bathroom scene had been exactly the kind of conversation she'd hoped to stumble upon, but the details were still so sketchy. There was something happening in the bank that Jane was not aware of and they wanted to keep it that way. The Chief Financial Officer was out of the loop and that fit their plans, reassured them that their jobs were safe for now...

Was that enough smoke to convince her editor to start hunting for the fire at Preston Bank?

Mulling over the conversation she'd overheard, Cassie made a beeline for the ocean. Staring at water might inspire a creative idea on where to go next.

If it didn't, at least she'd still be sitting next to the ocean.

Cassie decided to head for the palm-lined bay walk that took her past her favorite smoothie place. "No skipping lunch today, Miss Shirley," she murmured before sipping her large banana-grape-kiwi-spinach-pineapple-mango drink with an extra shot of some kind of *superfood* seeds. Delicious, but violently green, which should convince everyone it was healthy.

The wide-open space of the shaded bay walk was quiet, but she could hear kids shouting nearby. Green grass sprawled on one side, and the expanse of the ocean covered the other. Not even the inconvenience of her notebook and the small laptop she carried when she interviewed for stories weighed her down.

Cassie was looking for the perfect bench to finish her lunch and zone out with the waves, when she spotted Jane Wynn.

Who had apparently found the perfect bench with the same plan in mind. Her smoothie was a deep purple. That alone convinced Cassie it was less healthy but more delicious than her own.

"Is this why you couldn't talk to me this

morning?" Cassie asked as she dropped the tote that had been digging into her shoulder onto the bench. "Too busy?"

Jane closed her eyes. "Who told you how to find me? I've been careful not to let anyone know where I was going. My secret's out." Then she pointed at the drink. "Did you go with a superfood, too?"

Cassie held up her lunch as if it was a trophy. "I did. I feel very virtuous right now."

Jane pointed at the bench. "You're here. Might as well tell me what you need."

Cassie slid onto the bench. When she'd asked to speak to Jane, she'd had no motive except to build their connection. When Cassie interviewed people for stories, they always started out stiff, nervous, a little worried about what they should say. She knew how to ease that. Funny stories of her own usually worked. Showing her interviewees that she was as much of an outlier as they were and totally unconcerned about it loosened them up.

Jane, on the other hand, gave the impression of being a woman who had everything together.

"I was only going to stick my head in to say hello. I know you don't have a lot of time for chitchat." Cassie sipped her drink and stared out over the dark water at the edge of the bay walk. Zoning out here could be so simple. If Jane didn't want to talk, zoning out together could build the bridge Cassie needed for a scoop.

As soon as she thought that, Cassie froze. A scoop? As though she was building a friendship to manipulate someone into giving her information.

"Did you get a bad chia seed?" Jane asked before laughing. "The look on your face right now."

Cassie cleared her throat. "Yes. Superfoods are dangerous."

They both stared out at the water for a minute.

"Brent Preston as a high-school student." Jane didn't turn her way as she spoke. Was she trying to convince Cassie that whatever was coming next was unimportant? "Tell me about that."

Cassie set her smoothie on the bench. Should she assume Jane would want to hear about the golden boy of Sawgrass High, or should she go with the truth?

"Well, he was Mister Popular. Quarterback,

played basketball, good student. All the girls loved him," Cassie said.

"Even you?" Jane asked.

If Cassie needed to prove her credibility as an awkward person, this would do it. "Especially me. All those movies where the nerd pines for the jock and has the fairy-tale makeover so that he sees her inner beauty that was there all along and falls in true, deep, everlasting love?" Cassie sighed. "That was me… without the makeover and the happy ending."

Jane faced her this time and wrinkled her nose. "Uh oh."

"Now? It's easy to laugh about it." Cassie shrugged. "My version of the makeover never came, so I had this idea to rescue Brent by planning our senior prom. It was the class president's responsibility, but Brent…" How could she say this without telling the whole truth?

"He's not great with responsibility," Jane said flatly. "He is very good at getting other people to do the heavy lifting, shall we say?"

Was she referring to herself?

"Exactly. It was a scramble, but I learned a valuable lesson. Brent Preston was never going to fall for my inner beauty. Which was fine. Because it was a lot easier to see him as he was, a charmer without much substance." Cassie wanted to scrutinize Jane's face closely to determine the impact of her words. Was Jane doing some pining of her own for Brent? Or was this a professional venting about a typical, clueless boss?

The urge to test either by asking questions about the dynamics at Preston Bank was strong. The ethical implications were still… undecided.

"Yet you're still here, saving him from his latest bit of responsibility." Jane brushed her long, dark hair over her shoulder. "He has a real knack for pulling that off, doesn't he?"

The urge to confess her plan to find a source inside the bank for Dan's story via planning the reunion was strong, but Cassie wasn't sure what that would do to her chances of convincing Jane to confide in her.

Honestly, at this point, she didn't want Brent to find out that Cassie had turned the tables to use him. He might tell her to stop organizing the reunion.

Cassie didn't want to lose the built-in excuse to talk to Marcus, either.

"This time, I offered to help because I want to reconnect with friends. I can't leave something important like this in Brent's hands." Cassie tried to inject a kernel of the truth, hoping that it might ease her concern about her motives.

Jane didn't answer that but stared hard at the drink in her hands.

"It's sort of like if you have a job you like or even coworkers who depend on you, you step up to do things that aren't technically your job because if they don't get done, a lot of people will be hurt." Cassie realized that fueled a lot of her decisions: jumping in because she could, and other people would be hurt if she didn't. If she was right, she and Jane had that in common.

But that didn't mean taking care of things that weren't their responsibility didn't become annoying sometimes.

"I get that. It's good I work next to a park with a view of the water though." Jane shook her cup. "And superfoods can't hurt."

Cassie crossed her legs as she tried to find something encouraging to say. She'd come down to the water for the same reason Jane had. Cassie wasn't sure what questions Jane was asking herself, but she was hoping the ocean would have the answers. "Sometimes it helps to remember that bad days don't last forever." She sipped her drink. "My mom used to tell me that." Cassie had held on to that with both hands some days.

"Yeah, I—" Jane shook her head. "You're right. I'm good at my job. The fact that my boss is oblivious to anything but his own agenda is frustrating, but it's not a reason to quit."

Cassie schooled her features carefully. Brent had an agenda? If Jane was talking about quitting…

"You fell for him at sixteen, when you could be forgiven for bad decisions." Jane patted her chest. "I had to wait until I was thirty-three and working for the man." Before Cassie could commiserate with how Brent could sneak in under a woman's defenses, Jane added, "And it would all be okay if he'd go back to ignoring me. But no, Brent turns to me, the closest woman around, to present a fake date. I have to go to a high-school re-union that isn't even mine because I couldn't figure out how to say no when he asked me to be his plus-one." Confusion was written all over her face. "Why would I say yes? High-school reunions are terrible even when they're your own."

Cassie tilted her head back and laughed, grateful to have bonded over the only tie between them. "Well, I'll be there. I'll make sure we have good food." Cassie gestured to the ocean with her almost empty drink. "I'm looking for positivity here."

Jane's grin was a relief. Cassie had managed to accomplish something today.

The alarm on Cassie's phone went off. She grumbled as she dug through her tote to turn it off.

"Duty calls?" Jane asked.

"Yes, I have to get out to Concord Court to do interviews for another story." Cassie sighed. "But I should download the interviews I did at the bank first."

Jane nodded. "What do I owe you for keeping my secret bench a secret?"

The question burned on the tip of Cassie's tongue. *Do you know anything about rumors of loan fraud at Preston Bank?*

But she wasn't certain Jane would answer honestly. Was she mixed up in the fraud? Had she gotten involved fully aware of what she was doing or had her involved been a mistake that she'd only recently discovered. Maybe she was the whistleblower. How would she weigh a news story exposing problems there?

"You mentioned quitting. That was only because of your feelings for Brent, right? Everything else is good at the bank?" There. She was doing her duty to Dan's story without burning her connections.

"Pretty good," Jane muttered. "Coworkers are nice and professional, the bank and its assets are well managed—too conservative now and then, but solid overall." She shrugged. "I'll wait. Burn out doing favors for Brent to settle in comfortably, I guess."

"In ten years or so, jump in to take over whatever the former class president is supposed to do then. It's the best inoculation."

Jane's lips were twitching as she met Cassie's grin.

"You can trust me. I'll never reveal your bench to anyone." Cassie waved as she grabbed her tote. "See you soon." That was true. She'd have a chance to decide where her ethical boundary line was the next time she met with Jane. She had until the reunion.

Her reconnection to Marcus.
Her conversation with Jane.
The stories she was building for *Miami Beat*.
There was a lot riding on Cassie's shoulders.

CHAPTER EIGHT

MARCUS BRUSHED THE dirt off his knees as he stood to stretch. No matter how often he worked on the plantings at Concord Court, he was left with such a sense of accomplishment. He owed the place so much, and being able to do what he loved to pay some of that back was a blessing. When he'd left the Air Force, coming home had seemed straightforward. He could stay with his parents until he found a job and knew where he wanted to live.

But what kind of job had been the first hurdle to jump.

Being unable to clear that hurdle had left him sleeping in his old bedroom under his mother's worried stare until he'd buckled under the pressure and taken the advice of the kind grandmotherly lady at the employment agency. She'd given him a photocopy of a newspaper story about Concord Court, a bridge townhome community for veterans transitioning back to being civilians.

That one conversation had changed his life.

"You on your own today?" Sean Wakefield asked as he paused outside the Court's office. Wind stirred the flags forming a backdrop for the office building—the US flag, the state's flag and one for each branch of US military service.

"Yeah, I'll be back here with the crew next week to mow and clean up, but I wanted to put in color around the pool and the office. Thought it was going to be a quick job, but I got carried away. I love putting in annuals and refreshing perennials in the springtime." Marcus pointed to the new flowers. "Good to remind everyone the seasons do change around here before the heat gets too intense."

Sean stepped up next to him. "Red. I like red."

Marcus smiled at the guy who'd become a good friend in his two years at Concord Court. Sean was in charge of construction, repairs and the grounds at the court. He'd served, and he understood some of the challenges most veterans experienced as they came through.

But he didn't know a thing about plants.

"Red…" Marcus gestured at one option. "These reds? That's scarlet salvia. Good with sunshine and heat, attracts butterflies. The other red one, with the yellow tips, that's blanketflower. Should be low-to-no maintenance. Good for gardeners like you." Marcus clapped Sean on the shoulder.

Sean grunted. "That's what we have you for. Butterflies are good. What about bees? I heard they were in trouble." When Marcus paused, studying Sean's face to see if the guy was legitimately asking about pollinators and their health, Sean shrugged. "I watch the news," he muttered.

"And bees. Also, you know who else loves red?" Before Sean could give him the goofy answer that Marcus knew was brewing, Marcus said, "Hummingbirds. The purpley-blue ones are mistflower."

"What do they attract?" Sean asked.

"Me. I like them." Marcus laughed at Sean's snort. "Glad you'll be able to answer any questions that come up about Concord Court's new plantings. Make sure everyone knows that these plants are natives." He moved to gather up his tools as a car pulled in behind.

One glance brought him all the way around to watch Cassie slide out of her car. No suit today. That was a good thing. The suggestion of his father's that he should consider how his old friendship with Cassie might change instead of disappearing popped up at the oddest times.

He'd evaluated it, decided dating Cassie would be a colossal mistake—she'd let him down once already when he'd needed her more than he knew—and thought that was it.

But his brain wouldn't let it go.

His plan had been to finish early and get to his townhome before she got here. He'd lost track of time when he was playing in the dirt.

"Why does the look on your face tell me you know who this is?" Sean murmured.

Marcus didn't have time to answer that or to tell him to be cool before Cassie stepped up onto the sidewalk. This time, he knew better than to check his breath. Zeke still hadn't let that go.

"Hey, Marcus. I'm here to talk to Brisa Montero about the business lab for *Miami Beat*."

He watched her yank the tote that had to weigh half as much as she did over her shoulder.

"Good. I can show you in, introduce you."

He coughed as he noticed how Sean was watching them. "We should get together soon to talk about progress and the budget for decorations. I need to get out to the nurseries early next week to see what's available."

She nodded, but Sean interrupted as he stepped forward, his hand held out. "My friend here has lost his manners. I'm Sean Wakefield. I work here with Brisa." Marcus didn't appreciate that her slow grin matched Sean's lazy smile.

"He's also in love with Brisa's sister," Marcus said, "so there's that."

Cassie's expression didn't change, but the gleam in Sean's eyes told Marcus he might have revealed more than he meant to.

"Let me take you into the office," Sean said as he motioned over his shoulder. "This guy needs to get out of the sun. Also, a nap or some food. Does he seem cranky to you?"

Cassie's giggle reminded him of the way he'd been able to hear it over the crowds that filled the hallways of Sawgrass High. If Brent Preston had said or done anything she could applaud, Cassie acknowledged it, her smile flashing.

Had she ever giggled like that over him?

Marcus couldn't remember, but he did know how her real laughter sounded through to his soul.

"Could I stop by after this is over?" Cassie asked and dug her feet in to halt Sean's urging her inside. "We could make a plan for what to do next." She shifted her tote again. "About the reunion, I mean."

Marcus dropped the hand trowel he'd been using and took that pause to think.

What else could she be talking about, other than the reunion?

Surely Cassie hadn't been shooting down wild ideas about the two of them…doing anything else. Had his father planted that seed in her brain, too?

"Fine. Absolutely. For sure." Marcus pointed over his shoulder. "I live there." His townhome was on the back side of the complex, the first row of houses completed in the early days of construction.

"Will your truck be parked in front?" Cassie pointed at his truck, the bright red one emblazoned with the company's tree logo. It would be impossible to miss.

Getting around the awkward embarrassed lump in his throat took some work, but he managed to say "Yes. Back there." He pointed again. Was he afraid she'd forgotten so soon?

Luckily, Cassie nodded and let Sean usher her inside. Marcus closed his eyes to shake off the creeping embarrassment. If he ever did decide to pursue Cassie or any other woman, he was going to have to step up his game. It hadn't progressed much past his teenage years, where he'd needed a strong nudge to the ribs to understand a girl was into him.

Sad. Also, Sean was going to give him such grief if he didn't hurry home.

Marcus immediately dropped the hand trowel again.

When Sean stepped back out of the office, he clapped his hands. "I knew it would happen. It gets us all sooner or later, but I was beginning to fear you were going to beat the odds. Glad she finally showed up."

Marcus carefully stored his tools in the locked toolbox in the back of the truck and tossed the trash he'd picked up in the bag. Nothing left behind. That was the way Southern Florida Landscape Design would always do business. Come, make everything more beautiful than before and leave nothing else behind. That had been Zeke's policy when

Marcus started on one of the lawn crews, and it was good. No cigarette butts. No empty drink bottles. No wrapping or plastic containers from planting. No complaints.

"Are you trying to ignore me?" Sean asked in a scandalized voice. "You know that will never work."

Marcus sighed because he was right. Sean would keep poking until he got the answers he wanted. The guy was a great friend, but he was even better at pushing buttons.

"She's an old friend. Cassie needed some help planning our high-school reunion." *Because she's been in love with the school's golden boy since then.* He wasn't going to say that. It would make him sound like he cared. "In exchange, she's going to do a write-up about my business and the Concord Court business lab. She works for *Miami Beat*."

Sean tipped back on his heels as he absorbed the information. "Good website. I like to read this one column. Off Beat is the name. It's usually about characters around town. There was one about a pediatrician that dresses in superhero costumes and requires his staff to do the same. Can you imagine going into that office as a kid? The pictures were amazing."

Marcus propped his hands on his hips. "I don't know for sure, but if I had to bet this truck, I'd say that's Cassie's column." He wasn't sure how he knew, but there was no doubt in his mind that that was a job she would love and excel at, do whatever she could to keep. That pediatrician's story was one that would catch Cassie's attention. She'd always jumped in with both feet for anyone who loved kids, animals and underdogs.

It also was unsurprising that she'd have fans or that Sean, one of the best guys he'd ever met, would be one of them. They both had good hearts.

As expected, Sean's excitement was over-the-top. "What? No way! I didn't recognize her from the photo next to her column." He tilted his head to the side. "Could be the glasses, like an alter ego."

"I'm going to take a shower while I can." Marcus pulled open the driver's-side door. "Make sure she knows you're a fan. She'd appreciate the boost." There was something about the way Cassie talked about her job that made him think she didn't get enough recognition, especially from her father.

"Oh, I will, and I'll put in a good word for you." Sean blinked innocently.

"Don't." Marcus wanted to make it clear how firmly he meant that, but it would only fuel the fire.

Sean crossed his arms over his chest, prepared to wait.

"We aren't anything but old friends, not anymore. She stayed here. I joined the Air Force. She hated that and made it clear. Then, she pops back up when she needs help because of a silly crush she shouldn't have had at eighteen, much less now." Marcus made himself stop talking. Apparently, he was keeping all of that too close to the surface.

Sean inhaled slowly. "Well."

Marcus hoped that would be the end of the conversation, but he wasn't shocked that Sean leaned into the truck window after he shut the door. "I hear what you're saying. I also hear some of what you're not saying. She let you down. That's bad. I shouldn't have been so nice. I'll stop reading her column if that's what you want."

His lips were twitching when Marcus looked up. "No, you won't."

Sean chuckled. "No, I won't. But what I will do is tell you a story about a ridiculous mistake I made when I was young that I don't want anyone to remind me of because I hate that it hurt people." He frowned. "But I've grown. Matured. Almost as if that's what people do."

Marcus tightened his hands on the steering wheel and refused to acknowledge that he was understanding the moral of Sean's not-story.

He and Cassie had both been young then. She'd wanted what was best for him, but she'd gone about it the wrong way. It happened. It could be forgiven, even.

That didn't mean he should forget it and pursue…more with her.

"Just saying, she's cute." Sean stepped back. "Definitely cute enough to consider building a bridge to get over that past hurt." Then he held up his hand to wave with a big, cheesy grin.

Because he knew how annoying he was.

And how right.

Marcus was still shaking his head when he made it inside his town house and cranked on the shower. Hot water billowed out. It might wash away Sean's words, but Marcus doubted it.

That was the danger. Not ending a good friendship, but falling headfirst into love.

The steam of the shower snapped Marcus to attention. How long had he been standing there, staring at the question of dating Cassie but trying not to see it?

He had to hurry.

He'd get dressed and do some investigation. Her column at *Miami Beat* was important to her. If he understood more about her job, he could understand the new Cassie better.

Which was an essential part of working with anyone and had nothing to do with checking out a smart, kind and attractive woman to see if they might have things in common.

He wasn't going there with Cassie, but the urge to discover more about who she was now wouldn't be ignored.

CHAPTER NINE

WHEN BRISA MONTERO slammed to a stop in front of the Concord Court office, Cassie had to wait for the golf cart to quit rocking before she stepped out. The place was bigger than Cassie had expected, so having a ride that could zip up on sidewalks and whiz between buildings to check out the property had been exciting. Taking proper notes about all of Brisa's plans for the future of the Court and the veterans it supported had been impossible while the cart was in motion. Thank goodness she'd been recording the whole time.

"I've never heard of a bridge community like Concord Court before. Are there others in Miami?" Cassie smoothed back the hair that had been blown out of her ponytail and followed Brisa into the office she'd only seen for a minute before the golf cart roller coaster.

"Not like this, no, but there are similar places around the country." Brisa motioned at her computer. "A quick search shows they come in different shapes and sizes, but there are places specifically built to assist veterans in adjusting to their new lives. Here in Miami, vets can find support groups and employment counselors, specialty rehab and long-term care for older veterans, but my father wanted to build a place that did more. Two years to stay here and find the right fit, instead of having to take whatever job you can find. These vets are the kind of employees companies should be recruiting, but it can be a struggle to translate military experience to civilian skills." Brisa's hands never stopped moving as she talked, Cassie noticed. She was so striking, it was hard to look away.

"Some know exactly what they want to do. Others need to experiment. Mira Peters wanted to teach, but she needed to finish her degree. Concord Court gave her two years to do that without the struggle of also working to pay for rent. Wade McNally is a trauma surgeon. He had a job already lined up and would have had no trouble financially, but he's also got a family that needs time to adjust to his new life. We're learning to support them, too." Brisa straightened in her seat.

"There are so many things these veterans deserve. Job counseling and coaching were the first things we added, beyond our physical- and mental-health support team. I'm not short on ideas, just hours in the day to get them all done."

Cassie looked down at the bulleted list of services she'd managed to jot down. It was impressive. "And the small-business lab in the works?"

Brisa nodded. "Yes. That's a good story. It shows how veterans who come through Concord Court can contribute to the place. Marcus Bryant was Air Force. But, coming back here, he wasn't sure what he wanted to do, so he needed to research. Experiment. Ask himself where he wanted to put his talent and time. One of the rules here we have here is work or school. You have to do one or the other. He's an overachiever, so he did both, working on lawn crews and taking courses at the same time. Putting those things together reminded him of how much he loved drawing and planning spaces." She shrugged.

"The next logical step? For him, it was to start a small business, but that's not something they teach at our local university. I listened to him talk about business licenses and loans and marketing and so many details that were standing between him and being successful at what he loved." Brisa held her hands out as if to say *Voilà!* "Thus, the business lab was born. Connecting small businesses and supporting them with those details will benefit them all."

Cassie made notes as she listened, but it hit her over and over how little she knew about what veterans went through when they left the military and came home. War movies and news stories about returning soldiers formed her understanding of what military life was like, but as she listened to Brisa list the kinds of small businesses that were springing up now, it was impossible to ignore the multitude of different jobs and outlets serving in the United States military covered.

She'd never been far from home, or from her father and their caring neighbors.

And still, Cassie had struggled to find the job that fit her.

So she understood how critical Concord Court's support could be to create stable futures for these men and women who had sacrificed so much.

"What you're doing here is amazing," Cassie said. "What can the community do to support Concord Court? If you could ask for one thing, what would it be?"

Brisa pursed her lips as she thought. "We will always need volunteers who have the time to help the veterans or their families, and donations to support the programs we want to build. Like every other nonprofit, we're pushing to expand both things. But even simpler than that, I'd say hire a veteran. Big employers, small businesses and the average person who might need a website or an accountant or lawn care. Each one of these veterans has been trained to be the best, and I've learned over and over that when you give them a shot, they will beat your expectations. Concord Court will work hard to make the connection."

Cassie closed her notebook. "Every organization needs a spokesperson like you." It was amazing what they were doing here. Hearing Brisa Montero—who had previously been famous in Miami circles for her beauty, bad marriages and spending her father's money— speaking so compassionately and analytically about the veterans' needs and solutions was impressive.

"Why do I have the feeling we both know I've come a long way?" Brisa asked with a sunny grin. "Concord Court has a way of bringing out the best in people. That's why it matters so much to me. I've needed a lot of friends to get here."

Cassie added *down to earth* to her mental description of Brisa.

"I'll put the website and the phone number in the write-up." Cassie took one of Brisa's cards.

"Great," Brisa said as she turned to her computer. "I'd love it if you could include a quote from one of the veterans. Let me look up Marcus's email. He's been here since the beginning, so he could give you a great perspective, too."

Cassie cleared her throat. Should she go along and pretend she needed the information or…

Brisa glanced at her from the corner of her eye. "What?"

"I know Marcus. He's the one that prompted me to start the story on Concord Court." Cassie tried to keep all emotion under control and off her face, but she wanted to squirm under Brisa's careful study. "Actually, his mother bragged about all he was doing with Concord Court's assistance."

Brisa swiveled to face Cassie fully. "Interesting. Very interesting." Then she propped her chin on her hands, obviously ready for the rest of the story.

"We grew up as neighbors. Same apartment complex. Our parents are still there, so when I run into his mother, she tells me the news," Cassie said and fiddled with the spiral on her notebook.

"Neighbors." Brisa blinked innocently. "High-school sweethearts?"

Cassie laughed at the breathless anticipation in Brisa's voice.

"No, I wasted most of high school waiting for Brent Preston to fall for my wonderful personality. Marcus was my best friend. He put up with a lot, believe me." Cassie cringed. "The poor guy had more patience than I deserved, but I like to believe it was good training for dealing with his landscaping customers."

"Brent Preston," Brisa said slowly. "I mean, he's handsome, but not the sharpest, you know? I dated him for a stretch, and I don't think you missed much. I honestly can't remember the details." Brisa wrinkled her nose. "You've grown since high school, right?"

"In regard to crushes, yes," Cassie said firmly.

"Good," Brisa said as she raised her eyebrows. "Because when it comes to Marcus… watch out!" She pointed dramatically to punctuate her words. "Every time I see him, I search my brain for the right match. He's so good-looking, smart, funny. I wasn't there to guide you when you were a teen, but I am here now. Do not overlook Marcus Bryant."

Cassie opened her mouth to say…something, but she was lost as to what that would be.

Time to make an exit.

"Are you single, Cassie?" Brisa asked slowly. "Because I happen to know that Marcus is single, much to his mother's disappointment. He's weakening under my gentle attempts to set him up. I will win soon." One corner of her mouth curled up, as if she was laying out a tempting offer.

Cassie chuckled. "We have a bumpy history, Brisa. If you can find another option, I'm sure he'd be more receptive."

Brisa sniffed but finally waved her hand as if she was tossing in the towel for this round. Cassie wondered if that meant she was going to regroup and try a different angle.

"I'm headed over to talk to Marcus about this high-school reunion we're planning." *For Brent, so that I can investigate his company and write up an exposé.*

Cassie had a feeling she could trust Brisa with that information. Something about her inspired trust and immediately improved Cassie's mood, but she wasn't sure how much more she wanted to talk about Marcus with someone who called him a friend and had matchmaking in mind.

"I'm hoping I can write up a story on Concord Court for the About Miami section and then have a profile of Marcus in my usual column of interesting people." Cassie dropped her notebook into her bag and moved to sling it over her shoulder. "I appreciate your time. As soon as I know how much space my editor will give me, I'll come back with the photographer to get some shots. I'll call you to set up a time."

Brisa stood to walk her out of the office. "Great. We've only scratched the surface. If you're ever short on stories, I know plenty of interesting people."

Cassie laughed. "I bet."

"Did the caterer I suggested work out?" Brisa asked. Cassie's first call to set up this interview had netted three names she might be able to book for the reunion: a caterer, a DJ and a carpenter who might be available to do odd jobs. "She did our New Year's Eve party. Everything was good, but her barbecue sliders are delicious."

"I called all three and booked the DJ. The caterer and I haven't decided the menu, but I am definitely looking forward to the tasting she's setting up. I'll be sure to try the sliders."

As Cassie went to get into her car, Brisa muttered under her breath, "Marcus will be so mad at me."

Uncertain that she'd heard correctly, Cassie stopped.

Brisa bit her lip and then began to plead her case. "I'm the local matchmaker, a busybody who likes to set her friends up. And I'm good at it." She waggled her eyebrows. "I hear what you're saying about you and Marcus and the past. How do you feel about lawyers-in-training? Peter Kim will be one of the good ones, and if we don't get him a match, he'll never let me live it down. Would you be interested? So many great men around here."

"That begs the question why you haven't set yourself up," Cassie answered.

Brisa's face scrunched up adorably. "I would include my boyfriend as one of the greats around here. Let's have lunch sometime. I'll tell you that whole story. You will laugh, you will cry, you will understand how big my mess-ups can be, and you will know that I've gotten much better at matchmaking since." Her grin was infectious.

Cassie chuckled. She believed that story would be a good one. "For now, no matchmaking needed, thanks. But I'll keep you in mind." Cassie got into her car.

"Do you know where Marcus lives?" Brisa asked. Her faux innocent tone was also adorable.

"I'll find his truck." As Cassie backed out of the parking spot, she knew Brisa was watching. It had been a fun interview. Those usually turned into the best stories. She was sad she didn't have a great community like

Concord Court to go home to. It reminded her of growing up in the apartment complex and leading the pack of roving children with Marcus. They'd had some big adventures.

Finding Marcus's home was easy enough.

Knocking on the door was harder, but Cassie did it. There was no reason to feel awkward about it. She'd interviewed so many strangers. Talking to a friend should be simple, even if it was the first time she'd seen his house. When the door opened, she smiled. "Hey." That was an excellent opening line. Short. To the point.

"Hey." Marcus stared at her for longer than she expected. If this was how the conversation was going to go…

"Come in." He motioned her inside.

The way her heart kicked up speed was concerning, but she wanted to make sure she was the only one who knew it was happening. Small talk was the answer. "I'm glad to get the full tour, including your townhome. In my head, I had pictured squatty little buildings in a compound, built inexpensively and with no style, but Concord Court is exactly the opposite. The wrought iron fence and all the plantings around the pool are gorgeous."

Enough small talk. There was a fine line between pretending to be calm by talking and showing she was definitely not calm by talking too much.

"Brisa was the decorator. Lots of experience with nice things, but I think she also used all that experience to get good deals that matched her style." Marcus crossed his arms over his chest and stood in the center of the room. Was he nervous, too?

She moved to study the photographs grouped above the couch. His furniture was modern but comfortable, dark against the stark white walls. The photos were the only things hanging. Some were landscapes or architecture. "Where is this?" Cassie pointed at a picture of a city. There was a building rising above it with towers on all sides.

Marcus stepped up closer. "Istanbul, in Turkey. That's the Hagia Sophia." He glanced at her as if he was checking to see if she wanted to know more. "This part—" he tapped on the curved dome in the center "—was built in the sixth century. The minarets were added later." He crossed his arms back over his chest. "I didn't get to see the inside, not enough time, but it was awesome to see a building that old, still standing, still being used."

"Wow. So many amazing sights," she murmured as she studied the landscapes.

"I didn't collect many souvenirs, just pictures," Marcus said. "Eventually I got pretty good with the camera, managed to get photos of the places I wanted to remember."

"Big leap for a guy who had never even left his hometown before, I guess," Cassie murmured.

"Some people join up to see the world. I learned to enjoy that along the way." Marcus didn't move any closer.

Why did it bother her to see these snapshots of the life he'd lived while they were apart? For some reason, it brought back the argument they'd had, the last time she'd spoken to him, before he'd left her behind.

Determined not to drag all that up, Cassie moved over to the other photos. "And these guys?"

Marcus shrugged. "Friends. Guys I served with."

Cassie waited for him to add more, but he seemed content with that.

"Are any of them here at Concord Court?"

That was the easiest way she could come up with to ask what had happened to them. Cassie had spent time over the years worried about his safety. She'd never said anything to his mother or father about those worries, but with every Marcus update, she'd been reminded that he'd chosen a life that put him in danger.

"No, most are still in. I was the old man in the group," he said, his lips curled. "It's good to be around guys my own age here. Easier to keep up on the morning runs, too."

One quick glance was all she allowed herself to confirm that with the breadth of his shoulders and the power of his biceps, there was nothing physically that Marcus would struggle with, not even jogging with younger guys.

"Is it okay with you if we sit outside on the patio? It's my favorite spot." Marcus moved into his kitchen. "I've got tea and water."

"Tea," Cassie answered as she noticed his laptop was open. Her smiling face in the top-left corner told her it was the *Miami Beat* site, and the page he'd chosen was Off Beat, her space. "Are you reading my columns?" He would have to subscribe to get access to more than three. Maybe he'd searched and landed on this one from six months ago.

"Yeah, that one about the zookeeper who is having cheetah spots tattooed all over his body? It made me wonder how you track these stories down."

"Oh, Leo," Cassie said as she calculated how long it had been since that profile. "A genuine guy with too much love for his job." A year? How many columns had Marcus read?

Marcus held out a glass of iced tea. "Not sure how I could forget that guy's name is Leo."

Cassie tapped her finger to her lip and pretended to mull over the question. "Not sure what name his parents gave him, but it is now legally Leo." She sipped her tea. "And I get suggestions from all over. Interesting people quite often know other interesting people, if you can imagine that. We also have a tip line that sometimes turns up leads."

Which reminded her again of the story she was working on incognito, in a sense.

Marcus motioned for her to follow him. They passed a staircase and a bathroom to reach a sliding glass door to a shaded patio.

"I'm far enough away from the pool that it's nice and peaceful out here, especially in the shady afternoons."

They stepped outside, and Cassie was not surprised to see more modern style in comfortable outdoor chairs and a series of potted plants lining the longest edge of the concrete. She settled and realized some of the awkwardness had eased. This fit her expectation of what Marcus's home would look like.

"How often do you bring your work home with you?" Cassie asked and pointed at a large fern.

Marcus shook his head. "This is rehab only. The fern belongs to Tasha. Her mother-in-law gave it to her, so after she forgot to water it for most of its life, she brought it to me to revive."

"Big brother to the rescue, huh?"

"Always," he said dryly.

Cassie laughed. *Always* was right. He'd kept his sister and brother in line, and the rest of the kids in the apartment complex had followed suit.

"Do you ever get tired of being a hero?" Cassie intended her words to be teasing, a reminder of how often she'd needed him.

"Sometimes," he said before stretching to

grab his glass from the table. "Sometimes it costs more than I want to pay."

Cassie traced a finger in the condensation of her own glass. If she wanted to get her old friend back, she was going to have to find an approach to this subject. "I guess you've lost friends along the way." Her mouth was dry. Was she ready to hear the truth about how much danger he'd been in?

He grunted. "I lost my best friend before I even finished boot camp."

Cassie had to turn his statement over to view it from a couple of different directions before she could guess what he meant. "Are you talking about me?"

"Doesn't matter. It's not important anymore. If you have the budget for decorations, I'll text you after I line up the plants and materials we'll need." Marcus stared out over the courtyard walled on all sides by townhome clusters.

As if that was all he had to say.

The coldness between them had appeared in an instant, and it knocked her off her game. Her whole life she'd struggled with this, with being shut out. When it happened, Cassie could either wear herself out trying to guess what was happening between the lines...

Or walk away.

But if she let this go right now, she might never have another chance to reconnect with Marcus. Her hands shook as she placed her glass carefully on the table. "It does matter. It matters to me." She cleared her throat. "If you're bringing it up now, after all these years, it matters to you, too, despite what you said. So..." Where did she go next? "Tell me. Please."

Marcus rubbed the nape of his neck, still staring out over the patio. Whatever he was going to say, it was important. Cassie tried to prepare herself because his reluctance convinced her it would hurt, too.

"Joining the Air Force wasn't easy. I was afraid, but I needed to do something more meaningful than an introduction to composition and college algebra at that moment. Everyone else in my life—even my mother, who threatened to end it daily unless I remembered to wear a helmet and stop drinking out of water hoses because she wanted to protect me—understood why I joined." He sighed. "And then there was you."

Cassie tangled her fingers together. Distress over the emotion in his voice was sending tremors through them. "I begged you to stay here with me." She had. Her whole life, she'd either won people over with logic or charm or learned to do without. Begging had left her vulnerable, and being vulnerable was scary.

"Okay, but when you didn't get what you wanted, you told me to leave you alone. I could be a hero all by myself. That's what you said. *A hero*." Marcus didn't look at her, but his tone was bitter.

After all these years.

Because she'd hurt him.

When he'd responded with his own hurt, she'd faded away.

Was there any way to excuse herself for that?

All this time, she'd struggled with how he'd ignored her wishes and disappeared so easily from her life. If he'd thought of her as a true friend, he would have...

It was easy to see how her own pain had gotten in the way.

Cassie stood and faced him. "I'm sorry. I..." The lump in her throat choked her. "It's my dad and me, Marcus. I don't have any excuses, really, except..." She had to inhale slowly. "When you lose someone you love, it changes you. It has to. And at eighteen, you were my family. Watching my mom get sick and..." Cassie hated the tears. People tended to back away when the tears came out. "All I could imagine was the overwhelming grief I would feel if you were gone. I didn't want to lose you. I just... I messed up."

She was afraid to see what his expression might be, and she was out of strength to force him to respond, so she tried to smile. "And you still listened to me and agreed to help. Even though it involved ol' Brent. I guess I made you an offer you couldn't refuse." Was it too soon for a joke? Cassie dug around in her tote and pulled out Brent Preston's credit card. "So quick update. I've placed deposits on everything we needed to rent, along with the DJ and the caterer. I'll text you the total remaining for decorations and the name of the carpenter Brisa suggested for whatever projects we come up with. Email your receipts, and we can work independently until the day of setup." She didn't meet his eyes as she backed away. "Signs for your business and lots of business cards. We'll need those. Better not forget."

"Cassie, don't go. There's no need to split up now. We're working together fine," Marcus said. The chair scraped as he stood, and Cassie knew she needed to escape.

"No, this makes more sense. We both have plenty going on. Let me know if you need anything from me." Then she was moving back through his living room and hurrying to her car. She checked in the rearview mirror as she drove away. He hadn't followed her.

The choked noise she made wasn't quite a sob, but she was glad she'd managed to hold it in until she was alone. Controlling her emotions had been the key to a happy home. Her father's grief had pushed her to learn to cope with a sunny smile for his benefit.

Until she was alone.

All this time, she'd been mad and hurt that Marcus had found his new life and left her behind, but it was her fault. She'd hurt the boy who had been a rock for her, and any hope she'd had of getting to know the new Marcus was gone.

Her dad. *Miami Beat*. She still had those. Nothing had changed there.

So why did it feel like her firm, safe footing had dissolved? The threat of falling with no lifeline to catch her was what she'd hated when Marcus had left at eighteen. It hadn't been two whole weeks since she'd surprised him at the library. Why did losing him again so quickly hurt like this?

CHAPTER TEN

MARCUS HAD SPENT a lot of time in the Concord Court's pool area at midnight, especially considering it was off limits according to the rules listed on the sign attached to the fence. The table he and Mira had claimed the first time they'd met in the early days of the Court had served the not-really-a-therapy group that assembled there very well.

Veterans returning home usually had a lot on their minds. Some of them coped with that or insomnia or nightmares or a hundred other things by walking away sleepless nights or talking out their problems. This group picked up members who did both. People wandered into the pool area, and they never left but dropped in and out as needed.

He'd met his best friends around this table.

Some of his best friends. Tonight, the one friend he couldn't stop thinking of was there with him in spirit, too. Marcus wasn't sure he'd get the courage to talk about Cassie, but he needed someone to listen and hopefully untangle his thoughts.

Tonight they had a small group. He and Peter had taken their usual spots, and eventually Sean Wakefield and Wade McNally joined them.

"Reyna must be staying at the station tonight," Peter said to Sean. "You get lonely?"

Sean stretched back in his seat. "I had a feeling someone was going to need my wisdom, so I was bound by duty to answer the call." Then he shrugged. "And Reyna is on duty at the station tonight. I miss her and Dottie." Dottie was the dalmatian with hearing loss that Reyna worked with as part of her duties as a firefighter at the local stationhouse. She was also Sean's second love.

Wade sighed. "I couldn't sleep. My daughter's started hiding bridal magazines around the house. Gets a man thinking." He covered his face with his hands and looked like he could use some uninterrupted sleep.

"She's in elementary school, man," Peter exclaimed and then ducked his head when he realized how loudly he'd said it. "What's with that?"

Marcus shook his head at the incredulous look Peter shot at Wade. Peter had to be the smartest one at the table, but nine times out of ten, he needed extra clues to catch up.

"They're hints that she'd like to see a wedding," Wade said dryly. "She wants a stepmother."

Marcus laughed and some of the knot in his stomach that had tightened with Cassie's departure that afternoon relaxed.

"Oh," Peter said, "Right. That makes sense. Everybody knows it's coming. It's only a matter of when and how you make the proposal worthy of a Montero sister." Peter picked up his open bottle of water. "You can't pop the question as if you were asking her if she wanted to go shopping or on a trip. Monteros are proud...larger than life. They move on a different level."

The silence that met his pronouncement was funny, but Peter was absolutely correct. Wade might not be ready for the truth.

"Tell her to start hiding them in Reyna's town house," Sean grumbled. "My hints don't seem to be working."

Marcus kicked his chair. "Since when are hints your style, Wakefield?" They'd known each other a long time. Subtlety was not Sean's strong suit.

"Ever since I asked her to marry me and she turned so pale I was afraid it was fatal—" Sean picked up his drink "—I stopped asking, thinking gentle suggestions might ease her into it." He scratched at the label on the bottle. "Bridal magazines, you say?"

Wade nodded. "You can have them. I don't stand a chance. My proposal will be Brisa's third. What are the chances I can go bigger than Rich Guy Number One or Two?" Then he cursed out loud. "Correction. I'd be her third husband. Who knows how many actual proposals she's had?"

Marcus decided not to remind Wade of the fake engagement ring Brisa's last boyfriend, the football player, had given her. He didn't need the heartburn.

Silence stretched between them, Sean and Wade focused on their own thoughts.

Marcus and Peter exchanged a look. "Anybody got problems to talk about that are real problems? Not that being in so much love that you know happily ever after is a foregone conclusion isn't hard for you two to carry all on your puny shoulders." Peter rolled his eyes. "Some of us are out here, all alone."

"And some of us are not you, a guy who has a date with a different woman every weekend," Marcus said. "How sad for you."

Peter sniffed. "It's a lot of hard work. I am so busy."

Their low laughter might get them in trouble if anyone heard it, but it felt good.

"What about you, Marcus? How's the business?" Sean asked. No matter how goofy the guy pretended to be, he was the one who could zero in on someone else's worries. It wasn't always easy to talk about the things they discussed here. That's what made this group so important.

"Good. Got a great contract that guarantees projects on house renos for the next year. That makes it easier to look at longer or bigger jobs, not to mention make the garage and truck payments." Marcus slouched in his chair. He'd shared. No one would find it strange if that was all he had to say, but that wasn't what was keeping him up tonight. "Then there's the high-school reunion I'm helping set up. Enchanted garden theme, so it's like free advertising for my business.

Should get some contacts from there. I mean, I went to high school with these folks. That's a pretty solid connection."

Marcus didn't glance across the table at Sean. There was almost no way the guy would let it go, not after meeting Cassie on the sidewalk, but...

"What about Miss Cassie?" Sean asked in a singsong. "Why do I have the hunch that all that stuff—" he motioned vaguely at Marcus's head "—that I can see going on in there is about more than your business's bottom line?"

Wade tilted his head to the side. "Now that you mention it, he's usually the one who observes and comments, but he does appear to be deep in his head tonight." He braced his chin on his hand. "Tell us more about this woman."

Sean replied before he could.

"Old high-school friend. Reconnected to work on the reunion." Sean made the *Go on* motion with his hand. "We're all now on the same page."

Marcus ran a hand across his jaw. "That's pretty much it." Then he closed his eyes. "Except she was…my best friend, and still…" This was the part that had kept him awake.

"You know how there's one person who can absolutely destroy you, rip your heart to shreds?" Marcus asked. All three men nodded. "I didn't know it was her until she did it, and I thought I'd handled how I felt about it, put it in the past and moved on. Then she turned up, after all this time, in the same cheerful, kinda clumsy way she did at eighteen, and that hurt was back. A gross pain in the center of my chest. She doesn't seem to be struggling with that, though. Cassie picked up where we left off, roping me into her scheme to win the attention of the same guy she had a crush on in high school and making it seem so logical, like such an excellent plan to advertise my business, that we fell back into place."

"But you can't do that as easily because of the stuff you're still carrying," Peter said. "What did she do? Stuff you in a locker or something?"

Marcus glared at Peter.

"Am I also the only one at this table that had trouble in high school?" Peter asked before flopping back in his seat to mutter under his breath, "I was a late bloomer."

Marcus hesitated to tell them any more. The questions keeping him awake cascaded in a domino effect. Had he overreacted to her response? Had he been carrying around this baggage for no good reason? If he admitted it aloud and these guys confirmed his suspicions, then he'd also have to deal with the guilt about upsetting her that afternoon.

"Might as well get it off your chest," Sean said.

"You can say anything here. We've all already proven that," Wade added.

Peter agreed. "C'mon, let us help."

It was Peter's encouragement that convinced Marcus. When that guy got serious, everyone paid attention because it was rare.

Marcus inhaled slowly. "Cassie begged me not to go, not to join the Air Force, and said she couldn't talk to me if I did. Our whole lives, we'd been so much the same, but in one afternoon, she became someone else, somebody dramatic and selfish. I couldn't change my plans, even if I wanted to. Since she was my best friend and I was scared about boot camp and failing and leaving home and dying…" Marcus stopped as he heard how loud he'd gotten. "I needed her, and she let me down."

He tried not to fidget as he waited for their comments.

"Sounds familiar. I've tried to forget that terror of the early days. I had to stop calling home. My mother's voice, even if she was talking about the weather…hearing it would choke me up. Last thing I wanted to do was cry in my bunk because I missed my mother, but I missed her." Peter looked up at the dark sky. "Took a long time to earn my way back into her good graces."

Relief settled over Marcus's shoulders to hear someone else admit what loneliness and homesickness could do. Like bring them to their knees.

But it was hard to admit it to each other at the time or to the people at home missing them, worrying for them. It was a pain to hide, to swallow deep.

So Marcus had done that, but it hadn't solved anything.

"Oh, man, that is tough. They don't have any idea what we're going through, but it's almost like she made it about her, instead of you. That would be disappointing from your best friend," Sean said. "What did she say the next time you tried to talk to her?"

Marcus bit his lip. Yeah. That's what he'd expected. In one question, Sean had ripped the bandage off to expose the ugly scar. Marcus had messed up then. Chances were high he'd messed up again that afternoon. "She asked me to help her decorate for our high-school reunion."

The silence at the table should have given him time to brace for impact, but Sean's groan hit him in the abdomen anyway.

"This is classic. You hadn't spoken since that day she asked you not to go. You didn't tell her how it hurt then or two weeks later. You didn't tell her what you thought about her selfishness. You didn't say hello, good-bye or go jump in a lake for years," Sean said. "A miscommunication that should have been cleared up before you finished boot camp, but no, it festers, and instead of years of wedded bliss, you've got baggage."

"Wedded bliss?" Peter asked. "This is where things get interesting."

"We were friends, not in love," Marcus mumbled. It felt important to get the reminder in.

"She said something emotional and hurt-ful. You did something emotional and hurt-ful," Peter said, "but you were eighteen. Kids. Who didn't do that kind of stuff at that age?" He winced. "I hate to say it, but I wouldn't beat myself up over it, M. Kids make mis-takes, and they learn from them." He tapped his chest. "Ask me how I know that. So much experience."

"Is that all there is to it?" Wade asked. "Do you want to clear the air and dump the bag-gage, or are you trying to decide if you want her friendship?"

"Or her friendship and her kisses?" Sean added. "Because I am telling you, I have learned over the past year or so how nice it is if you can have both. That's when you start plotting gentle hints and surprise weddings, when proposing literally turns a woman into a ghost."

"When I mentioned it to her this afternoon, how hurt I was, she left in a hurry." Marcus stretched his legs out, restless in his seat. "I wasn't sure what to say. She had explained how losing her mother as a kid made it hard to see me go. Which makes sense, and I might have eventually figured it out for myself if

I hadn't gotten caught up in my feelings. I guess I'm not sure if it's better to keep poking at this wound or maintain my distance now and let it heal back over." It would be easy enough to simply plan, organize and set up the reunion decorations and leave it at that. Cassie would follow through with all her promises, the story in *Miami Beat* and promoting his business. They didn't have to hurt each other anymore.

But the image of her shooting trash at the can in the park came back so easily, so clearly, like there had been no time lost between when he'd last seen her at eighteen and this week.

"It's been years," Wade said slowly. "If that wound had healed the first time, poking it now wouldn't hurt a bit. That's what healing does, repairs the parts that hurt. Trust me, I'm a surgeon." His lips curled, but he didn't laugh. "Sounds more like you have wounds that won't heal until you clean them up. That's how it works in medicine. I assume it's the same here."

Marcus wiped a hand across his mouth and shot a glance at Peter. "No words of wisdom to add?"

Peter cleared his throat. "Here comes the wisdom. What if she was able to break your heart like that because she was your first love?" He held up his hands as if the men around the table were trying to interrupt him. "Love at eighteen, as I recall, was different. But what if now…you're looking for another Cassie, and there was only ever one of her?"

Peter slumped as if he'd exhausted himself.

Sean whistled quietly. "This guy… Speaks only nonsense until he opens up his mouth and hammers you with the hard questions."

Marcus laughed and said, "That's impossible. Nobody's in love without knowing they're in love." He and Cassie would have known.

The way Wade and Sean snapped to attention shook his certainty.

"The people who are in love?" Wade said. "I don't know if it's always the case, but it's commonly true that they are the last to know, my friend. Ask me how I know that." He tapped his chest just as Peter had.

Marcus would never have guessed all these guys would jump on the *Date Cassie* bandwagon, but if he'd wanted them to put the idea out of his head, they'd let him down.

"Listen, you don't like how things ended

this afternoon. Go talk to her. This opportunity landed in your lap for a reason." Wade tapped the table. "Forget what's down the road or way off in the future. What can you do this weekend to make you both feel better?"

Marcus considered that. "I was going to visit some nurseries, try to track down nice centerpieces that could also work as door prizes. I could get Cassie to come along."

"Excellent idea. Then figure out what comes next." Sean was the last one to stand and scoot his chair under the table.

Everyone was heading for the gate to exit the pool area when Peter added, "If this turns into another love story, I will be the only one all alone."

Sean slung his arm around Peter's shoulder. "No worries. You'll be next. We will apply all our attention to solving your inability to find the right woman. We will spare no effort. We'll call in the big guns, too. Mira could already know how to fix you."

Marcus was laughing as Peter began muttering under his breath again.

Whatever happened next, it felt good to have a plan, Marcus thought. He and Cassie would talk. He'd apologize for his own part in their distance.

And then…

He couldn't fill in that blank, not yet. But the warm feeling that went with the thought of seeing Cassie again made him wonder if Peter had always been this insightful and he just hadn't heard him.

CHAPTER ELEVEN

THE FIRST ORDER of business on Saturday morning was to find Cassie's home address. Marcus had her email address because she'd followed-up and sent him the budget. In the message, she'd included her phone number, in case there were *emergencies*. He wasn't sure she'd agree that needing more time with her, to untangle his mind where she was concerned, qualified. Marcus could call but…

He thought it was important to see her face-to-face to make his case.

After all, she might not agree to see him if he gave her advance warning.

That meant finessing the information out of his mother but without tripping any matchmaking alarms. So after his morning run, he waited until he knew his parents would agree it was an appropriate hour and dialed.

As the phone rang, he played through several casual approaches. "My son. What do you need?" his mother asked instead of putting either of them through the usual greeting and small talk. "I am about to beat your father and Brian at gin rummy. That means your father will agree to dinner at any place of my choosing and Brian will have a blind date with a lovely soprano from the choir. Let's make this quick."

Marcus checked the clock. Nine in the morning, and they were already into a high-stakes game of cards. "So, I'm thinking it'd be good to have Cassie's address." He crossed his fingers that she'd be distracted by her win, rattle it off and not ask questions until much later.

"Yes," she answered.

Nothing else followed.

Marcus pinched the bridge of his nose. There had to be an easier way to do this. "Would you, you know, give it to me?"

She sniffed in response. "I have a policy of protecting the personal information of the people I love, son. You know this. You insist on it, quite loudly at times." If he wasn't mistaken, there was a grin in her voice. It was going to grow.

He heard his father speak. "Is he asking about Cassie?"

As if his parents had already discussed this possibility.

Then there was more muffled whispering as his mother covered the phone with her hand. He tried to wait patiently until he heard Cassie's father say, "Give it to me. I don't have the same policy."

Marcus felt himself immediately straighten in his chair at the long pause that confirmed the phone was changing hands.

"What's this about, Marcus?" Mr. B asked.

The urge to pretend it was reunion business was strong, but he wanted to stick to the truth. "I have some things I need to say to your daughter. I want to say them in person, and then we need to get on with choosing plants." Blunt. Honest. That was Mr. B's style. It could work.

Her father said, "And then?"

Marcus cleared his throat. Everyone was asking the same question. Would he be able to answer it by the end of the day? Not if he didn't get the address. "I want my friend back, sir."

As he said it out loud, Marcus's shoulders

relaxed. Whatever else might happen, this was true. He didn't want to carry the weight of losing her anymore. They might never be the same kind of friends as they once had been, but he and Cassie were a great team.

Everyone could use a friend like Cassie Brooks.

He knew that. And he hoped the reverse was also true.

"Good. Girl needs you around. I'll give it to you. You ask her to stop over here before the reunion next week." Her father rattled off the address and silence followed.

Marcus almost punched the button to end the call, but his mother added, "She does need you around, but not as much as you need her. I am also looking forward to seeing my son dressed up for this party next weekend. You two will be going together, so don't disappoint your mother." Then she was gone.

Just like that. She'd gotten the last word. It was one of many talents she'd been born with.

For some reason, it was a funny quirk that morning instead of a funny irritation. The sun was brighter as he plugged in Cassie's address and made the short drive to a duplex on a residential street. As he parked, he knew exactly why she'd chosen the place. The street dead-ended, and on the other side was a small playground and paved area with a basketball hoop. One pavilion had been built, but there was no table underneath. Not that that would have mattered to Cassie because Marcus could see a half-pipe, a funbox, a roll-in, stairs with railings… She'd found a house with a skate park in the neighborhood.

The duplex had heavy 1970s ranch vibes, with a slightly slanted roof broken by a diagonal offshoot that formed a triangle with the mirrored portion on the structure's other half, long rectangular windows near the roofline and a large plate-glass window next to the front door.

Where Cassie was waiting for him.

The hedges were overgrown, but everything else was neat. Not exciting, but neat. Cassie had a hundred interests, but gardening had never made the list.

She stepped outside onto the small porch and watched him walk up the driveway.

"Did my mother warn you I was coming?" he asked, nervous again.

Cassie said, "Yep, she does that. You have to get her to make a specific promise, or she finds the loophole and does exactly what she wants."

Marcus nodded. "Right. Well, I'm glad I don't have to explain her to you. It's nearly impossible to do."

"Miss Shirley is family. It's not necessary to explain family." Cassie crossed her arms over her chest. "What's up?"

Now that he was here, Marcus was stuck. He didn't know how to begin to address what was between them.

To buy time, he bent down to pinch shriveled blooms off the beleaguered rosebush next to her porch. When he straightened, he said, "I'd like to talk. I was hoping we could do that as we choose some trees to rent. What do you think?"

She visibly relaxed, he noticed. "Okay. I don't like how things are between us, either." She pointed over her shoulder. "Let me grab my keys."

Marcus moved back to the truck, relieved that she was open to what he wanted to say. Once they were in the truck, he asked, "You all right to take the scenic route, or are you in a hurry?" He figured her answer would be a good indication of what his chances were of cleaning their wound.

"I've got time." Cassie put the radio on low and adjusted the AC vent to blow right at her. "Remember when your dad got you that old truck? You were mowing lawns as hard as you could to save enough money, and we walked home from the bus one day and there it was. A truck. At least three different paint colors, a missing fender and a bright red bow on top?" Her eyes danced at the memory. "Every kid who saw it was jealous."

"I was worried it wouldn't make it out of the driveway without breaking down," Marcus said as he tightened his grip on the steering wheel of the shiny truck he was driving now. "We went everywhere in that truck. Never broke down on us once."

"Your mama wouldn't let it. She kept your guardian angel on call." Cassie giggled. "Scenic route through Cutler Bay. I want to see if that shaved-ice shack is still open. If you had your skateboard, we could stop at the Palmetto Bay park. The good park." She waggled her eyebrows. Growing up, they'd skateboarded the old-school way, off every paved and convenient surface at the park or the apartment complex. Then, when they had transportation, they'd found skate parks.

"Left it at home, but you might have to teach me how to skate again. It's been a long time." Marcus glanced at her. "There's no way that shaved-ice place is still open. It was a disaster when we used to go there. Surely the city has condemned the building by now." They could get shaved ice at any number of proper, well-frequented establishments.

"They made the best pickle-juice snow cones." Cassie had rolled down her window to hang her arm out. "I never found another that good. Maybe it was the funk of that place that added something special."

Marcus grimaced. Somehow he'd blocked the pickle-juice snow cones from his memory. "Strawberry. Watermelon. Tiger's Blood. Ocean Breeze. Those are real shaved-ice winners."

"Bo-ring!" Cassie sang. "If that place is open, we're both getting snow cones." The matter was settled to her, so he drove. The winding highway that followed the curve of Biscayne Bay would never be the quickest way to make it to Homestead, but it was hard to worry too much about the two lanes that passed beautiful old homes. Enormous mature trees, some banyans that twisted back on themselves and returned to the ground, shaded the road and the bicycle path that ran alongside. Kids on brightly colored bikes, serious athletes on expensive road bikes and old couples taking their own scenic route on comfortable cruiser bikes formed a traffic jam on the path, but it was easy to remember how they used to be when he and Cassie were kids riding here for the pure fun of it.

Cassie's ponytail whipped in the breeze as if she was seventeen again. When he watched her happily weave her arm through the air currents, Marcus knew how special the moment was. This time, he could see her joy in the journey and the easy way she adapted to the world around her. No road rage. No stress about her to-do list. As a kid, she'd been the same, and he'd appreciated it without knowing how rare it was.

What if Peter was right? What if he'd been looking for someone like Cassie without knowing it ever since he'd lost her?

By the time he stopped the truck in front of The Nursery, his favorite place for native plants, the lump in Marcus's throat signaled that there was a whole lot more emotion involved in this thing between him and Cassie than he'd ever realized.

If he didn't get it under control, he was going to make a fool of himself.

"Hey, if it isn't Marcus Bryant, my favorite customer," Pascual Barrera yelled as he trotted out of the small office. The Nursery was open rain or shine, and customers had to be prepared for the weather because all the plants were outdoors. The man motioned them to the gate and stopped to grab his straw hat. Before Marcus or Cassie could argue, Pascual plopped hats on their heads, too. "Might not be August, but the sun will still get you."

Cassie shrugged and tapped the hat when Marcus glanced at her.

"What can I sell you today?" Pascual propped his hands on his hips as if ready for anything Marcus might say.

"We've got an event coming up. I wanted to rent plants for delivery next Saturday at Sawgrass High School and pickup on Sunday, or Monday if you prefer," Marcus said and waited for the argument. Pascual always had an argument.

"We don't do that. No renting. Trees get damaged. Too much work." Pascual waved his hand. "If you want to buy, you let me know." He turned to go but kept one eye on them to make sure they weren't giving up.

"You do rent them, Pascual, but only for me. Why is that?" Marcus asked as he took down one of the clipboards that had been pinned to the office wall. There was an order form attached.

"Because you're my favorite customer. A good customer." Pascual studied Cassie carefully. "For a wedding?"

Marcus shook his head.

"Oh, you're doing one of those house-staging things," Pascual said and wrinkled his nose. "Curb appeal to sell, but why not plant it? No rent needed."

Cassie stepped forward. "We're planning our high-school reunion. We had to decorate for our prom decades ago, but we got plants and flowers from another nursery then." She scanned the nearest plants. "They didn't have such a nice inventory to choose from. Surely we can work something out. I'd hate to go with second-best."

Pascual narrowed his eyes. There was no

way he misunderstood her compliment or her cagey move, but since both details were true, Marcus knew it was a solid tactic.

"Also, I recently signed a contract that will guarantee my company's landscaping residential projects for a year. You know I'm going with native plants." Marcus tilted his head to the side. "I'm not saying it's big business, but it's good, steady business. And it's going to grow. Events like this, where I'll be advertising my company, will benefit my partners." Marcus was relieved to get the hard sell over. In the early days, he'd struggled to be firm, to negotiate strongly for the best terms for himself, but he was learning with each job.

Pascual grinned. "Why didn't you say so? Steady business? Growing business? Music to my ears. The nursery is yours. Make me a list. We'll see what price we can come up with." He ducked his head to catch Cassie's stare. "We want to keep the customer happy."

Cassie was grinning as she marched away.

Marcus exchanged a glance with Pascual. "Yes, we do. Thank you."

"Always, my friend," Pascual called as he headed back to his office.

Marcus straightened his shoulders. It was now time to take care of the conversation that mattered most.

CASSIE STARED UP at a large palm tree as she waited for Marcus to catch up. She'd chosen the tree mainly because she could identify it. All of the other brown things with the green leaves? All she knew was the generic name *tree*.

"It will take a team of volunteers and special machinery to move that one. Better think smaller," Marcus said as he pointed. "Like this blue saw palmetto. It's hefty so it gives us a good backdrop, but it's not impossible to shift."

Cassie turned her head to study it. "It's… spiky. Is that enchanted enough?"

When Marcus frowned as if he was confused but also giving her question deep thought, Cassie felt the warm glow his respect had always given her. He was the expert here, but he never once waved off one of her questions because she knew less than he did. Marcus treated her and everyone else the same. He listened, he considered seriously, and then he answered. Clients would love him.

But they might be spending all day outside in the sunshine if he asked her opinion on every choice.

"I can definitely see this type working outside, as the entry you talked about." Cassie poked around the next batch of trees, trying to imagine if they'd suit the gym.

"I like your fresh take on things. This is how it went the last time we did this, too." Marcus's lips were twitching. "Keeping me company like you did then."

Cassie was happy to follow him down aisles of plants and to wait when he jerked to a stop to make note of the perfect shrub or tree or…whatever. He was muttering about "aromatics that might cover the gym-sock smell…fetterbush, marlberry." That was new since the first time they'd done this.

It was also unbelievably cute to hear him mumbling, like a mad scientist concocting the perfect experiment.

It was important work that she didn't want to interrupt, even though what she wanted to know most was what they were doing here together. When his mother had called, Cassie was certain she and Marcus were going to hash out the past that he'd brought up the last time they spoke. When she could stop crying and be fair, she knew he deserved more time to talk this through.

Realizing she'd hurt one of the most important people in her life had rattled her.

Making it right was important, but Cassie couldn't come up with an answer to how, no matter how often she turned the problem over in her mind. If Marcus had an answer, she wanted to hear it, but she couldn't start the conversation.

Cassie's plan before Marcus had shown up? Pretend that everything was normal, good, okay.

Lucky for her, that came naturally when she was with him.

They finally reached the farthest fence of the nursery. Pascual and his office were tiny in the distance, and Marcus was studying his list, his bottom lip pinched between his fingers. "This might be too much, but it's better to have more than enough than to be scrambling." He pointed at the bench she'd claimed in the shade of coral honeysuckle vines that had taken over the fence. "Wonder if he'd let us prune his honeysuckle vines. We could put it in the photo backdrop if people want to have a romantic-couple shot." He scooted onto the bench next to her, still jotting notes.

"Romantic-couple shot, huh?" Cassie asked. "Right here." She could hear the laughter in her voice. He would, too, when he returned to the real world.

She could tell when it happened. His head popped up, and he turned to her. Was he going to apologize or make some funny remark about the romantic part when they had never been romantic in their lives? Whatever it was, he swallowed it and set his clipboard down carefully.

Cassie couldn't stand waiting anymore. Instead of pretending, she wanted everything to actually be okay between them.

"I'm sorry for what I said then, Marcus. I was hung up on how much I needed you. I never once imagined how leaving home and joining the military would mean you would need me." Cassie had thought about nothing but this ever since she'd left Marcus's townhome. "That's not how we worked, you know? I followed you. I looked up to you. You looked out for me and your siblings and the kids in the apartment complex." She shook her head. "None of that matters now, though, and it wasn't right then, either. You were a kid yourself, even if standing next to you made me stronger no matter what was going on. I don't want to make excuses. I hurt you. I'm sorry."

Saying everything she wanted to was such a relief. Whether it made a difference or not, she wanted him to know she truly regretted it. "I've missed you so much."

He raised his eyebrows. "Missed trailing behind me in the hot sunshine while I talked to myself and the plants? I know how to show the ladies a good time."

Hearing him refer to ladies, as if he might have decided to take a date to a nursery like this, caught Cassie's attention. Had he done that? If she'd ever thought about it, she would have identified this as *their* thing.

Like lazy road trips through Cutler Bay were their thing.

She'd never done either of these things with anyone else. She hadn't wanted to. Had Marcus?

"I need to apologize, too. We were young. We didn't know how to deal with all that..." He paused, and Cassie wondered how he'd fill in the blank. Whatever it was between them, it had been important enough to both of them to nurse hurt feelings when it was over. "We had so much emotion. That's what kids are, right? Drama and emotion." He waved a hand to brush that off. "You were too important to me to let go, but I got in my own way, and then I held a grudge against an eighteen-year-old girl. I haven't gotten much smoother since then, to be honest." He rubbed his forehead and snatched off the straw hat to fan some breeze between them. "Definitely not my best look."

"I don't know. The hat works for you. Rugged. Farmer-y." Cassie tried to give him a seductive look but ruined it by giggling.

"I meant getting my feelings hurt. You know that." He plopped the hat onto his head. "I know I make this hat look good." They grinned at each other as the moment stretched out.

"Are we okay, then?" Cassie asked softly. "Friends?"

Marcus studied her face for so long she started to wonder if she had something on it. Was he staring at her lips? The urge to lick them had to be controlled.

"Friends. At the very least." Marcus wrinkled his nose. "You know how someone puts an idea in your head, and you blow it off because it's so silly. It can't be true, and so you go on. And then someone else, completely unrelated, mentions the same thing—like some cosmic coincidence. So while you can ignore the first one...the second one hits differently." He frowned. "Does that ever happen to you?"

Cassie remembered how Dan's question about connections at Preston Bank had seemed to line right up with the social-media notification from Brent Preston. Was that the universe at work like Marcus was suggesting? It had led her to this bench, sitting beside him and repairing one of the biggest hurts in her life.

"Maybe. I think I know what you mean." Cassie bumped his shoulder. "Why do I get the feeling Miss Shirley is involved?"

His laughter was deep and slow. She'd heard it so often in the past that it was familiar, but it had been a while since she'd been this close, this connected to him, so it was also brand-new.

"My dad made the suggestion, but the two of them are definitely plotting together. They think we should go further than being old friends and acquaintances," he said.

"I'm okay with that. You were the best friend I ever had, Marcus. I'm happy to have you in my life again." Cassie wanted to explain how it felt, the ease and the comfort that blossomed inside. "I missed my friend. I hope we can rebuild that."

He studied his hands for longer than she expected. Was it a hard question?

"More as in…dating." Marcus groaned. "I thought it was silly, but now…" He shook his head. "Do you think we were in love when we were kids?"

Cassie straightened. "What? I mean, I loved you. But romance?" She raised her eyebrows at him. "Do you?" Granted, she'd thought herself in love with Brent Preston, so Cassie at eighteen had been a horrible judge of men and romance in general.

Given her recent relationships, she might not have gotten much better.

"That was my reaction, too." Marcus pointed at her face. Cassie wondered what it was doing. Shock had taken over. "Then one of the guys at Concord Court asked me if the way we left things then…if it would have hurt so much if it hadn't been love."

Cassie stared hard at the dirt under her shoes as she considered that. "I don't know. Family can hurt like that, too." She could remember a few times when something her father had said made her think her heart was breaking. She'd pieced it back together, and now she was pretty protective of it.

"Sure." Marcus picked up his clipboard and tapped it on his leg. "Let's go negotiate with Pascual. We're going to pay more than we should because he is doing me a favor, but I'm going to talk him into letting me come in on Saturday morning to trim and tame this honeysuckle. We can use the flowering vines to cover part of the entryway into the gym or in the photo backdrop, somewhere we need color." He raised his eyebrows as if wanting her approval for the plan.

At this point, he had her okay for whatever he wanted to do. What she needed was time to wrap her head around his question. "I like it. I'm in. You let me know if I need to charm Pascual at all, and I'll give it my best shot."

He stood. "Guy doesn't stand a chance. We can't lose."

Cassie trailed behind him to Pascual's office, glad for wide-open paths because she wasn't able to watch where she was going. Marcus? He'd dropped his bombshell, taken her off-the-cuff answer in stride, and appeared to have settled the question of anything else between them.

He'd had more time to evaluate the possibility, sure, but was it that easy for him to dismiss?

She'd never met anyone else who got her like Marcus had. She'd certainly never dated anyone who had the power to hurt her the way he had.

If they'd been in love then, what did that mean for them now?

CHAPTER TWELVE

MARCUS TRIED NOT to stare at Cassie as he pulled into her driveway, but the mood between them had changed while they were at The Nursery. Possibly it had happened at the bench, which he'd suggested as a romantic prop for photographs. Their easy chatter and walking down memory lane had died out, and Cassie had settled into deep thoughts.

He'd floated the idea of more between them, but then shot it down with an easy explanation when she'd confirmed his doubt. She loved him like a friend. No romance. That was easy. He could let it go.

"You okay?" Marcus asked as he parked. "Are we okay?" More than anything, he wanted to make sure he'd accomplished his first goal: healing the wound between them.

Cassie smiled. "Yeah. Just thinking about what I should pick up to take over to my dad's for our Saturday-night date."

Marcus wanted to push because he didn't trust her answer, but things were still so fragile between them. "Standing date night. I'm jealous."

"Oh, you should be. My date is grouchy, eats whatever you set in front of him without saying thank-you and falls asleep before the end of the movie he wanted to see. It's what every date night should be." Cassie folded both hands over her heart as if it were so romantic.

"I know he appreciates your visits. He mentioned that to me when I was over having Wednesday-night dinner." Marcus ignored the twinge at the fib. Cassie's father had pretty much implied his daughter could do more.

Her raised eyebrow convinced him she already knew, but neither one of them wanted to poke too hard at the flimsy lie.

"Movie night with my dad is still more fun than most of my real dates. I keep thinking eventually one of these guys will click, but not yet."

Marcus wanted to ask more about that, but she'd answered the question that they were simply friends. So her dating should have no impact on him. At all.

"Dating isn't going too well for my dad, either. Your mother has introduced him to three women. There was something fatally wrong with each of them." She rolled her eyes. "One wore a perfume that made him sneeze, but he thinks *I* should be more tolerant. You should have heard the grief Daddy gave me when I ended things with a nice man because of the way he texted." She held out both hands. "I couldn't help it. Everything was some kind of abbreviation. It was like deciphering a top-secret communique to figure out what time to meet him and where."

Marcus bit his lip as relief and the glow Cassie had always brought bubbled up.

Even her side-eye was cute. "You think that's a silly reason to stop dating someone?"

He slowly shook his head.

"Silliest reason you ever ended things. Go." Cassie pointed at him.

As Marcus flipped mental pages, Cassie narrowed her eyes. "Don't lie, Marcus."

Eventually, he made his decision. "The only woman I've dated since I've been home wanted to move to Orlando to be nearer to the amusement parks."

Cassie blinked.

"She was interviewing with a rental-car company, preparing to pack up and go." Marcus stretched his arm out across the back seat and waited.

"How long did you date?" Cassie asked.

Marcus closed his eyes as he calculated and felt the smooth slide of her hair over his hand, like silk. "Two months? When she got the job offer, away she went."

Her frown was intense. "That's not silly at all." She huffed out a breath. "Your lives were going in different directions. That's all."

He nodded. "I feel like that's how all my relationships end. I'm perfectly happy, but life kicks up, and we spin in different directions."

Cassie put her hand on the door, ready to leap out of the truck, but she met his stare. Marcus waited for her to acknowledge what he was saying. Life had gotten in between them, too. That was all. He could let go of the hurt if she could, too.

He was not prepared for her launching herself across the front seat, her arms wrapping tightly around his neck before he knew what was happening. Once his brain caught up to the hug that had already started, he wrapped his arms around her back, pressed his nose close to her shoulder and settled in to enjoy her weight against his.

Cassie was back. What a relief!

"Thank you for being my friend, Marcus," she whispered. "Then. Now. I'm so happy you're back in my life."

Something cracked in the center of Marcus's chest, something in the area of the wall he'd put up to protect himself from her brand of hurt. She'd always been able to lift his mood and see the positive side.

Cassie would decide where they went now. At least he'd voiced the idea of them dating. He'd give her some space and time to examine the question of love. What if her first answer had been right, and they had loved each other like close friends?

Marcus wasn't viewing her as a mere friend would now, but he'd be patient. He wanted her to make the best decision for herself. It was enough to know that he'd be seeing her again.

CASSIE HURRIED TO her father's door, fifteen minutes late because her whole day had been out of whack ever since Miss Shirley had texted her a warning that Marcus was on the way over. She juggled the pizza box as she dug into her pocket for the keys but saw the note stuck to the door.

At the pool. Cassie read it and wondered if her father had been replaced by a look-alike at some point. He'd always loved to swim, so that fit, but the water might still be too cool.

Then she realized the anniversary of her mother's death had passed that week. Some years, grief swamped her like the loss was brand-new, but this year, with so much going on, Cassie had felt vaguely...off, a little out of step. It was a relief to understand what was going on, even if she hadn't named it on the day.

Retirement would mean her father had no such distractions.

Cassie mentally kicked herself for not realizing that earlier when she might have helped him through the day. That was her role, and she'd failed. What could she do about that now?

Since it was past dinnertime and her stomach would testify to that, Cassie carried the pizza with her as she hustled to the pool. Her father was sitting in one of the loungers, completely relaxed, as he stared up at the sky. The tablet she'd given him specifically to read her column in *Miami Beat* was on the table beside him, and he'd brought two sodas with him. "We're dining al fresco tonight, eh?" Cassie asked as she plopped the pizza down. "Should I have dressed for the occasion?"

Her father pointed at the other lounge chair. "I saved you a seat. Sit."

Cassie did and tried not to panic. This was out of the ordinary, but that didn't have to mean something terrible was coming.

"Do you remember the summer we moved here?" he asked, his tone casual as if it was an idle question. "You were so small. Just tiny, but you had this huge personality. That was your mother coming out in you, that personality." He clasped his hands over his abdomen. "Been missing her this week, I guess. Seemed right to come out here."

Cassie waited to see if there was anything else coming before answering. "I do remember. My whole world was upside-down, but I did love this pool." They had eaten dinner out here every night she could convince her father to do so for months, heat or not.

"Bet you wish I had more of your personality than hers." That would have made her teenage years easier, anyway.

Cassie folded her hands to match her father's.

"No way. That personality, your pointed chin, how your eyes sparkle when you're about to do something you shouldn't. I like seeing her in you. Makes it impossible to forget her. For a long time, that got me through the day. I had to keep going because there was this little girl, all that was left of the woman I loved with everything I had, and she needed me." He stared at the calm pool.

Cassie blinked as she absorbed what he was saying. Her father's grief had overshadowed so much of her youth that it was impossible to ignore, but there were joyful moments, like burgers around the pool and him sneaking her and Marcus money for the ice-cream truck and so many small bits here and there. She'd learned to always be sunny for him, and when she couldn't, she would pretend as well as she could. Still, he'd worried. He'd worked hard, and he'd raised her alone.

"Okay, then I bet you wish I could stop needing you to take care of me some days,"

Cassie said slowly, the ache in her chest familiar. Was there any worse feeling than knowing someone you love is disappointed in you?

He grunted. "Have you ever needed me, kid? I mean, really needed me? You fell often enough, but you never broke anything. You won over the throng of kids that could have made your life difficult. You paid for your own college, and every time you've been knocked down by some job, you pick yourself up and start climbing again." He tapped the pizza box. "And you bring me along with you, so I can worry and keep a check on your too-big ideas. All that time, I thought I was keeping you alive, but it might be the other way around now."

Cassie swung her legs over the side of the lounge to sit up because this was a conversation she needed to remember. "Daddy, are you dying? Hit me with the bad news. I'm ready."

His eyes snapped to hers before his laughter rolled out, loud and long. "Dying? No. Why?"

Relieved, Cassie stood to grab her drink, opened it and took a swig. "We don't talk like this, that's why. You are quiet. I act like a clown and try to lighten the mood. That's what we do." She opened the pizza box, took a slice and offered it to him.

"No, *we* don't usually talk like this." Her father accepted the pizza. "I don't." He took a bite.

Cassie tried to wait patiently for him to chew.

Eventually, he said, "You hear about these dating apps?"

Cassie took her own defensive bite and pointed at her mouth to show him she couldn't possibly answer. After a few moments, she relented. "You think I haven't tried them, Dad?" Cassie did not want a lecture from the contented widower about how she had to put herself out there. "They're...not great." Nor was she going to explain how low dating had sunk, either.

He frowned. "Not you. Me. Shirley's setting me up, but these ladies are all..." He lowered his voice and checked over his shoulder to make sure Marcus's mother wasn't lurking somewhere behind them. "They're nice, Cassie, but I don't want to sing in a choir to get out of the house. You know?"

It was a good thing she'd already swallowed her mouthful of pizza because Cassie would have inhaled sausage and olives down the wrong pipe and might have keeled over right there by the pool. Cause of death? Choking and two-for-one toppings.

Cassie cleared her throat. "Shirley might find you more suitable ladies if you cooperated with her. Tell her what you want to do to get out of the house. She might know someone who enjoys that." She rubbed her forehead. "Or...try the dating apps. Go for it. Just be careful, okay? There are a lot of... unsavory types out there." It was easy to picture her father as a wide-eyed innocent in the shark-infested waters of modern dating, but his frown convinced her he didn't want to hear any more warnings.

"We can make a pact to get out there. Let's set a bet. First one with three new dates gets to set the other one up with a person of their choosing." Cassie pulled out her phone. "How do you feel about being the subject of a series for *Miami Beat*? We could make this big. Father and daughter points of view on modern dating, me hunting for a suitable match for you."

Her father blinked slowly. "Because you're sure you'll win?"

Considering her experience with dating, there was no way she'd bet money on it, but she had more recent history than he did. Wouldn't she win?

"I do not want to be the lonely-hearts column for your magazine. You don't need my help there, and we both know it. Your column is the best thing in it," he said as he pointed at the tablet, "but I wouldn't say no to a bet. First one to get three new dates sets the other one up." His slow grin worried Cassie. Should he be that confident he was going to win?

Had she been played?

Then she realized what he'd said about her column. He was reading it. All the times she'd waited expectantly for him to say something... What if he'd been waiting for her to ask?

That was what she'd done with Marcus, waited for him to come after her.

She had to stop waiting and go after what she wanted. Cassie wanted her father to love what she wrote, but she'd have to show him that. And Marcus...

She stared hard at the hand her father offered

her before shaking it. "Fine. We have a bet. Eat your pizza while we watch the sun set."

He held up one finger. "I'll be with you in one moment." Cassie watched her father pick up his phone. When he only glared at it, she almost offered to help, but he finally poked the screen and held the phone to his ear. "Hi, Erin. This is Shirley's friend, Brian. She mentioned you enjoy Sunday brunches. I haven't done that in a while, but…" He stopped to listen. No matter how long Cassie held her breath, she couldn't make out actual words from Erin's side of the conversation. "At eleven tomorrow? It's a date. I'll see you there." Then he ended the call and dropped his phone in his shirt pocket. "You're already behind."

Cassie had to remind herself to close her mouth, which had dropped open in shock.

When he held out his hand for the pizza box, Cassie shook her head. "No, we aren't going to let you off that easily. You want pizza?" She motioned with her chin at his tablet. "Tell me which of my columns you've liked the best."

He narrowed his eyes. "Fine. No contest. My favorite story was about the girl who taught herself harmonica so she could join her mother's blues band on the road." He blinked. "What a good daughter."

Since that story was the third or fourth column, Cassie decided to give him points for remembering and dropped the pizza box in his hands. "Okay. Least favorite."

"You don't expect me to answer that," he said as he opened the box. "All right, it was the snake guy. Too many boa constrictors in that house trailer. I hope you didn't go inside."

"Why don't you ever talk to me about these, Dad?" Cassie asked. She'd been desperate for him to approve...and he did.

"I wanted you to aim high," he said, "But lately I've realized some people are just happy, they find it wherever they are. You are one of those people. That job makes you happy, and I'm glad of it."

"Are you sure you're healthy? You aren't dying." Cassie wanted this so badly to be real and a new phase of their relationship. He'd lived for her, then she'd done her best to care for him.

"Not dying. Gonna be living every day," he said. "Got a bet to win."

Cassie chewed her pizza and tried to ignore

his smug grin. The sense of impending doom she felt about losing to her father was strong, but if this was what it took to see him happy like this, she'd go along and be out-dated by her father.

And if the idea of Marcus being her first date immediately came to mind, she dismissed it.

That wouldn't keep her from counting on him to be her reunion date, though. Had her father forgotten that was coming up? Didn't matter. All was fair in love, war and friendly bets with family members.

CHAPTER THIRTEEN

ON MONDAY, CASSIE watched the *Miami Beat* staff photographer direct Brent Preston so that they had a couple of different shots to choose from for the story about him and the family bank. Working with a guy who understood his best angles must be quite a change for Nelson. Normally, the subjects of their stories were either hesitant to have their photos taken or giddy at the opportunity to be featured. Brent had been there and done that so many times that he moved naturally from one cool pose to the next.

"All right. I know we've got some good ones. I want to get other shots of the building, the bank in the lobby, the sign outside." Nelson handed Brent the standard photo release. "Need your signature. We'll use shots for the feature on you. The others will be kept on file for future opportunities."

Cassie waited until Brent had signed with a

flourish. She'd been up all night trying to find a way to come at Dan's possible story from a new angle. The conversation she'd over-heard suggested Brent might be involved in whatever it was about, but what should she ask to get more information? This was her prime opportunity. Unfortunately, no man-ner of questioning was going to turn up a lead when there was no story to follow.

"I'll meet you at Southern Florida Land-scape Design. Don't be fooled by the sign out front. It says *German Auto*. They haven't had a chance to change it yet," Cassie said as Nel-son finished packing up his bag.

He gave her a thumbs-up and left Brent's office.

"You'll never guess what I found." Brent held a CD pinched between his finger and thumb. "High-school photos."

The cringe that shook Cassie was instant. Did anyone want to be caught off guard by high-school photos? "Of what?" Maybe they were photos of Brent. That would be fine. In fact, they'd add some unique color to her stories.

"It's the yearbook archive, so anything they took pictures of that might have made it into the yearbook. You know there are prom pictures on here." He held the CD out to her. "You want to borrow it?"

She did. She really did. There might be legal issues to iron out as to who owned the photos and whether they could be tracked down to get permission to use them, but the headache could be totally worth it.

"Can I?" Cassie asked with the smile she'd flashed at Pascual. It had worked better than expected there, but she had no faith in its power over Brent. He'd never been influenced by her wiles before.

"You bet. You can owe me a favor."

Cassie waited for the realization to hit him. How many favors had she already done him without calling any in herself? But the point went right over Brent's head.

"Great. Nelson's on tap to take photos at the reunion, a group shot of the three of us and atmosphere shots. This is going to be a great story." Cassie carefully slid the CD inside her notebook. No way was she leaving this office without it. The bigger question was whether he was ever getting it back. She needed to inspect the photos to see if any of her belonged out in the world.

"Three of us?" Brent asked as he stood. Their allotted hour had come to an end, obviously, and he was moving on to the next item on his agenda.

"You, me, Marcus. The organizers." Cassie packed her tote up and slung it over one shoulder.

"Ah." Brent shoved his hands in his pockets. "Don't know much about Bryant. How is his business? Sounds like cash-flow problems if they can't put up new signage. That's free advertising down the drain." His tone was curious but distracted. "I run into people from school all over town, here and there at functions, but he never was one of the guys."

Cassie paused. The impulse to defend Marcus boiled up. "He joined the Air Force. No way could he run into you at your country club, and he was too busy to follow you on social media." She didn't roll her eyes, but she wanted to. If she was hoping to trade on her relationship with Brent Preston to get a source for Dan's story, she wasn't being smart about it.

Brent raised his eyebrows at her.

She didn't blame him for being surprised.

This might have been the first time in their lives that she'd ever snapped at him.

Cassie wasn't going to feel bad about it.

This certainly wasn't the first time he'd *deserved* to be snapped at.

"Sure," Brent said slowly, "I only meant that most people that have any connection to me at all hit me up when they need a loan or a charitable donation or a sponsor for their kid's baseball team. That's all. Guy with a new business needs good loan terms. Calling up an old friend would occur to a lot of people. And Preston Bank, my bank, has pretty generous loan approval policies for people I can vouch for. My friends can rely on me."

Was that a hint of loan impropriety? Would it be enough to cause the bank trouble or build a new story?

Cassie wondered whether she should apologize or double down.

There was no way Marcus would ask Brent Preston for anything. The poor guy had listened to her pine for Brent forever. But she didn't want to lose this thread, either.

"For that matter, I haven't heard from you, Casserole. Even my ex-fiancée called me up for a business loan, and I was afraid she'd set my boat on fire after I ended the engagement. I guess a low percentage rate and waiving the collateral limit convinced her to move on with her life. Well, that and the prospect of jail time, perhaps. Jane wasn't thrilled when I pushed that loan through." Brent braced one shoulder against the doorframe. "Never needed a mortgage, Cassie?" He smiled, but it didn't reach his eyes. Was Brent Preston feeling used by people who claimed an acquaintance with him?

Snorting at that irony wouldn't improve the situation, so Cassie refrained. "Not yet. You're at the top of my list to call when I do."

He nodded. "Home ownership is a core investment. You should look into it."

Cassie thought about explaining to him that her dad still lived in the apartment he'd struggled to afford as a single parent. Her own job history… Well, now she might be secure enough to trust she could fulfill the terms of a thirty-year mortgage, but it still seemed like a huge step. She bought used cars and paid cash when she did. Would she ever sleep again if she had a house payment every month?

His easy advice reminded her of the wide gap in their history and experience. She and Marcus understood each other. She and Brent? They had never spoken the same language.

"Good advice. Thanks." She was ready to be done with the interview, and she'd be glad not to have a reason to speak with Brent Preston once the reunion was over. "I'm going to stick my head in to say hello to Jane and leave her my receipts. See you on Saturday?"

"Bright and early," Brent said before he disappeared into his office.

Jane wasn't at her desk, so Cassie took the elevator back down to reception.

"Could I leave this for Jane?" she asked the receptionist, the same beautiful model-type who'd been there every time.

The woman took the envelope with a nod. "Certainly. I will see that she gets this." Her lips curled up at the edges, so Cassie trusted it was a smile and returned it.

She was prepared to leave when the woman added, "Brent has told us about the upcoming story in *Miami Beat*." She smoothed her hair back over her shoulder. "Your photographer took my photo. I would be pleased to be included."

Cassie paused and turned back. "Great.

Can I get a quote about working here at Preston Bank?"

The woman pursed her lips. "Of course. I have been receptionist here for three years. In that time, Brent has assisted with many problems." She wrinkled her nose for a split second before everything smoothed out. "Or he had someone else do so, I suppose."

Cassie made a few notes. "Oh? That's wonderful. How does Preston Bank support its employees?" Was this it? Was this beautiful woman going to drop the crumb she needed?

"So many small ways, but the largest way is by providing an immigration attorney to navigate citizenship. I came to Miami at seventeen. Every day I sit here behind this desk, with my US citizenship, my completed GED and my associate degree, I remember how much Preston Bank has done for me." This time her smile was broad, genuine.

"And that is because of Brent Preston." Cassie wondered if there were deeper sides to the man. Surely he'd matured as he'd aged. It happened to them all.

"Well," the receptionist said slowly, "it is because of the people he hires, for certain."

She inhaled slowly. "Good people surround themselves with good people."

The click of Cassie's pen was loud as she closed her notebook.

Almost as loud as the click in her brain.

Because the receptionist had articulated the nagging problem in the back of Cassie's brain. Everyone she'd met at Preston Bank had been friendly and overwhelmingly positive about her story and what they knew about the bank.

Brushing that off as a PR decision, an attempt to polish the bank's image for the story to be sure good press followed, was the easy reaction. Cassie had gone with that at first.

But even Jane Wynn, who was irritated about the extra job duties she never signed on for and annoyed that Brent saw her as a crutch instead of a woman, had been positive about her job at the bank.

As a final Hail Mary, Cassie said, "It's rare for someone so handsome to be so kind, wouldn't you say? Do you happen to know if Brent is dating anyone?" She batted her eyelashes, hoping the receptionist would believe she was asking for herself. When the younger woman frowned, Cassie added, "Asking for a friend."

The receptionist sniffed. "No, not since he ended his engagement, I do not think."

Cassie waited. Surely the younger woman would say something about…something.

But she didn't. Eventually, after they'd stared at each other for an uncomfortable amount of time, the receptionist added, "I think if he liked you, he would have asked you already."

Resigned, Cassie agreed. The receptionist was one thousand percent correct.

And there was no story brewing here.

Her big break? It wasn't coming.

Deflated and relieved, Cassie dropped her notebook back into her bag. "Check out my column in *Miami Beat*. If you can find an angle, some kind of unique…"

"I've been reading them." The receptionist pointed at her screen. "I make high-fashion doll clothes," she offered.

Cassie paused while she absorbed the order of those words and rearranged them in her head until they made sense. "High-fashion doll clothes." She pulled her notebook back out. "Tell me more."

The receptionist's eyes lit up. "Oh, I love fashion. Paris Fashion Week, New York... I love them. I want to see every photo, every recording, every story about new fashion lines." She shrugged. "And then I recreate my favorite items." She pulled out her phone, navigated to the photos and offered it to Cassie. "Here are some of my completed designs."

Cassie took the phone and scrolled through some of the shots, amazed the further she went in. There were miniature gowns, fabulous hats, tiny handbags. The dolls were in various sizes, and the outfits were tailored perfectly. So many questions percolated in her brain that Cassie knew this was a winner. She put her bag down and dug around until she found her wallet. She'd remembered to replenish her business cards, so she offered one to the receptionist. "I want to write about this. Can you call me next week so that we can set up a time for an interview?"

The receptionist's slow grin was beautiful. Cassie wondered if she'd ever walked a runway herself and made a mental note to ask that question when she had the opportunity. At this point, Nelson was going to beat her to Marcus's office, and neither man would be happy about wasting time.

Cassie's huge grin as she hurried through the building's lobby surprised the security guard by the entrance. He smiled back but then watched her closely all the way through the door, as if she might be up to something.

Back out on the sidewalk, Cassie hurried through the drizzle and wished she'd remembered to put an umbrella in her bag. At least she'd completed all of the work where her appearance mattered. Marcus would have seen worse than her wet hair. Brent and the receptionist might have been traumatized by frizz.

As she drove, she tried not to worry about telling Dan she'd failed to turn up a good lead at Preston Bank. The doll-fashion story was going to make for an excellent column. The receptionist's background, her success here and the unique hobby all added up to an interesting read.

Was Dan going to be as happy about that as she was? Maybe not, but Cassie was energized. She was also looking forward to seeing Marcus again. A little rain couldn't bother her.

CHAPTER FOURTEEN

MARCUS LEANED AGAINST the outside wall next to the window with the fresh new South Florida Landscape Design logo and tried to figure out what to do with his hands. If the photographer ordered him to "look natural" or "relax" one more time, he was going to stomp inside and lock the door behind himself.

At least Cassie had finally shown up.

The troublemaker who'd signed him up for this was heckling him from a safe distance.

"You can't frown in every shot, Marcus. Didn't know you were signing up for modeling lessons when you agreed to do the story, did you?" she asked from her spot perched on the tailgate of his truck. "Smile with your eyes. You can do it!"

Nelson had first posed him next to the truck, but he'd been dissatisfied with the glint of setting sun on the metal. Or something. The photographer hadn't actually articulated his problem, but he had muttered about losing the best light and something about the golden hour.

Marcus knew he was already skating on thin ice with the guy so he'd interpreted the impatient pointing as a scenery change and moved to lean on the wall.

"I thought we'd do action shots." Marcus crossed his arms over his chest and ignored the click of the camera. "Like I would work, the photographer would shoot, the end."

"We tried that," the guy who'd introduced himself as Nelson muttered, "but that office of yours is a black hole. Photography needs light."

"We could have tried a job site. I mean, I could be *working*." Marcus shifted and heard more clicks. They had started out with him at his drafting table. They'd switched on every desk light and overhead light, and Nelson had not been satisfied.

"We're lucky the rain stopped or we'd have to reschedule," Nelson added as he lowered the camera.

"So lucky," Marcus said in response. He almost meant it, too. Now that he knew how much he hated this, he definitely wanted to get it all over with that afternoon. No rain checks.

"Maybe the shots from your party will be better." Nelson shrugged at Cassie. "I've done the best I can here."

Marcus pinched the bridge of his nose and gathered his patience. "Then I guess I can get back to work."

Nelson handed him a piece of paper. "Sign this first. Standard release." Marcus pulled out the pen he kept clipped in his pocket for estimates, turned to face the brick wall and scrawled his name on the bottom line.

"*Miami Beat* thanks you," Nelson said. "I'm going to take exterior shots of your garage while I'm here." He didn't wait for agreement but headed around the building. Zeke had ducked out there as soon as the photographer had strolled in, so Marcus had a feeling his partner was going to be signing his own release form before Nelson was done.

"He's good at his job," Cassie said as she hopped down off the tailgate. When she turned to slam it shut, Marcus noticed she was wearing real pants. Not jeans. She was dressed as Reporter Cassie, not his old friend Cassie. They were blending together more and more.

Since he had a hunch what the professional

clothing meant, Marcus asked, "Seen Brent lately?"

The way she paused in gathering up her stuff answered his question. "Why?"

Marcus motioned at her outfit. "I can tell a difference in how you're dressed. At least it's not a suit this time." Ready to get out of the humidity that was building now that the rain had stopped, Marcus opened the door and motioned her inside.

"You don't like my suit?" Cassie asked as she breezed past him. "I keep it on hand for important occasions. I thought it worked for me, even if it's tighter every time I put it on."

Marcus ran a hand down his nape. This was when he wished he had better skills, more game, like Peter. If he wanted her to entertain the idea of something more than friendship, he should insert a smooth line here.

Marcus *really* wished he had one.

"The suit was great. Showed your legs." He realized there was a better way to say that when she frowned at him. "I mean…" He cleared his throat. "You looked great in the suit. You look great today." All he'd done was fill the air with more words, none of them…great.

"I was at the bank, getting research for the

story. I dressed like a professional. I was talking with people in the executive suite and down in the lobby branch, not just…" Cassie raised her chin. "I'm not trying to impress Brent Preston, if that's what you're implying."

Yeah, that guy. Did she believe that there was any other reason to change how she dressed every other day for her job than to impress Brent Preston?

He should point out the problem, but the right words wouldn't come.

Probably because his brain was too busy thinking about how pretty Cassie had been the last time she'd stopped in here, and today—even though she was giving him a hard time, and he was forgetting every word but *great*. Marcus grunted as he took his seat at the drafting table. "Right."

Why did it matter if she wasn't being completely honest about why she'd volunteered? It didn't.

There was something about this crush that she'd carried the whole time they were kids that irritated him. He didn't want her to be interested in impressing Brent Preston. Marcus picked up his drafting pencil and twirled it in his fingers as he tried to come up with a subject change.

Brent would never see Cassie for who she was. Besides, she'd learned all she needed to know about him when they were kids. Then it hit him.

Even without Brent Preston around, there was no guarantee Cassie would have looked at Marcus any differently. Cassie didn't wear the suit or worry about professional hair for him.

It wasn't Marcus she wanted to impress. Never had been.

"I'm serious, Marcus." She plopped down across from him and pulled her laptop out of her tote. "I have no feelings for Brent Preston except for a slight bemusement at how oblivious he is to some of the things he says." She was shaking her head as she opened the laptop and pulled out a CD.

"Like what?" Marcus braced his elbows on his desk. If the guy had said something rude to Cassie…

She grimaced as she met his stare. "He loaned me this CD of pictures and told me I could owe him a favor." She snorted. "Can you even imagine? Forget what we're doing right now to help the guy, but over a lifetime, can you imagine forgetting all the favors other people have already done for you?" She bugged her eyes out.

The faces she made were cute—the old, animated Cassie shining through, even if she was dressed differently than he remembered from their days in the park or bike riding. She turned her laptop to face him. "Let's take a walk down memory lane. Maybe I do owe the guy a favor."

Marcus scooted closer until their shoulders brushed. He stared hard at the screen and knew she was busy navigating the folders stored on the CD. That left him plenty of time to enjoy the smell of her perfume, something light. Was it floral? He breathed slowly because he wanted to remember it.

"Prom. This is the good stuff." She turned to face him. The widening of her eyes told him she hadn't realized how close they were standing together until that second, but she didn't shift away. This close, he might be able to count the freckles that dotted her nose and cheeks. "Your deep brown eyes have always been the best eyes." The way she blinked convinced him she meant it even if she hadn't intended to make the confession.

"Best?" he asked, uncomfortable in uncharted waters but determined not to let this moment pass.

This moment did not feel like friendship.

"In books, eyes are *piercing* or *knowing* or..." She licked her lips. "I don't know. Sometimes they dance."

Marcus smiled slowly. "Like the moonwalk? My eyes do not dance."

Her huff of breath stirred between them. "No, but when I look into them, I see...understanding. Or kindness. I can see a good soul who looks at me and appreciates the real me."

Deflated, Marcus leaned back a bit. "Doesn't sound sexy. Explains a lot about my trouble with women."

Cassie rubbed her forehead. "It's the hottest, sweetest thing I've ever seen in a man's eyes, which might explain as much about my trouble with men."

Before he could press the opening wider, Cassie cleared her throat. "Let's see if there are any pictures that we can use in the story. I'd love to show how far we've come." She opened up the first folder and started clicking through. After a minute, she stopped. "Look at this."

Marcus realized he'd been watching her, not the slideshow, and turned his attention to whatever it was that she was pointing at. "Do you remember Brent having frosted tips in his hair?" She covered her mouth with one hand to muffle the giggles coming out. "Was that still a thing the year we graduated?"

Marcus studied Brent as high-school quarterback and golden boy. In this photo, he was holding a helmet with one hand. They'd won the homecoming game that night, and the head cheerleader, Mercedes Esposito, was kissing his cheek. Where had Marcus been at that moment? Probably searching for Cassie, so they could go get food. He'd always been starving after a game.

Indeed, the tips of Brent's spiky haircut were a light blond.

"Must have been. No way Brent would be caught lagging behind in men's trendy looks department." Marcus leaned one elbow on the desk to bend closer. "This is pretty much how I remember him. Winning, and girls throwing themselves at him."

He gave her the side-eye to make sure she understood who he meant.

Cassie muttered, "I was helpless in the face of good hair and confidence. Don't blame me."

They were both silent as she continued

moving through the pictures. Eventually, she came to one that captured the backdrop of the stage. There were people dancing, and it was the perfect time-capsule snapshot. "So much satin!" Marcus watched Cassie study the photo carefully. "And there's Mercedes." She tapped the screen. "I remember being so jealous of her gown."

"Not her date?" Marcus asked and held up a hand as Cassie narrowed her eyes at him. "She and Brent were pretty tight."

"I was over him by the time we made it to the actual dancing. Do you remember the splinter I got when we were carrying in that backdrop we painted? The thing must have been two inches long and stuck in the meaty part of my palm. Terrible." She held up her fingers to show him what a four-inch splinter might look like, but if he remembered correctly, hers had been under an inch. "You got it out for me."

Of course he remembered that. He could draw Cassie's dress, though, without missing many details. He took his notepad out of his pocket, determined to see if he was right.

"Would your Dad have let you get away with that two-piece tummy showing style?" Marcus asked as he drew. Her dress had been deep blue, not navy but a true indigo—sometimes blue, sometimes purple. The dress top had wrapped around her neck, leaving her shoulders bare, and followed her curves to her knees. He frowned. There was some kind of shimmer but...

"Are you kidding? I could have told my dad everyone was wearing bikinis to prom and he would have waved me through the door as long as he didn't have to go shopping for one. I got my dress the week of the prom." She turned to stare at him. "Do you understand how wild that is? The week of? All the good stuff was gone! I didn't know how much I could spend, and I wanted him to..." She shrugged. "Doesn't matter. My date seemed to be okay with it."

She wrinkled her nose at Marcus. They'd been each other's dates, mainly because no one else had asked, and it made sense because they were working so closely on the prom together.

He glanced up as she flipped through more shots. There were some posed carefully in front of the Enchanted Garden sign they'd spent hours adding glitter to the night before prom. Each boy stood behind his date, arms wrapped stiffly around the girl's waist where she rested her hands, corsage displayed beautifully. The prom pose.

"Does it bother you that you don't have any of those romantic dance or kiss stories about your prom?" Marcus asked. He'd seen the moments in more than one movie, enough to know that while he'd had a good time, the whole event had been extremely low romance.

She sighed. "A little, but what I really miss is having those awkward, posed pictures that parents take and then pull out to embarrass their kids for years afterward. My dad wasn't up to that, either."

Marcus frowned. "I have some. My mother took about a hundred pictures of me as I adjusted my tie." It had never occurred to him to ask why she hadn't done the same for Cassie. They'd loaded into his beater truck to go to the dance together. There had been opportunity, and his mother had always been so careful to help Mr. Brooks. "My mama fell down on her job."

Cassie waved a hand. "Oh, it's fine. It's not a big deal now." Her tone almost matched the words, but Marcus wondered how many other things she'd missed because of her mother's death and her father's grief. "She probably expected me to crash the party in my jeans and flip-flops, anyway." She glanced at him. "A few days ago, I had this sweet, out-of-the-blue conversation with my dad, and it made me realize that..." She shrugged. "I guess I tried so hard not to burden him that I ended up... hurting us, by not asking, demanding, speaking up more." She groaned. "Then and now, I could do a better job of talking. It wasn't that he didn't care. He didn't know, and I didn't speak up. Being mad at him because of that is silly."

Marcus realized she was putting his gut feeling into words.

He'd been hurt by Cassie, but she hadn't known that. She was right. Getting mad about that without doing something about it was pointless.

Was this growing certainty that she'd been his first love, even if they hadn't known it, and might be his last... Was that something else he owed it to them both to say aloud?

"I do remember thinking how pretty you looked in your dress. It was blue." Marcus wanted to make sure she knew that someone had seen her. "What do you call that where it goes up around your neck?" Faces weren't his thing, but he decided to give it a shot.

"A halter." Her frown was cute, but Marcus wasn't sure what to think about the realization crossing her face. Had she never considered that he'd seen her as a girl, a woman? She bent closer to the screen. "Nope, I can't tell that my dress has a halter from the photo. You remember that?"

"You wore your hair down. You could barely walk in the high heels, but I seem to remember they were blue, too." Marcus hadn't thought about that night in years. He added strappy heels to his drawing. Why was it so easy to pull up a detailed memory of staring down at her on the dance floor? "We only danced to one song." He waited for her to fill in the blank and tried not to be too disappointed when she raised her eyebrows, telling him to get on with it. "Aerosmith. 'I Don't Want to Miss a Thing.'"

Her eyes lit up. "Oh, man, it was. Such drama. Angsty teens slow-shuffling to that song from the asteroid movie. The guys who worked on an oil rig or something who were going to save us from the asteroid, right? The song was better than the movie." She shook her head. "Can you believe we were ever that young? That is so sweet to think about now."

She was right. It was sweet, life before everything changed, before they knew where their lives would go.

Cassie leaned back. "Let me see if I can guess what you were wearing. A tuxedo. Black." She rubbed her temples as if it was all coming back to her. "You'd gotten your hair cut, and your shoes were pinching your toes."

"We were all wearing black tuxes, but the toe part convinces me you remember something, anyway." Marcus had learned a painful lesson about rented shoes that night.

Cassie went back to scrolling through the shots on her computer. "I'm going to build a slideshow that we can run on one of the gym walls of these old pictures. Surely we aren't the only ones who enjoy strolling down memory lane."

Marcus stared at his sketch. Was he going to show it to her? Not yet. He slipped the notebook into his pocket.

"Good. Before Nelson showed up, I negotiated a low price on orchids from one of my usual flower guys. They'll be white, pink or purple. I thought those were the most enchanted colors." Marcus batted his eyelashes at Cassie to make her giggle and ignored the flutter in his chest when it worked. "I've ordered white ceramic pots to dress them up. What else do we need for the centerpieces?" He preferred simple, but he wanted Cassie's opinion.

"That's going to be perfect. The tables are black. The plates and cups are white with silver plasticware to mimic the real thing. We've got a classic, minimalist theme going here." She brushed off her shoulders to show how good a team they were.

"I'm bringing in pops of color on the stage, and around the food tables and the photo backdrop. I've got hibiscus coming in, some small flowering trees. For the name tags, I ordered gardenias." Marcus hoped it would be enough.

"I love the smell of gardenias. Good choice for the gym. And the twinkling white lights. That makes every night more special." Cassie took the CD out of her computer. "I reminded Brent today that he's the master of ceremonies. We are not responsible for any scripted banter, Where Are They Now? games or any additional engagement." She held out both hands. "We'll get the decorations up, the food there, the DJ prepared and then hand Brent the keys, leaving us plenty of time to work the room to make sure everyone there knows about your business and to dance to as many power ballads as we like."

Marcus cleared his throat. For some reason, it felt important to remind her that they were different people now. Not kids. This could be about more than business for them. The night could include some enchantment for themselves, if they wanted it to. If she wanted it to...

It seemed he'd already made his decision. Did he remember he was the one who'd wanted nothing to do with her before all this planning started? Yes, but nothing was the same anymore. There had to be a sense of *them* in some way afterward.

"Hey, you like food." She pointed at him as if she'd just remembered that. "Want to check out the caterer's samples with me tomorrow night? She's got a small restaurant over in Coconut Grove. Brisa told me to request the barbecue sliders, so I did, but I'm not sure what else there will be." She bent closer. "Come on. Food on Brent Preston's dime. You know you want to."

He did. Mainly to see Cassie with barbecue sauce on her face, but having Brent pay for it was a bonus. "I'm in. I haven't been to Coconut Grove in a long time. Should I pick you up?" He was testing the waters. But even if they were just going to be friends after this was all over, he'd offer to do the same.

"I'll have to go from the office. Do you know where that is? I can text you the address," Cassie said as she slid her laptop back into her bag. "I don't mind meeting you at the restaurant if that's easier."

Determined to be cool, Marcus shrugged. "It's no problem. If Coconut Grove is the same, parking can be a hassle."

She bit her lip. "I hate street parking." When she nodded, he stifled the urge to punch his fist in the air in victory. "My office, around five-ish?"

"I'll see you then." Marcus grabbed the handles of her tote before she could put it on her shoulder and motioned her toward the door.

"I can get that. I carry it all the time." Cassie held her hand out, but Marcus waited for her to understand he was going to carry it for her this time.

Eventually she rolled her eyes. "Okay, strong man. Just for that, I'm not even going to pretend to offer to climb up the ladder to string lights."

"I'll take that as a promise. Our insurance isn't good enough to cover any mishaps," Marcus murmured as he opened the door and waited for her to slip past him.

"We don't have insurance," Cassie said. He wanted to believe her tone was breathless.

"Exactly. You're making my point for me." Marcus grinned at her as he yanked her car door open as soon as she hit the button on her fob to unlock it.

Then she did it.

When they were kids, there'd been one move that Cassie did when she was flustered, irritated, on the verge of annoyed with him. She stepped up close and put her hands on his cheeks to stare up into his eyes.

She intended it to be intimidating, to prove how serious her threat was.

As a kid, he'd always been knocked sideways, when she did it.

As a man…

"Marcus Bryant, you listen to me," she said in her best mean tone, which might have worked if she'd honestly been mad. "Don't you spoil me. Nobody opens doors for me anymore."

A lifetime ago, he would have backed away, given her some tough words about doing what he wanted, and they'd have been on even footing again.

Now? He was going to take his shot. Never knowing the right thing to say meant that he would not miss the one opportunity when the words appeared.

Marcus slipped his hand around her waist and watched the teasing slip away. "Too late. Besides, you deserve more, Cassie."

Cassie's mouth dropped open. Then she pointed a finger. "You're messing with me." She stepped back, and he regretted having to let her go. She hopped into the driver's seat, hauled the door closed and started the car, but plopped back against the seat when he slowly raised the tote bag so she could see what she was forgetting.

Then she opened the door again. "Thank you. I was going to get it."

Sure, she was. He wanted to say something about how easy it was for her to forget things when she got rattled, but he was enjoying the show. He didn't want it to end.

So Cassie had never imagined anything between them before. She'd said as much at The Nursery, but he was hoping she'd at least need to take a serious look at what might be between them now.

When she dropped the tote on the passenger seat, he expected her to screech out of the spot and drive quickly away. Instead, she paused and tightened her hands on the steering wheel.

Whatever it was that was going around in her mind, he desperately wanted to hear it.

Eventually, she licked her lips and stared hard out the windshield, very obviously not at him. "If we were *in love* in love, don't you think we would have known it there at prom? Teen romance in the air, all the hormones raging, emotions flowing."

Marcus waited until she was brave enough to face him. "I did, but then I asked myself…"

He hesitated. There was a lot on the line between them because she had been his best friend in the world and could be again.

Or she could be so much more.

Cassie wasn't looking away from him, either. She wanted to hear what he had to say.

"I asked myself, What if that's when I fell for you? What if seeing you that way, seeing you differently, with shoulders and legs and everything—" He waited for her to smile at him. "What if that's when I fell in love for the first time?"

She didn't have an answer except a slow exhale, but she met his stare for a long moment before finally closing the door.

Marcus tried to relax as he returned to the office. The quiet inside was nice, but it left him with too much time to think about what could happen next.

CHAPTER FIFTEEN

THE THIRD TIME Rosa called her name, Cassie managed to snap to attention. She'd been staring hard at the prom dance-floor photo and thinking about… Well, she'd been stuck on Marcus and his last words since the second she'd heard them.

Also, she had listened to their prom song so many times on repeat that it had become an earworm that would not leave her alone.

"Sorry, Rosa," Cassie said as she rubbed her eyes. "What do you need?"

The older woman took her glasses off. "You aren't yourself today. Did something happen?"

Something other than the best friend who'd gotten her through her impossible teenage years turning the entire universe upside down? Oh, not much.

"Didn't get much sleep last night." That was an understatement. She'd stared at her ceiling and chased every single possibility down a rabbit hole. When she did fall asleep, her dreams ran wild. Finding the love of her life in her best friend seemed no more a longshot than being Aunt Cassie to her best friend's twin daughters. Marcus and Preston Bank's beautiful receptionist were apparently going to have a lovely family and name their children Chips and Salsa.

Dream after dream followed. It wasn't always the same mother, and sometimes the kids' names were actual names.

Somehow, in every scenario, Marcus had ended up with twins.

And Cassie was in none of them.

"Dan wants to see you." Rosa motioned over her shoulder at his office. "Why he couldn't tell you that himself, I do not know. I expect it's a power move." She said the last two words loudly enough that Dan had to have heard them from his office, but there was no response. Since Cassie had sent him an early draft of Marcus's profile and an outline of points that would become the knit-fashions-for-dolls column if he gave her the go-ahead, Cassie wasn't surprised he wanted to see her.

She hadn't sent in the story about Brent Preston yet. It seemed like a good idea to lay some groundwork before she did, to let Dan know she'd worked the angle of his anonymous tip but turned up nothing.

Normally, she waited for his verdict restlessly, nerves making it hard to focus on anything else until Dan gave her feedback.

Today, she'd gotten lost in what-ifs.

What if she told Marcus she wanted to see if love was a possibility now? She couldn't say whether high school had been their first-love story. Maybe she didn't know what love felt like.

What if she told him she didn't want that? Their friendship had meant the world to her. It could again, but if he wasn't happy with that decision…

What if twins ran in his family?

What if she stuck her head in the sand for as long as possible and waited for it to all just…stop?

"Today, Brooks," Dan called through the open door.

Cassie and Rosa exchanged an amused look before Cassie stood and marched into Dan's office.

"You called?" she drawled as she sat down across from him.

"Why are you wearing a dress?" Dan's narrow-eyed expression made it difficult to guess what his judgment of her fashion choice might be.

Cassie crossed her legs and shoved the memory of Marcus's verdict on the last time she'd worn a skirt out of her head.

"I have plans after work." Which was true. They were with Marcus, which should have no impact on what she chose to wear. But as she went through her closet that morning, nothing else had seemed right. "Still got my comfy shoes, though. Got a story you need me to run down?" She kicked up her foot to show her classic white sneakers.

He pointed at the computer. "The landscaper guy? That's a good story. Balanced, with good context. He's a friend, huh?"

Cassie didn't blink at how perceptive her boss was. This wasn't the first time he'd read between the lines. "I tried to be objective, but yeah, we were neighbors and friends growing up." That didn't do their friendship justice, but she was going to try to sell it to Dan to avoid any probing questions.

He nodded. "You write like someone who knows him, that's all. Move ahead with the story about Concord Court. Try five hundred words with a few photos and all the links. We'll put it in the Places section in next week's edition."

"Five hundred words?" Cassie asked. There was a lot of story to cover and not much ground.

"Try, Brooks." Dan rearranged the papers on his desk. "You'll send me twice what I ask for, and we both know it. It's the internet. No one wants pages. For that, you need to write a book."

"You'll cut twenty-five percent, and we both know it." Cassie blinked innocently at his glare.

"That's my job." Dan pointed at his awards. "Some people think I'm good at it."

Cassie bit her lip to contain her amusement. Dan was predictable. On some days, it was cute. Today must be one of them.

"This other story? The model who's a knitter?" Dan tilted his chin down. "No idea how you found her, but this is going to be good. Move forward with it. I want a draft next week."

Cassie was afraid her grin was smug, but it couldn't be contained.

"All right, all right, I admit you're getting pretty good at this." Dan sighed. "Maybe a book's not out of the question. Not sure how it would be structured, but you have some interesting stories all wrapped up in this Off Beat column of yours."

Cassie blinked as she caught her breath.

Dan had always appreciated her writing, but she'd never expected anyone to say anything like that to her. After years of struggling to find her place, it was amazing to know that she wasn't the only one who knew she'd found it.

When she didn't answer, Dan waved a hand in front of her face. "Hello? You still with me?"

Cassie cleared her throat. "I wouldn't know how to go about getting a book published. And the structure…" How would she tie all these unusual, wonderful stories together into one book? "I've always thought we could do a compilation called Lessons from the Off Beat. You know, look back at where these characters started and include an important lesson they've learned. It might be inspirational to people who don't always fit."

Cassie had thought of it. She'd never spoken it aloud. To anyone.

"Some might call a compilation *a book*, Brooks. You figure that part out. I'll assist with the rest." Dan stretched back in his chair. He didn't point at his awards or remind her of his success, but the familiar statement about how good he was at his job was part of the air in his office, always there. "I'll still cut twenty-five percent of the words you give me."

Excited and overwhelmed at the possibilities that immediately exploded in her mind, Cassie stood.

"Itching to run out into the world and get started," Dan said slowly. "Don't quit your day job yet. I don't have anyone else who does what you do."

The words pierced through the happy haze of excitement and caught her off guard. Swiping away tears as she turned to face him, she saw his eyes widen.

Then she remembered how she'd tried and failed to get Dan the story he wanted.

"You know, I've been trying to find a lead

on the Preston Bank anonymous tip for a couple of weeks." Cassie shifted from one foot to the other and attempted to will away the heat in her cheeks. "I did go to school with Brent Preston, and I knew he was going to need help with the class reunion, so I volunteered. I wanted to grab this chance to build this big story, something I could show to my father. Something printed in an actual newspaper that he can hold in his hands before he tosses all of it except for the crosswords." Cassie shrugged. "But I couldn't do it. I'm not much of an investigative journalist at all."

"You never have been." Dan folded his arms over his chest. "That's not a bad thing. You are a storyteller. World needs storytellers, too."

Cassie knew he meant to sound positive, but that didn't match what she'd been telling herself. Journalism mattered. Breaking the important stories could change the world. She'd told herself for years her job was meaningful because it was journalism-adjacent, not quite there but on the fringe.

Her disappointment must have shown on her face.

Dan grunted. "We're all storytellers, Brooks.

Every one of us. Journalists have to focus on truth, dig to find facts to support our views, explore all sides of the story and be objective. We tell hard stories that people can't look away from, but that's not the only kind of truth out there." He braced his elbows on his desk. "Storytellers lead us to the truth for ourselves. You have to use some facts, but understanding human emotion is just as critical. The warmth of your stories changes the lens from *Look at these strange people who do weird things* to *Be amazed by how passion for something can transform lives*." Dan cleared his throat. "Both are important. Both are hard to do well. But sometimes your storytelling, that personal connection, is the only way to change someone's mind."

Cassie couldn't stop the tears at that point. Dan had managed to take the one skill she knew she could rely on and elevate it to something to be proud of. "You might have a touch of that ability yourself."

His chuckle was rusty. "That's part of being an editor, for sure."

"Well," Cassie said as she dabbed at her eyes, "I managed to find the knit-fashion story after conversations with the receptionist at Preston Bank's corporate offices. She and everyone else I talked to only had solid things to say about their employment experience. If there's anything being hidden there, it's being done very well. The closest I got to a lead was a conversation I overheard in the bathroom that might suggest Brent is involved in something that's not common knowledge, but I have no idea what it might be. He did say he pulls strings to get loans approved for friends, but I'm not sure I'd call that fraud, not in the family business."

"What made you decide to attempt this story?" Dan asked. "All I wanted was a contact."

Cassie rubbed her forehead. "Brent Preston and I have history, but I didn't think he'd be a great person to give you the inside scoop on the bank. I knew he'd open the door for me. I was volunteering to do his work for our high school reunion, after all. That was kind of our thing."

She knew she'd chosen the wrong words when Dan's eyebrows shot up. "A history, huh? You run in Preston circles?"

The distance between the truth and what Dan thought *history* meant made Cassie laugh, and it felt good. "Absolutely not. Our history was like the popular guy who pays the nerd to do his homework, only Brent never directly paid out any money except to cover expenses. He was charming enough to get all that done for free." Cassie grimaced. "I had the biggest crush on him for…forever. Until I had to save him by planning the whole prom in weeks." She pointed at the computer. "Marcus Bryant saved me while I saved Brent. That's the kind of friends we were. Marcus and I have history, too. Real history."

Dan pursed his lips. "This reunion story you pitched, that was your way in the door?"

Cassie hadn't submitted an outline, just floated the idea in their planning meeting. "Yeah, and we're going to need to do a feature on Brent Preston, too." She wrinkled her nose. "Sorry, boss, it seemed like the best cover, a way to move around the bank and ask questions without automatically alerting anyone who might want to hide something."

Dan gave her a slow clap. "I am impressed. Hustle. Sleight of hand in the name of the story. That's journalism."

"Too bad I couldn't find the story." Cassie wasn't sure what she'd expected from her boss. Disappointment, perhaps. That was what she imagined when she pictured telling her father about it.

Marcus would be relieved she'd been telling the truth all along about being over her crush.

Dan shrugged. "Most likely means there is no story, Brooks. You can't make them appear by magic." He pointed at her desk. "The tip line? Ninety-nine percent of the time it's good for your stories, not mine. But that one percent is enough for me to take every tip seriously. That's part of the job we do, too, but it doesn't change the fact that when there's no story, there's no story. Nothing to beat yourself up over, not ever." He held both hands out. "All you can do is give it your best shot, and move on to the next thread that needs to be untangled."

Cassie frowned. "You know, I like you, Dan. I appreciate you." That was a lesson she needed to learn, that giving something everything she had mattered, even if it didn't always work out as she expected. If she could get that, really take it in, her whole life would be easier.

"Aw, you like me." He smiled, a genuine smile. "Not many people will say that."

Cassie was chuckling as she crossed the floor back to her desk. A quick check on Rosa convinced her that his assistant had been eavesdropping on every word. Her happy expression partly explained how Dan had managed to keep his beleaguered assistant all these years.

A good heart could earn loyalty and make it easier to ignore annoying habits.

With renewed confidence in her stories, Cassie made another review of Marcus's column. The picture Nelson had managed to get between Marcus's glares and his frequently moving his hands was perfect: the company's logo was clear, and Marcus was focused on the camera and seemed ready for anything.

That was who Marcus was to her. Focused. Steady as her heartbeat and ready for any challenge.

"Are you expecting a visitor?" Rosa asked. "Someone at the front desk is asking for you."

Cassie checked the time and jerked. She'd lost track, and it was after five o'clock. "Oh, buzz him in. I'll go meet him at the door."

As she stood and carefully smoothed the

skirt of her dress down, Cassie was aware of how Rosa watched. Dan was undoubtedly observing from a safe distance, too.

Being careful not to show any unease, Cassie walked slowly to the glass door that marked their offices and smiled as Marcus waved on the other side. Then she realized how awkward this visit could get. Should she have met him in the parking lot? Maybe. Was it entirely too late to worry about that now? Definitely.

"Hey, I need to grab my purse and we can go," Cassie said as she opened the door.

"Got time to show me around?" Marcus asked as he craned his neck to stare over her shoulder. "I'd love to see your office." When his gaze returned to her face, he was doing it again, giving her that warm, open stare that convinced her he cared for her. His eyes. They were dangerous.

"Sure." Cassie had to clear her throat to get rid of the large frog. "Not too many people still here tonight, but you can get the quick tour." All of a sudden, every step she took felt as if she'd forgotten how to walk. Marcus shouldn't have this much of an effect on her.

Good thing she'd dropped the heeled sandals back in the closet that morning. She needed to keep her feet flat on the ground around him.

"This is Rosa. She keeps *Miami Beat* up and running." Cassie waved a hand and waited while Marcus introduced himself. "My desk." She pointed and glanced out of the corner of her eye to see that Dan had come to perch in the doorway of his office. With his bedraggled tie and messy hair, Dan was the picture of *The news never sleeps*.

"This is my boss, Dan O'Malley, and those are his awards." When she realized how much waving she was doing, Cassie knotted her fingers together in front of her.

"Ah, the reason for the nice outfit replacing the jeans and running shoes. It all becomes clear," Dan murmured before shaking Marcus's hand. Cassie would have told him that it was inappropriate to make comments on her clothing in front of others, but his shark-like grin told her she was going to hear about Marcus's visit and everything to do with it, including her dress, at some later time. She'd fight with him then.

"We're on our way to Coconut Grove to see a caterer. I'll talk to you both in the morning."

Cassie grabbed her purse, shut down her computer and grasped Marcus's hand to tow him out of the office. The longer they stayed, the more Rosa and Dan would have to tease her about later. A quick getaway wasn't a good solution, but it was the only one she had at the moment.

When they made it outside, Cassie took a long, deep breath.

"When you do quick tours, they're *quick*," Marcus said as he moved in front of her to open the passenger-side door of his truck. "Afraid they'll say something embarrassing or I'll say something embarrassing? Which is it?"

"Both," Cassie replied as she climbed in. The urge to tell him again she could open her own door was strong, but he'd closed it before her tangled mind could put the words in order.

"Buckle up."

Cassie hadn't managed to come up with one sensible bit of conversation by the time Marcus expertly wedged his truck between two luxury sedans outside the restaurant in Coconut Grove.

"If your caterer can afford this kind of real estate, how good is her pricing?" Marcus asked before he got out of the truck. Cassie had intended to be out on the sidewalk before he made it around, but he winked at her as he opened her door. He knew her plan as well as she did.

"I did a little research today. This is her father's restaurant. She started her own catering business after she got out of the Army. Sounds like she's doing the same thing you are, building business contacts." Cassie smoothed her dress again, relieved to have found a neutral topic.

"Excellent choice," Marcus stated.

Cassie glanced up, ready to thank him for approving her decision to go with the caterer Brisa had recommended, but she noticed the appreciation on his face. Was he talking about how she was dressed or the caterer?

If he was looking at her like that, did it matter? She would happily accept it every time.

Something had changed between them, but she couldn't name it yet. If Marcus had ever looked at her like that before, with appreciation and heat, she'd never seen it.

Had anyone ever looked at her like this?

No way. It felt too good. She would re-member.

"Are you flirting with me?" Cassie asked as she smoothed her hair behind her ear and wished for some way to tie it up. Wearing it down had been a nice, fresh change that morning. This afternoon, it was strange, like the rest of Cassie's world.

"I was. I was trying to flirt with you." He sighed. "I've always wished I was better at flirting, at having a smooth conversation with a beautiful woman."

Cassie frowned. "We don't flirt. We poke and tease and sometimes encourage, but mainly we give each other a hard time."

He shoved his hands into his pockets. "Some people call that flirting, I think." He shook his head. "If you're not interested in… us that way, it's okay. No problem. But we should give flirting a shot, at the very least." He raised his eyebrows. "I mean, how will we know if we're any good at it, otherwise? Practice makes perfect or something like that." His innocent expression wasn't fooling her.

"I just don't…" Cassie wasn't sure how to finish that. There was so much to say, but she didn't have the words.

"Listen, when I asked you about high school and the first-love stuff... Forget it. Water under the bridge." He crooked his arm and waited for her to slip her hand through. "Let's go eat some fancy food that we aren't paying for and let the rest sort itself out later."

Cassie smiled because he was adorable. There was no other way to say it. Adorable. The kind of guy that it would thrill her to sit down for an awkward first date with. "You're going to keep flirting, though, right?"

"I'm going to try. You let me know if I ever succeed." He winked at her again! Marcus Bryant winked at her.

It was silly and charming and a little out of character.

She loved it. She loved every minute with him.

Cassie was starting to wonder why she'd spent so much time worrying. He was absolutely right. The past wasn't going to change. The only decisions to be made were about their future, and it seemed he was ready to take a gamble to see what it might be. Trusting him was easy, natural.

Maybe it was herself she couldn't quite believe in.

If that was the case, Cassie needed to fix it fast. She couldn't be responsible for hurting Marcus a second time. Just then, she knew she owed it to both of them to be all in for exploring how Cassie and Marcus 2.0 turned out.

CHAPTER SIXTEEN

As Marcus followed Cassie into the shadows of Quill, a restaurant he'd heard other people rave about but had never expected to visit, he tried to let go some of the tension that had settled in his shoulders. He'd wanted to push the idea of more than friendship with Cassie further, but he hadn't prepared himself for how it would overwhelm him emotionally if it seemed to be working.

All signs were pointing to success. He wasn't her brother. Tonight Cassie seemed to be catching on. Even better, he knew he had her attention. She might have brushed off the suggestion of deeper feelings before, but the way she'd watched him that afternoon convinced him she was taking this seriously.

That was all he could ask.

The cool interior of the restaurant gave him time to catch his breath, a welcome relief.

Marcus wanted to be steady, certain for

her. That was who Cassie had always needed him to be.

Cassie glanced over her shoulder at him as they threaded through tables toward an empty private dining room. On any other occasion, Marcus would have been impressed with the romance of the place. Quill was distinctly Mediterranean in design with arched doorways and stucco walls. A large skylight occupied the middle of the restaurant, and the afternoon sun lit a large, tiered fountain right in the center.

Marcus imagined the background of flowing water would add intimacy to any date, and the candles in wrought iron sconces around the room would cast a rosy glow. Marcus made a mental note to bring Cassie here for a date as she held open the carved door to the private room.

Once he'd closed the door behind them, the gentle restaurant noise faded.

"Christina, thank you so much for giving us this opportunity to taste what you're planning for the reunion menu. I'm sure you know better than either one of us what makes for memorable party food," Cassie said to the woman who'd led them through the restaurant.

At *memorable*, Marcus raised his eyebrows. Was that the right goal? *Tasty* or *great* or even *filling* would fit better.

Cassie murmured, "Brent said 'unique and memorable.'" Then she shrugged, her eyes gleaming as they met his. The two of them would have been happy with a classic veggie tray and tasty spinach dip, but not Brent.

"I'm happy to do it! Any friend of Brisa's is a friend of mine, and she's told me more than once how much Marcus has contributed to the Concord Court business lab." Christina brushed her bangs aside and patted her messy bun. "The web designer they connected me to? The difference in traffic to my new site compared to the bare-bones one I threw together… It's amazing. I'm happy to make another Concord Court connection and get great publicity in the process." She slipped Cassie a card. Marcus was impressed with how smoothly she did it. "Thank you for coming early. My father gets annoyed if I'm in his kitchen when the dinner rush lands." Her smile was beautiful as she pulled cloches off trays that lined one wall. "First step of my business-expansion plan is a commercial kitchen of my own. Did you have to come up with that for your business plan?"

Christina rested her hand on his shoulder as she waited for his answer.

Marcus cleared his throat. "I didn't know to do that until I was applying for the bank loan, so it's definitely something to think about." When she didn't step back, he glanced at her hand and then over at Cassie who was not smiling, but her eyes held an amused gleam. "It's also a good measurement of progress. If you set the goals and the timeline to reach them, you know you're moving in the right direction. We wanted an expanded truck fleet and an office space by the end of the first year, and we made it. That feels good."

"I bet it does." Christina squeezed his shoulder. "A kitchen of my own would be a dream come true." She waved a hand. "Where? No idea. Someplace inexpensive and yet up to my standards—so it's imaginary is what I'm saying."

Marcus said, "I get it. We bought a garage for the landscaping business. Needs a lot of work, but it's a solid step."

Christina pointed. "That's it, exactly! I'm happy to see business building, and I like that I can reliably pay the waitstaff, but it does keep me up at night, the jump from where I am to where I want to be."

Marcus knew that firsthand. Every bit of reliable new business that came on board made it easier to sleep.

"No desire for your own restaurant?" Cassie asked absentmindedly as she leaned closer to what appeared to be the barbecue sliders.

"Take one. No, I'm not thinking of a restaurant yet. It's hard enough to step outside of my father's reputation to get this done. With a restaurant, I'd never escape the comparisons." Christina nudged Marcus forward and then turned to pour them each a glass of water from an icy pitcher. "Try everything. This is what I'm proposing. Everything here is finger food, but it's also substantial enough that it feels special. That's what I always want to go for." She frowned. "I should have asked before this… Are you having a bar at this party?"

Marcus turned to Cassie as he realized they'd never once discussed a bar.

Her frown confirmed that she'd never thought of it either, but it faded as she chewed slowly. "This is delicious, Christina." Bliss.

That was the expression on Cassie's face. "Do you happen to know any bartender who might be available to work on short notice? And could possibly take care of getting the alcohol?" Cassie reached for another bite.

"Try the cheese puffs. They have pancetta in them." Christina pulled out her phone and quickly texted. "And that focaccia? It has blue cheese and grapes, which you don't expect but you'll never forget."

Everyone was quiet as Marcus and Cassie worked their way in a leisurely circle around the trays. An occasional "Yum" or "Wow" broke the silence until they heard a ding on an incoming text on Christina's phone.

"How do you feel about serving a good rosé and having cold IPA, cans or bottles depending on your setup, as alcohol options. Water and tea at the serve-yourself station. That way, one bartender can handle the setup, and you'll be supporting my friend Will's efforts to get his brand-new IPA out in the world." Christina grinned slowly. She knew she had a good option, a last-minute solution to a problem they hadn't known they had. "He'll quote you a price if you have an estimate on attendance."

Marcus did quick mental calculations. "No budget for an open bar."

Cassie frowned, but then picked up another cheese puff and grinned.

"That makes it even simpler. Now you have a cash bar with a set price for each drink. Easy-peasy." Christina clapped her hands and texted Will.

Cassie met his stare and shrugged. "This was not a problem we had with prom."

They grinned at each other. He took the barbecue slider she held out. They both happily chewed while they waited for Will to answer. Christina said, "One hundred dollars set-up and tear-down fee, and fifty dollars an hour for anything over three hours."

Cassie didn't even hesitate. "Done. What he sells he keeps, and he cleans up after himself." She dug around in her purse and finally pulled out a business card. "Tell him to email me an invoice, and we'll get him paid. Doors open at seven, but we'll be there all day so he can set up whenever he likes." Then she frowned and pulled out her own phone. "That carpenter, have you got him working on something?"

Marcus swallowed his fourth cheese puff.

"He's building the arches outside, but I wanted him mainly for setup. Gonna need someone else to climb ladders, someone who is not you."

She shook her head, but her grin at his poke was cute. "Right. I'm going to see if he can find or build a small bar and put some wicker or rattan, something garden-y, on it."

Christina finished texting her friend the details while Cassie worked out a deal with the carpenter. Marcus took the last bit of focaccia and enjoyed every bite.

"Max sent a thumbs-up emoji, so he's on board with our plan." Cassie slipped her phone into her purse.

Marcus sipped his water.

"You don't seem too worried about all this last-minute organizing and troubleshooting," Christina said as she stacked the empty trays. "I like that. It's pretty unusual to find, though."

"We want a night to remember. We're well on our way." Cassie shot Marcus a smile as she handed Christina the last empty tray. "Everyone we're working with came with a stellar recommendation. The night will come together."

Marcus could see the urge to argue on

Christina's face. She might want to mention that she was the only person who knew Will, and neither he, nor Cassie, knew Christina personally to trust her recommendations.

If Marcus was worried about the reunion, he would point out those things himself.

But that was how Cassie had always worked. People trusted her to complete everything she promised to do, so she gave everyone else the same grace.

That also made her a great friend.

He'd seen her do it at eighteen, planning the senior class's most important party as if it was a straightforward task. Tonight? It was a pleasure to stand back and watch her work her magic.

"So what should I change?" Christina asked. "The grape focaccia? I knew it was a risk, but sometimes it's fun to play with what everyone expects. That's when you stand out." She picked up a file and a pen. "Do you want to discuss a substitution?"

Cassie met Marcus's stare.

They used to be able to communicate wordlessly, but it had been so many years since they'd spent all their free time together.

Still, it was easy enough to shake his head.

"Keep it. Keep everything the way it is. This is going to be a great party, Christina. Make sure you bring plenty of business cards. The staff photographer, Nelson, will get shots of you and your food." Cassie paused in front of the door. "I don't suppose you'd be willing to give us the recipe for the focaccia?"

Christina tilted her head to the side. "Give *you* the recipe or…"

"No, *Miami Beat*. I order in." Cassie grinned. "But I'd love to try to get you extra room in the magazine. I might be able to sell my editor on including a recipe, and we could list your contact information. It's not a guarantee, but…" She shrugged.

Christina beamed. "Yes. I can do that. Count me in." She clapped her hands in delight. "A paying job *and* free advertising. I love Concord Court."

"Hug Brisa Montero the next time you see her. She's a good friend to have on your side," Marcus said.

"I'll let you know about the recipe." Cassie opened the door.

"And you'll let me know when the issue is online?" Christina asked. "I want to link to it on my website. My web developer tells me that's important." She leaned closer. "And I'd like to show it to my dad."

Cassie pointed. "Definitely. I will do that. Dad opinions can be super important."

Marcus followed Cassie as she navigated the busy restaurant and came to a stop on the sidewalk.

"She's good, isn't she? We both owe Brisa our thanks," Cassie said as she twisted to survey the funky storefronts lining the street. "Why don't I come here more often? I love how this feels like old Miami, so much culture and history."

Marcus made a show of checking his bare wrist. "It's still early. Do you want to grab a drink and take a walk through Peacock Park?"

Her eyes darted to meet his. Was she going to call an end to the night already?

What if he hadn't been on her mind the way she'd been on his?

Then she smoothed loose strands of hair behind her ear. "I'd love to."

CASSIE KNEW IF she squeezed the sweaty bottle of water in her hands any more tightly, the lid was in danger of popping off like a champagne cork. Being so nervous was silly. This was Marcus. Still, she was struggling to make conversation. Strolling through the park next to Biscayne Bay was nice as the sun was setting, but she wanted less silence.

"Do you know what they call a group of peacocks?" Cassie asked.

Marcus shook his head.

"An *ostentation*." He didn't express shock or interest, but she nodded vigorously as if he were positively delighted by her comment. "A group of alligators is a *congregation*." She cleared her throat. "So is a group of crocodiles." Was this what she was left with? Word trivia?

Desperate, she asked, "Do you think I can write a book?"

Marcus paused and then met her stare directly, holding it. "You can do anything you want to. I know that. Is it sometimes impossible to follow where your conversation is going? Yes. But yes, you can write a book."

Cassie realized she'd known his answer before she asked the question. If she asked her father, he would want her to lay out all the obstacles first, think logically about the short-term and long-term outcomes she'd face.

Dan had done some of that. Marcus didn't ask what kind of book, what her idea was or what her end goal would be. He answered the question she'd asked. Could she do it?

His answer had always been *yes*. No one would risk a friendship like that unless they were sure of the outcome, would they? But she was a risk-taker! Why couldn't she make a decision here?

Marcus guided her out of the way of a pair of joggers and motioned to a low retaining wall where they both sat. From here, they could watch the art class going on in the shade of large trees lining the park's grassy field. Six or seven kids were seated on the ground, painting canvases and themselves.

"Do you know what I like about you?" he asked.

What she wanted was an easy joke that made light of the question. Absolutely nothing came to mind, so she shrugged.

"You don't hesitate." Marcus stared out over the water. "Back there with Christina, problems came up, you evaluated possible solutions, and you made a decision. Not everyone can do that. Some people agonize over all decisions, big and small, but you step back, consider and then act. It's impressive."

She liked that he was framing it as a good thing. "Not everyone sees that as a positive trait." When she realized she was twisting the neck of the bottle, Cassie forced herself to set it down.

"You mean your dad?" Marcus asked. He didn't look at her. That made it easier to answer honestly.

"He's had to rescue me from those quick decisions more than once, especially when I was a kid. And he doesn't forget." What was a group of elephants called? That would have been a clever way to deflect, to keep the conversation from getting too serious. "For that matter, you have, too."

"Everybody needs help now and then, Cassie," he said. "People miss out on good stuff because they can't make the decision to go after it. That's not you. You're fun to watch in motion."

She frowned. "Like a pinball in a machine, bouncing here and there."

"Like someone who's living her life today, not in the future or the past." Marcus twisted his own bottle. Was he uneasy, too?

"I've been afraid to ask this, so if you don't want to talk about it, please don't. I think, as your friend, you should be able to talk to me about your Air Force time. I was a spoiled kid, but I'm not anymore." She turned to face him. "Before we tackle any bigger questions, we should make sure this one's settled."

He scooted back to lean on his hands in the grass. "I'll tell you anything you want to know. I worked in airfield management. When I was deployed, I spent all my time on airfields, not much time in the air, unless you count moving from one base to another."

"How was it?" Cassie asked.

"It's definitely not what I pictured when I enlisted." He shrugged. "Pretty much everyone I knew signed up because they felt like they had to do something. There were a few cowboys, determined to head straight into battle. Then there were the rest of us—young, scared, but ready. Instead of becoming a jet pilot, I learned everything there is about airfield operations. Safety hazards. Dangerous conditions. How to raise my voice so that cocky pilots listened to my instructions. It was something I never imagined, but I was good at it. And it was important. I liked that."

Cassie was embarrassed at how different his description of his days was compared to her worst-case imagination at eighteen.

"I'm not a hero with my name in the news, but it made my mama happy to have me on the ground," he said lightly.

"Of course you're a hero," Cassie said, leaning over to get in his face and make sure he understood her. "You made a sacrifice I could never make. You are a hero." When she realized how close she was, Cassie eased back. "You've always been a hero to me, too."

Marcus didn't move, but his hand wrapped around her wrist. "Is that enough about me?"

Cassie shook her head and brushed away her hair when it draped across his cheek. "I'm a reporter. I always have more questions." She rolled her eyes. "Actually, my boss called me a storyteller, but he meant it as a good thing." She tried for a saucy grin to make it clear that she was happy about the description. "My dad will want to know if the title comes with a raise."

Marcus didn't react to her little joke, but she didn't have another to follow it up with, so Cassie pulled her hair back to the side.

"We love our parents, but they can't live

our lives for us." Marcus's thumb traced circles on her skin. Cassie wasn't sure he knew he was doing it. His expression was serious. Being the center of that attention was exciting and reassuring. "My mother was convinced going into business for myself when I got home was the perfect way to waste all my experience, my education and my time. I should have tried to get hired at an airport, earned good money and found the woman of my dreams to give her more grandchildren immediately. But I've done a lot of working for other people. I have this shot to work for myself and do something I could love, and I'm willing to roll the dice on it. If it fails, I'll have to listen to her say *I told you so,* but that's no reason to give up."

Cassie fought the urge to brush a bit of grass off his chest. They were friends, not used to casual touches. Except for Marcus's fingers on her hand.

"I did it in the wrong order. I went after this dream and that dream, and I've lost track of what plan I'm working on now. My dad? He's been there, done that. Times like this, I wonder what my life would have been like if my mom was with us. If he hadn't been so knocked down by grief. Maybe he'll have the energy to be excited for my wins now." She sighed. "But I love him. I might even be getting closer to understanding him. Like with the prom pictures. If I'd told him to have a camera ready, he would have done it." Cassie wanted to make sure Marcus was with her, so she waited for his nod. "And my columns… I have been so irritated with him because he doesn't celebrate them with me, but we had dinner, and I realized…" She tipped her head back. "I made the same mistake with him that I did with you. I was hurt so I withdrew. All I had to do was ask, and my father was ready to talk about my columns. But I've waited so long for him to do something that isn't him, to gush over my writing."

"When I ran into him last week, he seemed…sad. I'm glad he decided to make a change." Marcus's expression was heartfelt. "Things don't change much around there, but your dad, my parents, might need new blood to liven the place up. He could use some excitement."

"I'm relieved to see this change in him, even if the idea of him on a dating app can stop me in my tracks. I'm so happy to see the spark, but at the same time, I'm mad at myself for missing the signs that he was struggling, lonely. Retirement is new. I should have known all that time would lead to sadness. I swear, I have one skill. I look around for people who need help and I help them, but I failed my dad. And when I think about how I let down my best friend…" Remembering it all over again made Cassie's heart ache. "It was an eye-opening pizza dinner, for sure." Her shoulders slumped, but she managed not to jerk when Marcus wrapped his arm around them to squeeze. She didn't want to scare him away.

"It's something special about you, but it's not all you are. He's an adult. I was, too. At some point, we have to learn to ask for what we need. Why does that take so long?" Marcus's slow smile was sweet and too much at close range. "Don't forget that you're a jumper. Jumpers are rare. The rest of us, who dip our toes in the water, are impressed and afraid of jumpers."

Cassie stared down at his hand on her shoulder and then up through her eyelashes to meet his gaze.

"I'm trying to learn to jump. Do you want

me to stop? Move my hand?" he asked, and she realized that how bad they both were at flirting could work in their favor. They might have fewer misunderstandings.

"Did you realize that Christina was letting you know that she was interested in you when she touched your shoulder in the restaurant?" Cassie asked. She already knew the answer.

He rolled his eyes. "No way. She was just…"

Cassie waited for him to realize the truth.

"That's my luck. When I'm already wrapped up in someone else, a woman finally shows interest." Marcus shook his head sadly.

Cassie giggled at his dejected look.

Marcus's hand slid across her back, and he bumped her shoulder with his. "You jump in until I want you to, I guess. This whole thing about being more than friends caught me off guard, but if I could hold your hand while I jump, I'd be ready to try."

"And this is the one time I can't leap before I look. Not with us. It's too important. I've missed you for too long to mess us up again." Cassie understood what he meant. They'd changed places here. She was too scared to jump. "If it makes you feel better,

I've been spending a lot of brain power and time wondering if you were right about us in high school. We were so young. What did we know about love then?"

He braced his elbows on his knees. "I asked you the wrong question, then."

Cassie picked up her water bottle. "What's the right question?"

He raised an eyebrow. "Right here, right now, could we fall in love?"

The panic that swamped her surprised Cassie. No words would come, and she was certain everyone in Peacock Park could hear her racing, pounding heart.

"The way your eyes widened!" Marcus waved his hands. "Scratch that. Forget I asked. Take a deep breath. Can't have you fainting on me here in the park."

Cassie realized her mouth had gone completely dry. Maybe he wasn't exaggerating about her classic response.

"Easier question. Will you be my date to the reunion? I'll make sure to request some Aerosmith, and we can shuffle in a circle like old times." Marcus stood and held his hand out. "That's it. We don't have to know forever. I can settle for that, can you?"

Cassie wasn't sure she believed him. Was he saying that to protect his pride?

"I want to, but we're going to have to call it a date." She bit her lip. "My dad has had a kind of…awakening, thanks to your mother, and he made me a bet. The first one of us to go on three new dates gets to set the other one up, and he's already winning. He cheated! He called the woman your mom was trying to introduce him to and set up brunch!" She hoped her scandalized tone was setting things back to normal between them. The fluttery, restless sensation that his interest in her as more than friends stirred up was hard to live with. "Will you be one of my dates?"

Marcus frowned. "I asked first. I mean, I called it a date. The panicked alarm in your ears might have been too loud for you to hear that." Then he grinned widely.

Relieved that she didn't have to make any life-altering decisions there beside Biscayne Bay, Cassie slipped her hand in his. "Nobody I'd rather shuffle slowly and mime singing a power ballad with than you. My best friend."

He paused. "Best friend."

Cassie fought the urge to jump in and say that it didn't mean anything except she didn't want to ever lose him again, that she was still thinking about the love question, but she didn't ever want to feel the way she had the last time they'd argued… There were so many things to say, but none of them answered any questions.

It was nice to walk next to Marcus while the sun sank. She'd missed him for so long and had told herself that she was fine without him.

Now she knew that she hadn't been fine. Her life had been less than it could have been because he wasn't next door, around the corner or at the other end of the phone line.

How would she ever recover now that she knew what she'd be missing if they went for more than friendship and it didn't work out?

CHAPTER SEVENTEEN

MARCUS STOOD AT the bottom of the ladder and tried not to think about how high the other end would be. The view from the bottom was one thing; once he made it to the top, he'd better not look down at the wooden gym floor. Max Duplaix, the carpenter who'd shown up bright and early to help with anything and everything, was right next to the ladder, hands on his hips as he stared up at the gym ceiling. The fact that Max was shaking his head slowly confirmed that Marcus would be the one defying gravity.

Was Brent Preston or the success of the high-school reunion worth this?

No way.

But it was easy to imagine the look on Cassie's face when she saw the lights strung up like stars. Enchanted.

"Hand me the first string," Marcus muttered.

"Me, I don't believe we need lights up

there, boss," Max said slowly. "Maybe…" He turned right and then left. "We put 'em on the tables. That's better. No ladder involved. How many extension cords we got?" He was ready to race off to work. The guy might not want to climb the school's gigantic ladder to reach the gym ceiling, but it wasn't because he wanted to rest.

"This is the most important part," Marcus said firmly, prepared to convince them both and get moving. He'd rearranged all his plans for the setup so that he could get this done first. He didn't trust Cassie not to skip up the ladder. Because it had to be done, and she wouldn't want anyone else taking the risk.

Marcus might survive a fall, but he'd never make it through watching Cassie fall from that height.

"All right. We start in this corner. You stay down here and…"

"Pray. I'll pray for you, boss." Max nodded firmly.

"I was going to say keep all the cords straight and hand me things, but prayer works, too," Marcus muttered as he headed up the ladder, cords slung over his shoulder so he could begin attaching the twinkle lights that had better add a huge amount of enchantment to the garden he was building for Cassie.

As he climbed up and down the ladder, Marcus tried to focus.

Whenever his nerves caught him, it was easy enough to keep going. All he had to do was picture the delight that would cross Cassie's face. He'd seen it more than once.

When she'd managed a tricky wastebasket shot.

When they'd mouthed the words to "I Don't Want to Miss a Thing" on the prom's dance floor.

When she'd seen the picture of him in his uniform hanging in the office of the business he was building.

When she'd enjoyed her first bite of cheese puff with pancetta.

He wasn't sure there was another woman in the world for whom he'd volunteer to open up a musty gym at eight in the morning on a Saturday to risk his neck for twinkle lights. But he was almost certain what it meant that he'd do it for her after all these years.

The fact that she wasn't convinced they were meant for more yet...

Well, it was too early to give up hope.

So he kept climbing.

"That's it, boss. Last string," Max said as he made sure to plant his feet solidly on the ground to anchor the ladder. "Little over three hours. Not bad. Ought to come down in half that time."

Marcus paused in moving the ladder. They had to come back down, too. He hadn't even thought of that. "Listen, if anybody asks you about these lights, you tell them they were there when we got here. We don't know who put them up."

Max patted him on the shoulder. "Sure thing. How 'bout I string up the lower lights? Let's place the posts." The posts he'd built and painted black to blend into the shadows were easy enough to arrange. They hung the old-fashioned Edison-bulb strings to frame the dance floor. Marcus wanted to mark the space and give it the feeling of an outdoor party with atmosphere. Without turning out the overhead lights and plugging everything in, he couldn't be sure that he was getting the effect he wanted, but there was no time to worry about that now.

"As soon as Cassie gets here, let's go pick up the outdoor arches for the walkway." Marcus pulled out his notebook. "Honeysuckle vines." He'd forgotten his inspired plan to go cut live vines at Pascual's. He wasn't sure he had enough time, but he didn't want to let it go, either. "Do you have time to ride out with me to The Nursery to collect some vines?"

Max held out both hands. "Yours all day long, boss. You tell me."

"I wish I knew." Dissatisfied that his plan was missing perfection at such an early stage, Marcus shook his head. "We'll do the best we can."

Max said, "*Bien*, let's get the bar I built off the trailer and hit the road. Miss Cassie said noon." He tapped his naked wrist. "Almost noon?"

Marcus checked his phone. It was close. Everything was taking longer than he expected. That was a good lesson, but he would have appreciated it at a different moment.

They'd moved the lightweight bar to the end of the basketball court nearest the bathrooms when the doors opened and Cassie walked in.

Imagining her face when she saw the room in full effect later on was what his whole payoff was here.

"Marcus!" she exclaimed, "you…" She pointed at the ceiling. "Did you and Max hang all the lights already?"

Marcus ignored the funny celebration dance Max was doing behind her back and nodded calmly. Serenely. As if it was nothing. He was glad he'd finished climbing and clutching the ladder before she'd gotten here. That made it easier to pretend it hadn't bothered him a bit.

Then he managed to catch her as she launched herself at him, her arms open wide for a hug. "I can't believe it. Why didn't you tell me to get here earlier? I could have helped." Then she leaned back, her eyes narrowed in a mean glare. "You really don't want me climbing any ladders, do you?"

A slow grin spread across his face. Whatever came next, he loved being here with her like this. She was sure her plans were coming together perfectly and was clearly thrilled about it.

"Well, the rental company is in the parking lot, and there are a few cars, which I hope are Brent's volunteers. No sign of the man himself yet?" Cassie asked.

Marcus tilted his head to the side. Surely

she didn't expect Brent Preston to have shown up that early on a Saturday.

"Right." Cassie grinned. "What am I thinking?"

Aware of the ticking clock, Marcus pointed at Max. "We're about to leave to pick up and install the arches Max put together for the walkway. Then I need to get out to Pascual's. Meanwhile, his team is going to be delivering plants. They should be here soon." Marcus handed her his notebook. "You can follow these diagrams to show his guys where to place everything. I'll be cutting it close as it is." But he wanted live honeysuckle blooms.

Cassie flipped through the pages. "I can follow instructions, but I don't want you to miss this chance to put your touch on everything. Would another volunteer make a difference?" Cassie asked.

"We need everyone here." Marcus patted his pockets, already feeling lost without his notebook.

"Boss?" Max called from the door.

"Better go. I've got this." Cassie waved at a man wheeling in a stack of chairs. "If anything comes up, I'll call you."

Marcus stopped. If she needed him, she'd call him.

Just like old times.

Cassie guessed some of what he was thinking. "You may be sorry I have your phone number again. Go. I've got this. She squeezed his hand. "We have to finish setting up on time because we have a date tonight, remember?" One side of her mouth curved up. It was the kind of expression that convinced a man he could move mountains if he had to.

Marcus had a burst of energy at the promise and jogged across the floor to meet Max. That boost lasted through loading the arches and unloading them in front of the gym. It lasted through talking over the arrangement of lighting and plants for the arches and the outdoor registration table with Cassie's team of volunteers.

And about halfway to Pascual's, Marcus realized he was enjoying himself.

No matter that he'd lost all control of the design.

Or that Cassie, who never hesitated, was weighing all her options so carefully.

This was his life. He was doing something he enjoyed, building a business to be proud of and reconnecting with the important people in his life.

It was a lot to accomplish on a Saturday, but he could thank Cassie for a big chunk of that.

He was going to make this a night to remember for the two of them.

Then she might be ready to jump in with both feet.

CASSIE KNEW THE grin on her face was completely inappropriate for sweating while she arranged and rearranged tables and chairs to her liking, but the happiness that glowed in her chest made it impossible to do anything else. Things were behind schedule, but everything important about this reunion was right on time.

Marcus was here. That was enough.

"Hello, we got some plants for you," Pascual yelled from the doorway.

"Oh, good." Cassie waved him in. "The florist with the orchids and the smaller bushes has been here, but we've been waiting on the main event." She pointed at him. "That's you."

The man puffed out his chest. "Away we go, eh?"

Cassie studied the first potted tree Pascual's crew rolled in and flipped through the pages until she decided it belonged on the stage. As each plant entered, she referred to Marcus's sketches, crossed her fingers that she was reading them correctly and gave direction. There were more plants than she expected, and her confidence at matching shrub to drawing started to falter.

Once they were all in place, she stood in the center of the gym and turned in a slow circle while she studied all the arrangements and chewed on her fingernail.

"Good?" Pascual asked, one foot pointed at the door. He was ready to move on with the rest of his day.

"Should I call Marcus to be sure?" she asked. "I could put him on and show him everything over the phone."

Pascual tapped his watch. "Late, you know?"

As Cassie checked the time, Pascual took the notebook from her. She watched him walk to every arrangement. At one point, he shook his head and switched two shrubs out while he muttered under his breath. Obviously, she didn't recognize her plants well enough.

When he was satisfied with the setup, he

marched back over to her. "We're good. Marcus will be happy." He dropped the notebook but scooped it up before she could reach for it. He frowned at the notebook and then held it out to her. "What's this?"

With a sinking feeling that they'd forgotten a critical part of the set-up, Cassie took the notebook and saw instead a drawing of a girl. She was wearing a dress that might have been Cassie's prom dress.

Cassie couldn't look away. She then remembered that he'd sketched something while they were looking at photos in his office. He'd been describing her dress.

He'd been drawing it at the same time.

"Looks like you." Pascual raised his eyebrows. "Not the face, but the rest."

Cassie laughed, glad Marcus wasn't there to hear his art criticized. He'd always struggled with faces. This one wasn't completely faithful to Cassie's actual features, but overall, it was good. Sweet.

And it was like the artist had captured who she was better than how she looked.

"What's this?" Pascual asked as he tapped the top-left corner. "Moon? Looks like a big rock gonna crush you."

"That is an asteroid." Cassie nodded firmly as Pascual scrunched his face, obviously confused. "Yep. An asteroid." The background behind her was space, but the stars Marcus had drawn in made her think of the white lights he'd shown up hours early to hang.

Only a fool would hesitate to take a chance with this man.

Cassie had been a fool before. She'd been a fool for Brent Preston, but she was over that. She was not a fool anymore. "Good job." She patted the man's shoulder. "You and your crew have made this party special. Thanks, Pascual."

Pascual nodded broadly. "You can count on us. Make sure you tell Marcus that. He's going to be big in business soon." The hand truck he was pushing squealed as if it was seconding his statement, and they both laughed. "Good to know the right people, eh?" He motioned with his head toward Brent Preston who had shown up for the last hour of setup and not one minute before.

Cassie would barely have time to get home to change. Dancing the night away in shorts that were smudged with plant dirt and gym smells and who knew what else was not going to work.

"We'll be back about the same time tomorrow to pack everything up." Pascual leaned closer. "Maybe you and I could brunch beforehand?"

Cassie's phone vibrated as she registered what he was asking. Pascual was asking her out. What a charmer.

"Unless you and Marcus…" Pascual held up his hands. "Of course you and Marcus! Man does not go to all this work for some referrals." He whistled a happy tune as he strutted off, and Cassie was glad her non-answer hadn't poked holes in his confidence. She was also glad to have the chance to absorb the shock of his answer.

Marcus had done this not once but twice… for her. He'd worked this hard for her, no one else.

If she had to guess, he wouldn't have volunteered the first time, much less the second time, especially since Brent Preston was still involved.

The same Brent Preston who had done none of the hard labor but was managing to soak up the accolades like dry soil.

She rolled her eyes, then pulled out her phone to see a text from her father.

Need some help. Can you come by before six tonight?

Cassie sent him a thumbs-up emoji. He never asked for help. For that matter, he never texted, either. Of course this would be the time when he did. Had he forgotten her reunion? Probably, but she could go and give him a hand with whatever it was and ask Marcus to swing by her dad's to pick her up for the reunion. Miss Shirley would appreciate the chance to see Marcus in a suit.

She hadn't realized how long she stood there staring at her phone, imagining grownup, handsome Marcus…a man she was going to date. Marcus in a suit. Then Brent said, "Goofy grin on your face, Casserole. Your boyfriend?"

Cassie shoved the phone back into her pocket. "All right, everyone. That's it. Thank you for your time and effort. Doors open at seven. Go home and put your dancing shoes on." She waited until people started moving toward the gym doors before asking, "That's *all* you have to say to me?"

He smirked. "Great job. I should have led with that."

At the very least. Cassie inhaled slowly. She was almost through here. There was no need to start a fight, not anymore. "Thanks. Marcus had the vision. Make sure to tell him he did a great job, too."

She headed for the door. No way was she going to waste precious time on Brent when she could be doing her hair and makeup.

"Is he still involved? I didn't see him around," Brent said before he trotted to catch up with her. Cassie turned all the lights off and dragged Brent through the doorway before he could get the full effect of the lighting. She didn't have time for him to be impressed, not now.

"He's been driving all over southern Florida," Cassie said as she pointed at the blooming vines that Marcus had dropped off for the volunteers to arrange over the arches leading into the gym. "Going the extra-special mile."

"For me?" Brent asked, his charming grin lopsided.

At that question, it all hit Cassie, everything that Marcus had done to build this special night.

"Nope, he did it all for me." The thrill that spread through her at admitting that out loud stole her breath. Grand gestures had all but disappeared, especially in the modern dating world. This was, by far, the biggest sacrifice anyone had made for her since…the last time he'd done it.

How clueless could one woman get? However her evaluation of whether she'd loved Marcus at eighteen turned out, there was no question in her mind that he'd loved her.

She'd had the love of an amazing boy who had become an impressive man, a true hero.

Why would she even hesitate to see where that could go?

"You need to be here no later than a quarter to seven to make sure all the volunteers are in place at the registration table." Cassie handed him the key ring and made an executive decision on the spot. "Plant guys will be back tomorrow around noon to pick everything up. You'll need to possibly hire someone brave enough to take down the lights."

"Hey, wait. That wasn't our deal," Brent said. "What about the favor you owe me?"

Cassie stopped in her tracks, his words catching her off guard. She bent over in the parking lot, giggling until she cried. "Favor. I owe *you* a favor?" When she managed to catch her breath, Cassie wiped under both eyes and inhaled slowly to catch her breath.

"I thought you were getting your story and Bryant's business and…" Brent twirled the key ring. "What's so funny?"

Cassie tipped her face up to the afternoon sun. "Let's talk favors. How many times did I copy down your homework for you? And you remember that time you needed somcone to sneak you into homeroom? Who pretended to faint to get you in the door?" Cassie closed her eyes and wished she could cut those memories out of the playback of her high-school years.

The only consolation was that she would never be caught doing that again.

"I don't owe you a single favor. Marcus will get business from this because he's good at what he does. So will the caterer and the bartender. They don't, in fact, need favors, either, because I brought good people together." Then she pointed at the key ring. "But now that I've done all the heavy lifting, you can handle the rest. I am going to have the best night of my life, so I'm calling us even. All those favors you owe me? Tonight is going to make up for every single one."

Marcus was going to take the day off tomorrow. Neither one of them was climbing the ladder to reach the gym ceiling again, not for Brent Preston.

"Oh." Cassie turned around and moved closer. "Don't think of dragging Jane Wynn into the cleanup. Show some character and treat her better than you did me, Brent." Cassie wouldn't betray Jane's secret.

And his sputtering? That was the icing on the cake, but she wasn't coldhearted. As she backed out of her parking spot, Cassie called, "Pay the high school's custodian twice what he's worth to go up that ladder." She'd slip Max Duplaix's number into Brent's pocket later on, and then she'd warn Max that he was going to get a phone call and he should negotiate an exceptionally good rate for himself.

Brent's best quality was being generous with his money, a valuable trait for a banker to have. Everyone could profit with her plan.

But the best part was that she and Marcus could just…be. They could be young again.

They could dance. They could yell power ballads at each other. If everything went the way she expected it would, they could be more after the evening was over than they had been before.

Because there was nothing like watching a man start work early on Saturday morning, hustle all over town to go the extra step to build a truly enchanted garden, complete with a vine-draped walkway, and know that he would do it over and over again.

All for a girl who'd once hurt him like no one else could have.

Whatever happened next would happen, but there was no way for Cassie to ignore the fact that Marcus was worth the gamble.

CHAPTER EIGHTEEN

HURRYING TO HER father's apartment was doing her hair no favors, but it was distracting her from the excitement that made it impossible for Cassie to relax. That was a problem she needed to get under control before Marcus showed up. A sweaty brow and frizzy hair were not the impression she wanted to make on their first date—the first real date where they both knew it was a…thing.

"You definitely need to come up with a better description than *thing* before you talk about it out loud," Cassie muttered to herself as she opened her father's door. It hadn't closed completely before she raised her voice to yell, "I'm here. What do you need help with?"

Her father came down the hallway. "All the neighbors know you're here, too." He was wearing…clothes. Nice clothes. Dark pants. White shirt. "This okay for a dinner date?"

He held his arms out, a silk tie dangling from one hand.

"Where did you get that tie?" Cassie asked. This was not her father's normal style. At all.

"Every Christmas, I give Shirley a gift certificate to her and her husband's favorite steak place. She gives me a new tie and a new button-down shirt. We all know it's tradition." He shook his head. "There's usually a woman's phone number tucked inside the pocket of the shirt."

Cassie covered her mouth with her hand as she did a slow turn around her father. "You look great, Dad, but you might be overdressed. None of the men I've been out with over the past decade have actually worn a tie on the first date."

He frowned. "Unacceptable."

When Cassie recalled the wrinkled T-shirts, sleep-crusted eyes and one-word answers she'd experienced on first dates, she was inclined to agree, but she didn't want to give him the wrong impression. If he was diving into dating, he might need an update.

Cassie took the tie he offered her. "I don't know about that, but...you will make a good impression like this. What do you want me to do with the tie?"

"Tie it for me. I've forgotten how." He motioned that it went around his neck as if she wasn't sure how that part worked. Cassie pulled out her phone. Internet video to the rescue.

After she'd watched three videos twice, Cassie managed a decent knot and smoothed the tie down his chest. "Erin won't know what hit her."

"Carmella." He smoothed one hand over his hair as he checked his reflection in the mirror that hung over the couch next to his wedding photo. "I wore a golf shirt for my date with Erin. I did iron my pants, though. Brunch seemed more casual than dinner."

Cassie plopped down on the couch. "You're on your second date?" Already.

His smug grin would have been cute if they didn't have a bet riding on this.

"Yep. One more's all I need." He rubbed his hands together, clearly counting his win already.

"How was brunch?" Cassie asked. "Where did you meet Carmella?" And why was it bothering her so much that he'd become the one who jumped in with both feet? Cassie hadn't known the trait ran in the family. Her father never seemed to jump at all.

"Her name and phone number were tucked in with this year's shirt and tie." He pointed at it in case Cassie needed an illustration. "I checked with Shirley first, to make sure Carmella was still single. She is." He held out his hands as if to say *Voilà!* No dating apps needed after all.

"I've been going about this all wrong my whole life," Cassie stated. "I should have been dropping big, broad hints Miss Shirley's way."

Her father sat down in his recliner, pinching his pants carefully to make sure they didn't get excessive wrinkles. "Oh, she's working behind the scenes for you, too. Don't doubt that."

Cassie frowned. "I haven't gotten any anonymous notes with names and numbers of eligible bachelors."

"That's because, for her, only one eligible bachelor will do." Her father tangled his fingers together, completely relaxed in his usual pose, while also being ready to go out on a date. Cassie was having trouble reconciling it all in her brain. "When I win this bet, she's already got your date planned."

"One bachelor." Cassie wanted to pretend she didn't know who he meant. This…whatever it was between her and Marcus was too fragile to be pinning everyone's hopes on. Neither she nor Marcus had any proven success with relationships.

"Dad," Cassie said slowly as she worked through the question in her head, "why now? Why does now seem like the right time to date? After all these years, I guess I expected you…wouldn't. Like, ever."

He didn't look at her as he asked, "Does it bother you?"

"No," Cassie said immediately. "No way. I'm happy. I've wanted this, but…" He'd seemed so stuck in his grief, so she'd never brought it up. Miss Shirley had been the only one doing that heavy lifting.

"Losing someone changes you, or it did me. My whole life narrowed down to one person. You. Keeping you safe was it. That meant keeping a good job and a roof over our heads and you in one piece. I could tell myself I was fine because I was accomplishing that. This year, I was sitting outside on…the anniversary—"

he glanced at her to make sure she understood what he meant, so Cassie nodded "—and Marcus came by his parents' for dinner. The gangly kid you used to run with was…grown. Fully grown and talking about his business and your career, and it was all so easy to see, how you two could fit." He shrugged. "Leaving me… by myself. Maybe that was enough, or it was the final straw, realizing someday you'd go to dinner with him, be part of the family. And I would be…in the same exact place."

"You're part of the family, Dad. You have your own spot at the card table," Cassie said impatiently because she knew there was no way Miss Shirley had ever excluded him.

"You know there's a difference between being like family and until-death-do-you-part family. You know you do." Her father shook his head. "Doesn't matter. I won't be the grown man trailing along behind his daughter because he had nowhere else to go."

"You don't need a girlfriend for that," Cassie said because her mouth wouldn't form the word *wife*. "And Marcus and I…there's nothing between us." Yet.

He raised his eyebrow, the perfect picture of skepticism. "No matter what, I've got to get myself out of this house. Erin, Carmella and Bev are going to help me with that. And hopefully I can help them in return."

"Bev." Cassie wasn't going to panic. Bev could have a packed social life and be booked up for…

"Tomorrow. Lunch. Bev." He held up three fingers and waved them.

Cassie had to laugh. She should have never made the bet. If there was one thing her father hated, it was losing.

His grin was pretty cute.

"Marcus is only one for me, so…" Cassie shrugged. "I should admit defeat. Go ahead and tell me what Marcus and I are doing." She could be a gracious loser.

"Oh, I don't know. You could see if that Preston guy is available tonight. You're beautiful inside and out. He'd say yes if you asked him to dinner, I bet." Her father waggled his tie at her. "Don't let him go like you did in high school."

"You're kidding, right?" Cassie asked. "I followed him around. No way he could have missed a crush that big." She huffed. "And all along, there's Marcus, being the absolute best of everything. I can't trust my taste in men."

Her father shrugged. "Good thing you can trust Miss Shirley and me and Marcus, unless the guy's less intelligent than I thought."

Cassie opened the small purse she'd packed to go with her dress. "Is it possible to fall in love without knowing it, Dad?"

He stared hard at her high-school graduation picture hanging over the television while he thought. "I think so. Or I believe it's possible to love someone more than you know until they're gone. When your world crumbles and your vision shrinks to a tiny point, you start to understand how much one person can mean." His sad smile was sweet. "Your heart is broken, but you also have this overwhelming gratitude that you had them for as long as you did. That's a struggle to overcome. You have to want to break out of that." He paused and looked upward for a moment. "And once you've had that, you're certain no one else will ever measure up. Some of us take that as a sign that looking is a waste of time."

He leaned back in his chair.

"Marcus asked me if it was possible that we were in love as kids. I don't think I was," Cassie said as she opened up the notebook she'd stuck inside her purse to stare at Marcus's sketch. "But he might have been. That means I've broken his heart once already. I'm afraid to do it again."

Her father was serious as he considered that. "It's possible that he loved you and didn't know it. And maybe you did break his heart." He squeezed her hand. "But you're both different people now. Who knows what the future holds? Also, he's a grown man. If he's okay with possibly getting hurt again, that's on him, not you."

Cassie smoothed her dress down. "Right. You're right, but I only want good things for Marcus."

"You better want good things for yourself, too." He tilted his arm to check his gold watch, the one he'd gotten for retirement after forty years with the same company.

She did. There was no question Marcus could be good for her. His steadiness, his strength and his ability to match her step for step while never losing sight of the goal or control of the situation meant he would always make her life better.

But what about his own life? Would he be content to follow her around and keep her from failing?

"How do I look?" Cassie asked, determined to hear what she needed to from her father. Without the prompt, he might never think to say it and she could use a confidence boost.

"Beautiful. Like your mother." He pointed at her feet. "Although I'm worried about those heels. You don't wear heels."

Cassie stared down at her feet and wondered if he might get better with positive feedback if she gave him more practice. Then she realized looking like her mother might be his highest compliment and decided to hold that close.

At the knock on the door, her heart raced again and Cassie had to take a calming breath as she stood and handed her father her phone.

"This time, I want you to take photos of me and Marcus." Whatever happened, she wanted the memories.

"Been practicing with the phone you got me. Erin likes to use funny GIFs to jazz up her texts," he said. Cassie paused with her hand on the doorknob. She had a lot of questions after that comment, but they would all lead her away from this moment.

Instead, she took another steadying breath,

fanned her face a few times to try to chase the heat away and opened the door.

There, on her father's doorstep, stood Marcus. He was dressed in a dark suit with a crisp white shirt. She'd seen him so many different ways through the years—mostly dirty, sweaty and happy because they'd run every spare minute when they were kids. At prom, he'd worn a tuxedo of some sort. The notebook she had in her bag reminded her that he'd noticed every detail of her dress that night. Noticed and remembered it still.

She hadn't done the same.

Cassie regretted that lost opportunity, but she was happy to have a chance to make a new memory.

He was perfectly framed on either side by his mother and father.

"I have my camera this time. We want to document this date for the grandchildren," Miss Shirley sang and motioned Cassie outside to stand next to Marcus under the arch that ran between their apartments.

"Grandchildren? I'm guessing she doesn't mean Tasha's twins," Cassie muttered out of the side of her mouth.

Marcus grunted. "No, she does not." They

shared a glance that surprised a laugh out of Cassie. She was nervous with Marcus, like she'd never been before, not even when she'd reached out to him after years of distance.

But the two of them had always been united against their parents.

"Let's get this show on the road. I have to meet my date in fifteen minutes," her father said and brushed away Miss Shirley's thrilled pats on the shoulder. "None of that. Let's get the kids fixed up first."

"Fixed up," Marcus said next to her ear. "Are they all in on this?"

Cassie didn't hesitate to answer. "Of course they are. We're going to have to split them up and end dominoes and cards, if we want to keep them from conspiring against us."

"Never gonna happen. We are family." Her father motioned them closer together and held up her phone. When he carefully poked the screen, Cassie told him, "Take more than one." She didn't want the single picture she had to be with one eye closed and her mouth hanging open.

Why couldn't men see that in the pictures they took? It was digital. The photo was right there.

Then she remembered Nelson was meeting her at the gym to take photos for *Miami Beat* and relaxed. Nelson would not let her down.

Marcus wrapped his arm around her waist and pressed his mouth closer to her ear. "You look beautiful tonight. All these years, and you've only gotten prettier, more Cassie-like."

She wrinkled her nose and knew without a doubt that was the photo her father had gotten.

"I hunted for a halter dress, but no luck. Fashion has changed." She ran her hands down the pale blue sheath that she'd settled on and realized she felt good in it. And she knew what he meant by *Cassie-like*. For the first time in a long time, everything was clicking.

"One more, children, and then you may be on your enchanted way," Miss Shirley called out as she looked for the perfect angle. When she was satisfied, she nodded. "Do not come home early."

Cassie chuckled as she took her phone from her father. "What kind of order is that?"

Miss Shirley smiled serenely. "A smart one."

"You, sir, come home at a decent time." Cassie pointed at her father. "Mind your manners. Don't keep Carmella waiting."

She pressed a kiss to his cheek, wrapped her hand around Marcus's and led him toward the parking lot.

When they stopped in front of his truck, he stared at her. "Thank you for getting me out of there quickly."

"Anytime you need me, I'm here for you." It felt good to say that to him.

But when he didn't return it, she realized the question of what they would be to each other was still lingering between them. At some point tonight, she was going to have to jump in with both feet...

Or risk losing Marcus again.

CHAPTER NINETEEN

MARCUS WAS SURPRISED by the emotion that bubbled up as he parked in front of the old gym. He was proud of what they had accomplished and hopeful that his hard work would turn into new business. The lot was filling up with cars, which signaled a bigger crowd for this reunion that only one person in the world could have talked him into attending. The fact that she was sitting next to him was contributing to the anxiety. The Cassie he knew was a girl who skated next to him, plotted low-level shenanigans and made him laugh. The woman he was getting to know still had traces of that girl, but she was also a professional with goals and dreams that might or might not include him.

Tonight in the cab of his truck, Cassie was brand-new. Flawlessly put together. No halter on this dress, but it was an icy blue and fit her perfectly. With her hair down and makeup that enhanced her bright eyes and her lips, Cassie was heart-stopping.

And very quiet.

That wasn't helping.

"You ready to do this?" he asked, his voice too loud in the silence between them.

"Almost." She fiddled with her bag and eventually pulled out his notebook. "I need to give this back to you first."

"Okay," he said as he took it and tossed it in the console. "Hope it helped with setup." Was she worried that the plants were in the wrong groupings? At this point, it didn't matter to him. No one else would know, either.

Marcus watched her stare at the notebook for a moment and waited for whatever was coming next. Eventually, she glanced at him. "I'm worried. That doesn't make a lot of sense."

He opened his door and hurried around to catch the passenger door as she slid out to stand next to the truck. "I'm nervous, too. Hold my hand."

Cassie rolled her eyes but slipped her hand inside his. He'd meant to tease her, but the connection between them worked to quiet the tumble of fears for Marcus. She needed him to be sure, so she could be sure.

"Ready to dance?" he asked as they walked up to the entrance.

"With you? Always." She grinned. "Are you ready to take your business referrals to the next level?"

He patted his jacket. "Pocketful of business cards to hand out. Ready as I'll ever be."

She squeezed his hand as they stepped up onto the curb in front of the arch that set the enchanted mood for the gym. Lights sparkled among the flowering vines. The coral honeysuckle flowers were holding up, which was a relief. He'd been afraid they'd walk in under shriveled buds. The arches were exactly what he'd pictured.

So was the expression on Cassie's face. Her eyes sparkled like the lights. "Look what you did, Marcus." Her voice was breathless.

In that second, Marcus knew he was invincible. He'd put that wonder on her face.

He pulled out his phone. He never wanted to forget this. "Let's take a selfie."

She stepped closer, and he moved to wrap his arm around her waist, his other arm stretched to take the photo. He showed her the phone to get approval on the photo and slipped it into his pocket when she nodded.

But he wasn't ready to step away.

"Before we go in and get tangled up in people and Brent Preston—" he said but lost the words he'd ironed out in his head when she stretched up on her toes and pressed her lips to his. The kiss was unexpected, but he caught her before she could leave. "Let's try that again."

"I'm sorry. I had to do it. I've been concerned about us and you and…" Cassie stopped talking.

Her eyes were locked to his as he kissed her the way he'd wanted to since she'd tripped back into his life. Slowly. The heat between them drawing them even closer while the world dropped away. Cassie's hands rested on his shoulders and when he remembered where they were well enough to stop, to take a breath, she sighed.

"Wow," Cassie whispered.

The tone, the dazed expression, that was all he wanted. Whatever happened next, he could work with that. "Let's go inside."

Cassie wordlessly slipped her hand into his, and they walked under the arches to the registration table. He filled out both of their name tags and pinned hers carefully to her dress with a gardenia blossom. They made conversation that he would never remember, but he handed out two business cards when she poked him to remind him.

Then they stopped in front of the doors to the gym. Cassie squeezed his hand. "This is it. Let's go get enchanted."

Laughter felt right, then. The nerves were gone. This was going to be fun.

CASSIE WAS SLOWLY but surely coming back to herself after the kiss of her lifetime when Marcus opened the gym doors. She was almost sure the sparkles in her vision were from the twinkling white lights strung overhead. Stepping inside took her breath away. The gym had been transformed. The edges were still there, enough to tie the place to memories of the school, but the old basketball court was a street party with a dance floor lit by a warm glow. Tables and chairs were clustered, some collecting old friends for catching-up conversation. Food and drinks were already popular with a short line snaking around the table. The DJ was playing something, but the volume would be low until Brent Preston finished his welcome speech. Someone had remembered to start the slideshow of old prom pictures.

"It's perfect." The relief was intense. "You did this, Marcus. Regardless of how many new clients you get tonight, it won't be enough. I could never have managed without you."

"Come on, Cassie. You have to know better than that. Plants and lights, that's me. Everything else is you. Don't minimize that."

Cassie frowned as she considered that. "I filled in the pieces every party needs. You made it special."

He started to argue, and Cassie desperately wanted to know what he would say, but Nelson walked up. "You want to take photos before the party gets rocking?"

Cassie nodded. "Yeah, let's grab Brent and get this out of the way."

What she wanted to do was get food, eat, hurry Brent through whatever nonsense he was going to say on the stage and then spend the rest of the night dancing with Marcus, laughing with Marcus and making sure everyone in the gym knew that Marcus was the best landscaper in Miami.

In that order.

The only way to get there was to knock out all the work.

Brent was standing near the bar, a bored Jane Wynn hovering next to him as his requisite date.

Cassie smiled at her. "I love your dress, Jane. I'm so happy you're here."

"Hey, thanks," Jane said as she perked up. "You did an amazing job with this event."

"Let me introduce you to the real magic. This is Marcus Bryant, the man behind Southern Florida Landscape Design. He did all this." She frowned at Marcus. "Your card. Give her a card." Then pointed as he followed directions. "Hold on to his card in case your house could use some enchantment, too." How many times was she going to say something similar that night? She'd say it a thousand times if it would push Marcus's business to where he wanted it to be. "Brent, you remember Nelson. He's going to get some shots, and then we can do the introduction and start the dancing."

Brent's grin was lazy. "I thought you said

you were done running the show when you handed over the keys, Casserole."

She bared her teeth. It might look like a smile, but she didn't mean it in her heart. "Not the important parts, Brent."

"Let's go out and take photos with the arches in the background. That is a beautiful setup outside." Nelson didn't wait for them to agree but headed for the doors.

As she and Marcus followed, she bent close to his ear. "If you have time, can you make sure Jane isn't standing around by herself? She's doing one of Brent's favors and doesn't know anyone here. She needs to be photographed with him, but I'm afraid he'll leave her hanging the rest of the time."

Marcus studied her face. "You bet."

Then she was working. Posing with Brent or Marcus or Brent and Marcus in front of the arches or the stage or the photography backdrop. She coached Marcus and Christina and her friend the bartender through their shots. She texted Dan to see if he would give her space for a recipe and a write-up of Christina's catering and ignored the grumbling she got but took the yes. She got a card from the bartender so she could mention his business, too.

Then it was time for Brent to get the show on the road.

She, Marcus and Jane stood near the stage while Brent stepped up to the spotlight.

"Good evening, Sawgrass Manatees, and welcome back." He paused for applause. "I am happy to see so many familiar faces." He tilted his head to the side. "Some of the name tags are familiar but the faces... Well, time makes changes, doesn't it?" His fake chuckle filled the space. "This is going to be a low-key evening. We'll eat, we'll dance, take a few fun photos, but I want each one of us to have a chance to reconnect. I've had the opportunity to catch up with some of you who've come through Preston Bank, but I'm looking forward to finding out more. You'll notice a photographer moving through the crowd. You can look for a story in *Miami Beat* coming soon about the reunion and my role in it." He glanced over his shoulder at the DJ. "With business out of the way, let's—"

Cassie realized he was going to skip over the critical business and moved toward the stage. When she noticed how big the step was, she had a bad feeling, but Marcus moved behind her to give her a boost up. She shot him a *thank you* look before she took the microphone away from Brent. "A few more items before the music starts. If you love the food, drinks and decor, you need to know who brought us this." She motioned to the small group next to the stage. "We've got our caterer and bartender here. Both are military veterans building small businesses through the lab at Concord Court. Please get a card or check out next week's *Miami Beat*. These beautiful centerpieces are also door prizes, so be sure to enter your name at the registration table and check to see if you've won before you leave tonight. And most importantly, the design of this Enchanted Garden comes from Marcus Bryant…" She clapped and everyone joined her. "A fellow Manatee, Air Force veteran and my best friend. While you're catching up with him, don't forget to get his contact info." There. She'd made sure to get the most significant info out there.

Then she thrust the microphone back at Brent and waited for Marcus to lift her down from the stage, his face a mixture of exasperation, amusement and pride. Cassie was almost certain she'd seen that expression on him before.

"Gotta watch the guy every second, or he will take all the credit," she muttered.

"You didn't introduce yourself, explain how much work you did or tell anyone about the column you write every week and should be proud of," Marcus said softly. "You're looking out for us. Who does that for you?"

Cassie frowned. "You do."

"I do." Marcus nodded. "He should." The glare he shot at Brent Preston was impossible to miss. "You shouldn't volunteer to do anything else for that guy. Ever."

She was prepared to vow solemnly to never do so or answer his phone calls again, but Brent stepped up and said, "And that, of course, was Cassie Brooks. But you all knew that. You might remember she used to go by the nickname Cas—"

She wasn't quick enough to react but Marcus sure was. He'd signaled the DJ and fortunately he'd cranked up the volume on the next tune to drown out the rest of Brent's words. Cassie whooped and raced onto the dance floor. She didn't need Brent to give her any of the credit for the reunion.

That was fine. She'd gotten something a

whole lot more important out of their deal. A life-changing something, if she had her way.

The anonymous tip about the bank was a bust, but she had three other stories, maybe more, and all that mattered was that Marcus was back in her life.

If she weighed it all out, she might actually owe Brent Preston a favor for that.

Oh, the irony.

Cassie watched the dance floor fill up and smiled at Marcus.

At the same time, they said, "Food." And then they laughed.

Cassie grabbed Jane's hand and yelled over the music. "Let's get food!"

Jane nodded, and the party started.

CHAPTER TWENTY

CASSIE WAS CAREFULLY working her way around the room, making sure she'd hit every grouping of people to promote all the small businesses that had contributed to the success of the night, with special emphasis on Marcus's work. She waved at him across the room. He and Jane were dancing as part of the group doing the electric slide. If their grins were indications, both of them were having a good time.

"These are fantastic," she said as she flipped through the photos Nelson had taken. He was getting ready to leave, his job done.

"I'm going to load the pictures up onto the internal site tonight. You can make your picks tomorrow or Monday before Dan gets in, and we'll be in good shape." Nelson took the camera back and carefully packed it in his bag. "This is a great party. You did good."

"Thanks. It's my last one. I'm never planning any other event ever for the rest of my life." She put her hand over her heart when Nelson raised an eyebrow. "I mean it. I'm out of the party-planning business for good."

"No weddings. Or baby showers. What about birthday parties?" Brent asked from behind her.

Nelson affectionately slugged her shoulder on his way out, and Cassie had to fight back the urge to follow. She didn't want to talk to Brent anymore, period. It was a perfect evening, and he'd ruin it somehow.

"I already told you that you'll have to find somebody else to take care of the cleanup, remember? I'm officially off-duty." Cassie crossed her arms over her chest. As good as she felt at this moment, she was susceptible to capitulating, and she couldn't let that happen. This time, Brent could handle things.

"No, I wanted to see if you'd like to dance, but I was waiting for a better song," Brent said as the dance tune ended and the DJ spun into a ballad. "That's more my speed. Waltz lessons did not prepare me for line dancing." He offered her his hand. "Want to?"

What she wanted was Marcus to be closer, but he and Jane were chatting with the bartender. She had no graceful way out, so she accepted Brent's invitation and followed him to the dance floor.

"I didn't think you could do it, but this was an amazing success, even better than prom, Casserole," Brent said as he put his hand on her waist and moved to the music. Seventeen-year-old Casserole would have died of sheer excitement to be standing this close to her crush. This Cassie was tamping down irritation. "That was impressive, but this is really special."

Cassie absorbed the compliment. It was nice to hear, nonetheless.

"Who would have thought, after all this time, your feelings would be strong enough to do all this work? For me?" Brent gave her the usual golden smile.

Then she realized what he'd said.

And she got angry. "Are you admitting openly that you knew how I felt when we were in high school?"

He scrunched up his face and bent closer to say, "Everyone knew! It was adorable."

Cassie closed her eyes and thumped her forehead on Brent's chest as the first wave of embarrassment swept over her. Then it was chased away by frustration and a good dose of annoyance. "You used it against me, didn't you?"

Before he could brush her off, she grabbed his hand off her waist and started pulling him toward the door. She had some things to say, and she wasn't going to pull any punches because they had an audience.

When they were outside, she pushed him around the corner of the gym and then paced back and forth while she breathed to calm herself.

"You cured me of that crush at seventeen, Brent. No feelings left, but if I had known that you thought it was *adorable* to use my feelings against me..." She had to stop and breathe through her nose some more. Then she realized the time had arrived to set him straight.

"I was on a story. *Miami Beat* got an anonymous tip about Preston Bank, a whisper about some kind of loan fraud. That's what brought me into your office, but I couldn't find any leads. I'm thrilled about that. I am. From every employee, I heard the same thing. Preston Bank is a good place to work. That is definitely something to be proud of," Cassie said and watched his face closely, searching for guilt.

Brent blinked. "I didn't know you had it in you, but I guess we're not so different after all."

The twist in her stomach hurt. This had been the fear in the back of her mind all along, from seizing her opportunity to approach Brent, her conversations with Jane and even…

"I was hoping that was true." Brent wrinkled his nose. "I called in the tip to…get your attention." He tried a pouty face as if he was such a lovable scamp. "You and I both know I had no shot of pulling this reunion off by myself, Casser…" He cleared his throat. "Cassie."

Words deserted her. Cassie could hear a faint buzzing noise in her ears. "Your tactics have gotten more advanced since we graduated."

He shrugged.

"Guess Marcus is your Cassie, huh? When you need help, you call on him and he rides to your rescue. It's great to have someone like that in your life, isn't it? Jane's good at that, too." Brent crossed his arms over his chest.

Cassie didn't understand what he was saying about Marcus, but Jane needed someone to fight for her.

"A smart man would understand what he has in Jane. Instead of looking for ways to use her feelings against her, he'd do his best to deserve them." Cassie shook her head. "She's too smart to be fooled for long. She's not me at seventeen."

He stared up at the sky. "You're absolutely right. About everything. My company is solid, the employees are respected and valued and Jane is too good to be fooled by me for long."

"Sounds…lovely. Why change, right? When Jane goes, there'll be another person behind her to manipulate." She almost wished she'd never continued this conversation. "I'll let you know when your story is coming out." She was ready to track down Marcus and tell him it was time to leave. They'd done everything they needed to do here.

Except…

"What did you mean about Marcus being my Cassie?"

"Right. Okay." Brent touched his chest. "It's good to feel better than me, right? But what if you were guilty of using his affection for you the same way I did? I mean, one look at the guy, and I can see he's in love. I don't know if I knew that when we were kids, but he never takes his eyes off you." He stepped up onto the sidewalk beside her. "When you jumped in here, who'd you call in for support? Him. What did he think about that? Not much, I'd guess. I figure Marcus Bryant wouldn't lift a finger for me." Brent grinned. "Would he? He's been chasing you long enough. Either stop running and let the guy catch you this time, or leave him alone."

Cassie watched Brent stroll back to the gym as Marcus stepped outside. Brent paused and offered Marcus his hand. She couldn't hear what they said to each other from where she stood, but Marcus eventually shook it. Brent clapped him on the shoulder and disappeared inside.

Avoiding Marcus until she convinced herself that Brent was all wrong wasn't an option, so Cassie straightened her shoulders and tried to act like her normal self.

"Everything okay?" Marcus asked.

"Yeah." Cassie waved at several couples

who were leaving. "Do you think the party is winding down?"

He didn't answer, and she was afraid he was going to push for answers, but he didn't. That was one of the things that made it so easy to be with Marcus. He never pushed.

"If you're ready to go, we've covered this crowd thoroughly. I tried to give Mercedes Esposito one of my cards, and she told me she had not one but two. You apparently gave them both to her at different times tonight." He smiled, but it didn't reach his eyes.

"I'll run in and say goodbye to Jane. Won't take a minute, I promise." Cassie waited for him to agree and then trotted back inside. The crowd was thinning so it was easy to find Jane. She was leaning against the bar, her chin propped on her hand, as she talked with the bartender.

The handsome bartender.

Cassie cut through the tables and chairs. "Will, you did a great job tonight…"

"Thanks for giving me a shot. Christina's hoping we can team up on other things." He glanced at Jane. "It's been a good night all around."

Cassie waited for Jane to seize her chance,

but Jane checked over her shoulder...probably to track down Brent.

"Will, are you single?" Cassie asked. She ignored the way both of their mouths dropped open. Eventually, he nodded, so she pulled Jane away. "Get his number. Go out on a date with him. Forget about Brent Preston, and make sure you really love your job. If the answer is not extremely yes, find a new job that you do love."

Jane snuck a peek at the bartender. "You think he's into me?" Cassie sighed, with frustration and understanding because she also struggled to understand when men were interested. It was so much easier to see it when she was watching from the sidelines.

"Definitely. He's working hard, and he's ambitious, with plans for the future. You are both of those things. Brent is neither of them." Cassie looked her in the eye. "Listen, I can't see the past or the future, but right now, I know you deserve better than Brent." She hugged Jane and turned to go, but she hadn't fully cleared her conscience. "I started this whole thing, the reunion, the story about Brent, to investigate an anonymous tip about trouble at the bank, hoping to grow my career." She rubbed her forehead, wishing for a better way to spill her guts but determined to get it all out. "You and I both know there's nothing shady happening at Preston Bank, although I did overhear a conversation between two women who were talking about getting approvals from Brent while you were out of your office because there would be no way to sneak them past you. No idea what that's about."

Jane sighed. "Was one of them a petite blonde? "

Cassie nodded.

"Brent asked them to plan a work party for my birthday. Two of my busiest loan officers were taking time out to plan a cake and balloons." Jane scowled. "Because that was too much for Brent."

Cassie gripped both of Jane's hands. "Seriously, love your job if you actually love it, but do not waste more time on Brent. I like you. I want to know how this turns out." She motioned between Jane and the bartender. "Call me!"

Then she was moving back through the crowd and wondering if she should have spent that time deciding what to say to Marcus instead.

"SOUNDS LIKE YOU'RE working with the wrong kind of trees in your backyard," Marcus said as he offered Juan Lee a card. "Give me a call, and I'll come out and take a look. Free of charge. Then we can discuss what would be easy to grow, something more drought-resistant but still strong enough to withstand Florida's storms." They shook hands, and Juan and his wife continued out into the parking lot. Marcus leaned back against his truck. He'd taken Cassie at her word and driven to the entrance to pick her up.

Then he'd settled in to wait.

He'd done his best to ignore all the questions running through his head. Watching her lead Brent Preston off the dance floor and into the shadows had shaken him. They'd been swaying to the music, talking closely, smiling before that.

What if Brent had finally come to his senses and seen what he was missing?

He didn't want to believe that Cassie could fall for that after all this time, but a handsome, rich guy would be difficult competition regardless.

When she finally came back out, he couldn't read her face, but he didn't want to have an important conversation there in the parking lot. He opened the door, and she climbed inside. Marcus carefully closed it and tried not to remember how he'd imagined kissing her again at the end of the evening, an Aerosmith tune in the air.

It wasn't long before they were next to her car in their parents' apartment complex, a weird tension that made conversation difficult. He asked, "Can I follow you home? To make sure you get in safely?" Which wasn't what he wanted to say. He was playing it safe.

"Are you going to ask what we talked about?" Cassie asked. "You want to know, don't you?"

Marcus shifted so he could breathe better. "I do and I don't. If he somehow came to his senses after all this time…" What? What would he do? Nothing. Marcus wanted Cassie to be happy. He would have bet anything there was no way Brent Preston could make her happy, but he wouldn't interfere, either.

She laughed, but it wasn't in amusement. "Not the way you mean, no. I confessed that I'd used this reunion as an excuse to get in touch with him. I didn't want to do that inside the party."

"You told me you were over Brent Preston. Didn't need another reminder like our prom."

Cassie seemed shocked at that. "Because it's true. I was researching a story for *Miami Beat* and needed a source inside the bank. The guy at the top seemed a good candidate." She stared at him hard. "But there's no story there. Nothing. I wanted him to know that the naive girl he was able to trick and use was onto him. But he called in the tip! He used me again, even as I was telling myself not to let it happen. Isn't that ridiculous?"

She covered her face with both hands. "That doesn't change how foolish I was about him, the fact that I bothered you with it every day or that everyone around us could see better than I could what was going on."

Being relieved and annoyed at the same time was hard to process, but eventually, Marcus said, "I wouldn't call it *bothered*, Cassie. You talked to me because we were friends. I wouldn't change that." Marcus realized that was the truth, too. How many times has she listened to him go on about his mom's hovering or… "Do not let that guy get inside your head."

"Too late." Cassie stared hard through the

windshield. "He said you were my Cassie, because you were in love with me and would do anything I asked—and I used you." Then she bit her lip but wouldn't face him. "He was onto something, wasn't he?" She picked up his notebook and opened it to the sketch he'd made of her at prom.

Marcus cleared his throat. "I don't know if this counts. I didn't know I was in love with you, so I understand if you didn't know it, either. How could you use it if you didn't know? Besides that, as my father pointed out to me recently, I was nearly grown then. I am grown now. I make my own decisions, so there's nothing you should feel guilty about."

Cassie scowled at him. "You don't believe that."

"I do. Before this reunion, I wanted to blame you for everything, for hurting me, but…you don't have it in you, Cassie, not to hurt someone on purpose." Marcus realized he absolutely believed it. "If you can, forget what we were in the past. Forget this night, too, the work we did. Wipe it all away. All you can do right now is figure out what you want to do next."

When she started to answer, he quickly

went on. "But not tonight. Tomorrow. Let's do something fun. Something only we used to do. I know, let's go to the good skate park. I'll meet you there in the morning." After he dug out his skateboard first. He wasn't sure where he'd stuffed it when he'd settled in at Concord Court. He'd find it. She'd skate circles around him.

That might be enough to buy one more day together. If he had to, he could keep finding ways to convince her to hang around for one more day until she forgot about Brent's words.

Cassie bit her lip. "I would like to skate with you again. I want to do everything we used to do with you again. I want to be us again."

He was ready for that and everything they'd never considered, too. "About eleven?"

Cassie nodded.

"I'm still going to follow you home to make sure you get in all right tonight." She started to argue. "I'd do that for any of my friends."

Eventually she gave in, and he kept his word. When she got out of the car in her driveway, he followed and waited for her to unlock the door.

"This isn't how I wanted this night to end,"

she said softly. The shadows around her door made it hard to see her face, but he could hear regret in her voice.

"I know what you mean." Marcus pulled his phone out of his pocket, pulled up his music and hit Play.

Her soft laugh as Aerosmith floated between them, much smaller and less robust than the DJ's version in the gym would be, but it lightened the tension weighing him down.

As long as he was standing in front of her like this, all was right with his world.

"I was planning to kiss you under artificial stars in a smelly gym. No way these real stars and this quiet night can ever be as romantic but..." Marcus waited for her to agree and relaxed when her arms slid around his waist. They swayed in a half-hearted attempt at dancing before Cassie pressed her lips to his. This kiss was as exciting as their first kiss of the night, but there was so much more to it. This kiss was about the future, who they were as adults, all the other stuff behind them.

And it was sweet.

When Cassie stepped back, she stared into his eyes silently, but she didn't speak. He understood. Everything had changed that evening, everything but who they were for each other. There were still big questions to answer, but neither of them could go back to who they were before they'd stepped inside that enchanted garden.

Marcus waited for her to go inside and wave in the window before he drove away. He thought about how she'd looked framed in the golden light as he drove back to Concord Court. Since it was midnight, he decided to see if there was anyone around the pool. He didn't want to talk or rehash his emotions, but he wasn't ready to be alone.

Sean, Peter, Wade and Mira were outside, but none of them were talking when he sat down at the table. "Y'all breaking up for the night?"

"Peter reminded me that tonight was the reunion, so I called out the expert in case she was needed." Sean motioned at Mira, who pretended to pick up a pen and paper like a therapist. "How'd it go?"

Marcus shrugged out of his suit coat and slung it over the fence. "Good. Place looked amazing. Lots of people were impressed and stopped by to talk about possible projects, so new business is bound to be coming. Everything Cassie promised came true."

"Cassie, the ex-best friend who grew up into a good writer for *Miami Beat* and who is also very cute." Mira's recap demonstrated how well she'd been brought up-to-date. "The one Peter is pretty sure you've been in love with for your whole life."

He glared at Peter. "You could have left that part out."

"Hey, she does her best work when she has all the details." Peter held up both hands as if innocent. "Besides, I needed the win. I'll be bringing up my shot of brilliance every time I can for the foreseeable future."

Marcus settled in and folded his hands behind his head. "Yep, it was brilliant. No way for me to ignore being fully in love with a woman who is not quite as convinced, now that you've pointed it out, so thanks for that."

"You are welcome," Peter answered.

Mira was amused as she said, "I'd say you've crossed the biggest obstacle, then."

"I have, but she's still at the starting block," Marcus said. "What's the use of winning the race when you're the only one running?"

Sean sighed loudly. "Welcome to the club,

friend. Except for Mira, who you have to admit has a unique case of dating her ex-husband, we're all in the same spot, waiting to reach the same place with the people we love. I did show Reyna a wedding magazine. She didn't throw it at my head, so we are making progress."

"I'm picturing an Elvis-chapel wedding, Las Vegas–style." Wade held out his hands. "Brisa's certainly never done that before. I'm not convinced that her father would ever forgive me, though, so I'm still weighing my options."

Sean grimaced. "Not a bet I'd take." Then he patted Marcus on the shoulder. "Cheer up. Falling? That's the hard part. You may have to wait for her to catch up, but she's going to be there with you, and that's all that matters."

Marcus scanned the faces of his friends seated around the table. Everyone agreed, and he knew it was true.

He'd spent a lot of time without her. Waiting for her to catch up would be easy enough.

CHAPTER TWENTY-ONE

CASSIE HAD ARRIVED at the skate park twenty minutes early. When she and Marcus had been kids, they'd thought this place was amazing. Then, it had still been crawling with skaters, all of them doing these amazing tricks. Now? Not so much. There were a few young kids and one dad, who was not that much older than she was, trying to show them how to kick turn. It was cute to watch them teeter away, make the attempt and celebrate when they didn't crash. She'd convinced herself to attempt the vert ramp when she saw Marcus arrive. Her neighborhood park had nothing as tall as this ramp, so it was exhilarating to pick up speed and land at the bottom of the stairs to meet him.

It made her heart race the same way the bold declaration she wanted to blurt out the second she saw him did. She'd thought about him all night. No sleep made things much clearer for Cassie.

He'd seen her at eighteen. He saw her now. Whatever risks they might face, Marcus was ready.

So was she.

"Jumped in with both feet already, I see," he said as he took the last step to stand next to her, his board under his arm. "Couldn't wait for me."

Cassie reached up to tighten her ponytail. "It's been a long time since I did anything this scary. I wanted to see if I still had it in me." Her words were breathless, a little weak, thanks to nerves.

Marcus raised his eyebrows, as if he understood that her words might have more than one meaning, but he didn't answer as he put his board down and pushed. Cassie sat on the stairs and watched him go through the park, gathering speed as he got more comfortable, carving out turns until he was ready to try a kickflip. Her worry dropped away at how easily he moved.

Eventually, he came back and said, "I've missed this. I can't remember why I stopped."

Cassie lifted a shoulder. "You needed me."

Was that technically true? Didn't matter. This was not the time for harsh reality. This moment was for bold intention. Eventually.

He pointed at her. "I bet that's it. I need you." He waited for her to acknowledge that he'd changed her wording. "Gonna take a minute to prepare myself for the bowl. That drop…" He scanned the park. "I remember how it feels to drop off the edge of the pool and hope the skateboard lands on a surface before your head does. It's thrilling and terrifying, and I need a minute to get there." Marcus eased down next to her.

Cassie bumped his shoulder and waited until he turned to face her. "Are we talking about your skating or my dating hesitation here?" He'd taken the lead, smoothing over the rough patch for her.

Because he always would.

Marcus blinked rapidly, one hand over his chest to show how shocked he was. "Whatever do you mean?" He banged his skateboard twice on the handrail, skaters' universal sign of applause for anyone completing an impressive trick.

Cassie laughed, happier than she could remember in forever.

Marcus grinned at her as he wrapped an arm around her back and ran his hand up to her nape. "I have an idea. We can trade lessons. You lead me through something scary, like that ramp you flew down a minute ago, and I'll do the same for you. You like arranging mutually beneficial agreements. I don't see a downside to this one."

"Are yours...dates?" Cassie asked slowly. "Because that's a win-win situation for me. No risk, high reward."

He frowned as he considered that. "Excellent point. I can tell you have more experience brokering these deals than I do. I appreciate your sense of fair play."

Cassie had no idea what to expect from him, not this way, but she could wait and watch him happily.

Then he held up a finger. "I've got it. You're still coaching me, showing me how to jump in feetfirst for the wild ride wherever my skateboard goes."

Cassie nodded, her lips twitching at the corners as she waited. She trusted him. She wanted good things for him. She wanted to be the best thing for him.

"In return," he said, "I am doing the same for you. These will be called *dates*, our parents will interfere, and we will be forced to plot against them. That's your job. You are in charge of all shenanigans." Cassie nodded, and he continued. "Also, kisses. I'm going to need—"

Cassie didn't wait for him to finish but pressed her mouth to his, her lips trembling. Marcus pulled her closer and waited for her to meet his stare. Then he kissed her again, their smiles turning into something deeper but no less happy.

When he pulled back, she said, "You might get some broken bones from this adventure."

"I can't see the future, but I know myself pretty well. I also know you. My parents show me what's possible over a lifetime. We won't rush anything, but we're going forward." He shrugged. "And I'm certain that there's no broken heart waiting for either of us. Every day we're together, we're in the right spot."

Cassie tangled her fingers through his. "This is a good plan. And we'll make sure whether or not we're in love is the last question anyone will ask."

He pressed his forehead to hers. "Right. There will be no doubt in anyone's mind about our love."

EPILOGUE

MARCUS SURVEYED THE CROWD that had assembled in Quill's dining room for the launch party of *Lessons from the Off Beat*.

Midafternoon sun filtered through the skylight to cast a glow over Cassie. She'd been seated behind the table on the other side of the fountain, talking and signing books, ever since she'd finished her reading. The subject of that chapter, the teacher who'd made time to teach American Sign Language to every student, was in a cozy huddle with Cassie's father off to the side. His parents were chatting with the caterer, Christina, about the cheese puffs she'd been circulating through the crowd. And his whole Concord Court family had taken over three tables they'd rearranged to sit together. He'd have to fix that, return it back to original and pristine condition, or Christina's father, the man watching closely from the doorway to the kitchen, would never forgive or forget it.

"You're pretty proud of yourself, aren't you?" Brisa asked as she offered him the last champagne flute on her tray. "I don't blame you. You should be proud of the party and of Cassie." Her eyes twinkled as she patted him on the back.

Marcus sipped his champagne. "You can't stop yourself, can you?"

Brisa fluttered her eyelashes innocently. "What? Who, me?"

"We discussed inviting the Coconut Grove business owners to the party." Marcus had doubted that many of them would jump on the invitation, but once he'd negotiated the use of Quill, he'd agreed to Brisa's suggestion. "I never expected turnout like this. You have to make every idea better, don't you?"

She gave him a regal nod. "It's what I do." Her smug grin was cute. "Honestly, personal invitations are huge these days. And when I walked into one of the galleries that caters to tourists, you know, the one on the other side of the park, I realized I knew other business owners in Wynwood who might also be interested in offering the book. Lots of tourists drop in, and Cassie's essays make a unique souvenir."

"Good thing you aren't busy at Concord Court these days," Marcus drawled, aware that she'd never been busier.

That was the kind of friend Brisa Montero was. Her own troubles disappeared when a friend asked for her support.

Brisa sighed. "Yeah, I've got to find the right person to take over the business lab. Sean is great. He's got the operation working flawlessly. Reyna knows how to reach volunteers, and I want to be able to build our programs. New things, not those we've already got in motion." She raised an eyebrow. "You don't happen to know a lawyer, accountant, or successful business mogul, other than yourself, who might be interested in a job, do you?"

"Can't talk Peter into taking it and working around law school, huh?" Marcus asked.

Brisa rolled her eyes. "No, he doesn't believe his schedule will allow time for school, a job, *and* spending time on his boat. The boat wins that battle."

Since he couldn't blame the guy, Marcus shook his head. "I'll keep my eyes and ears open for you."

Brisa hugged his arm. "I know you will. Go talk to your girl. She's finally done signing."

When he stepped up in front of her table, Marcus took a book off the top of the stack. "Can I have your autograph?"

Cassie picked up her pen. "The dedication wasn't enough, huh?"

Marcus shrugged. "That's for everybody else to see. I was hoping you'd write something just for me."

She studied his face as she thought and then bent her head to write a message before moving around the table to wrap her arms around his waist. "I can't believe you did this for me. How did you get him to agree?" She didn't make any obvious motion toward Christina's father but indicated with her eyes.

"It wasn't easy. I suspect Brisa played a part in that, although she hasn't admitted it." Marcus bent closer to Cassie's ear. "I was going to arrange a DJ or some kind of music, but if we aren't out of here by four o'clock on the dot, I'm afraid he'll call the police."

"All of these people. For my book," she said softly as she gazed up at him. Marcus would never forget the way she looked there, in his arms, in that second.

Then he remembered their audience and forced himself to return to Earth.

"I asked the guy who handcrafts kazoos from found wood and other objects if he could play our song," Marcus said, "but he snapped that he was an artist, not a performer."

Cassie laughed. "This is perfect." Then she tapped the book in his hand, so Marcus flipped open the cover.

"Should I wait to read this until everyone who knows us and loves us is not watching?" Marcus asked.

Cassie craned her neck to see that the whole restaurant had eyes locked on them. "Nah. They already know we're in love."

"'Never forget that I love you. Yesterday. Today. Tomorrow,'" Marcus read aloud. When he pressed a kiss to her lips and the room erupted in cheers, he knew they were keeping their promise to each other.

There was no way anyone could doubt their love.

* * * * *

For more great Veterans' Road romances from Cheryl Harper and Harlequin Heartwarming, visit www.Harlequin.com today!

Get 4 FREE REWARDS!

We'll send you 2 FREE Books plus 2 FREE Mystery Gifts.

Love Inspired books feature uplifting stories where faith helps guide you through life's challenges and discover the promise of a new beginning.

FREE
Value Over
$20

YES! Please send me 2 FREE Love Inspired Romance novels and my 2 FREE mystery gifts (gifts are worth about $10 retail). After receiving them, if I don't wish to receive any more books, I can return the shipping statement marked "cancel." If I don't cancel, I will receive 6 brand-new novels every month and be billed just $5.24 each for the regular-print edition or $5.99 each for the larger-print edition in the U.S., or $5.74 each for the regular-print edition or $6.24 each for the larger-print edition in Canada. That's a savings of at least 13% off the cover price. It's quite a bargain! Shipping and handling is just 50¢ per book in the U.S. and $1.25 per book in Canada.* I understand that accepting the 2 free books and gifts places me under no obligation to buy anything. I can always return a shipment and cancel at any time. The free books and gifts are mine to keep no matter what I decide.

Choose one: ☐ **Love Inspired Romance Regular-Print**
(105/305 IDN GNWC)

☐ **Love Inspired Romance Larger-Print**
(122/322 IDN GNWC)

Name (please print)

Address   Apt. #

City   State/Province   Zip/Postal Code

Email: Please check this box ☐ if you would like to receive newsletters and promotional emails from Harlequin Enterprises ULC and its affiliates. You can unsubscribe anytime.

Mail to the **Harlequin Reader Service:**
IN U.S.A.: P.O. Box 1341, Buffalo, NY 14240-8531
IN CANADA: P.O. Box 603, Fort Erie, Ontario L2A 5X3

Want to try 2 free books from another series? Call 1-800-873-8635 or visit www.ReaderService.com.

*Terms and prices subject to change without notice. Prices do not include sales taxes, which will be charged (if applicable) based on your state or country of residence. Canadian residents will be charged applicable taxes. Offer not valid in Quebec. This offer is limited to one order per household. Books received may not be as shown. Not valid for current subscribers to Love Inspired Romance books. All orders subject to approval. Credit or debit balances in a customer's account(s) may be offset by any other outstanding balance owed by or to the customer. Please allow 4 to 6 weeks for delivery. Offer available while quantities last.

Your Privacy—Your information is being collected by Harlequin Enterprises ULC, operating as Harlequin Reader Service. For a complete summary of the information we collect, how we use this information and to whom it is disclosed, please visit our privacy notice located at corporate.harlequin.com/privacy-notice. From time to time we may also exchange your personal information with reputable third parties. If you wish to opt out of this sharing of your personal information, please visit readerservice.com/consumerschoice or call 1-800-873-8635. **Notice to California Residents**—Under California law, you have specific rights to control and access your data. For more information on these rights and how to exercise them, visit corporate.harlequin.com/california-privacy.

LIR21R2

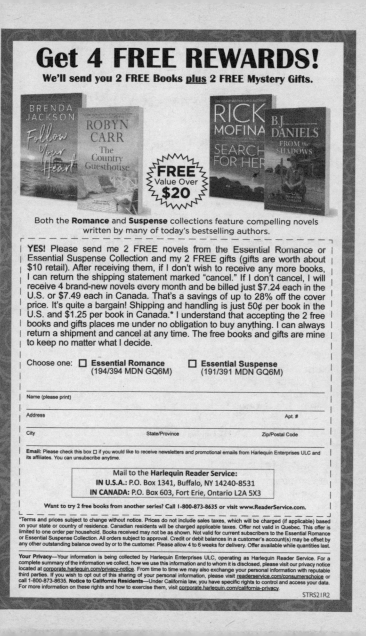

#415 THE COWBOY'S UNLIKELY MATCH

Bachelor Cowboys • by Lisa Childs

Having grown up in foster care, schoolteacher Emily Trent readily moves to Ranch Haven to help three local orphans—just not their playboy uncle, Ben Haven. The charming cowboy mayor didn't get her vote and won't get her heart!

#416 THE PARAMEDIC'S FOREVER FAMILY

Smoky Mountain First Responders • by Tanya Agler

Horticulturist and single mom Lindsay Hudson looks forward to neighborly chats with paramedic Mason Ruddick. He was her late husband's best friend, but he can't be anything more. Unless love can bloom in her own backyard?

#417 THE RANCHER'S WYOMING TWINS

Back to Adelaide Creek • by Virginia McCullough

Heather Stanhope wants to hate the rancher who bought her family's land. Instead, she's falling for sweet Matt Burton and his adorable twin nieces. Could the place she longs to call home be big enough for all of them?

#418 THEIR TOGETHER PROMISE

The Montgomerys of Spirit Lake
by M. K. Stelmack

Mara Montgomery is determined to face her vision loss without any help—particularly from the stubbornly optimistic Connor Flanagan. Can Connor open Mara's eyes to a lifetime of love from one of his service dogs...and him?

Visit
ReaderService.com
Today!

As a valued member of the Harlequin Reader Service, you'll find these benefits and more at ReaderService.com:

- Try 2 free books from any series
- Access risk-free special offers
- View your account history & manage payments
- Browse the latest Bonus Bucks catalog

RS20